★ ★ ★

A Journey
TO LOVE

JACKSON'S STORY

Book Two in the Journey Series

Cover design by germancreative
Edited by Wonder and Wander Editing Co.

The Journey Series is a steamy, closed-door romance.
Content Warnings: Coarse language, suicide of a loved one (off page),
PTSD, loss/grief, rape (off page), and violence. Jackson's story has hardships,
pain, heartbreak, and raw emotions. But there is even more inspiration,
hope, sweetness, perseverance, and unconditional love to balance out the
heartfelt story. Enjoy!

Follow me on Instagram and Facebook: @authoralexandragrace

Website: https://authoralexandragrace.carrd.co

The Journey Series by Alexandra Grace

The series is best enjoyed if read in the following order.

To hopeless romantics and fairy tale believers.

A Journey Spared (Book 1) Recap

U.S. Marine Sergeant Jackson Vane and his best friend Will were the only survivors in their unit of an enemy attack overseas. Jackson's extensive injuries resulted in four months of recovery in a London hospital and his unwanted discharge after eight years of service. Needing support, he had no other choice but to return to his childhood home in Richmond, Virginia.

Eleanor, his father's estate manager and the person who raised him, cared for him while he mourned the loss of his friends and career. Their special bond provided the medicine he needed to find a path forward. Avery, Will's cousin and Jackson's physical therapist, had loved him since she was young. She saw his return as their chance to finally be together. Her creative therapy helped him walk again, but he couldn't love her in the way she wanted.

After they broke up, Jackson continued his healing journey on his own until he could run long distances again (his first love). Running and spending time outside calmed his PTSD symptoms and energized him.

Before the explosion, he and his three friends traveled the world, seeking the next greatest adventure. When a mysterious feeling called him to leave Richmond a year after his father passed, he thought an epic journey would help him connect with the person he'd been before tragedy struck.

After brainstorming ideas, he decided to run from Richmond to Orlando, Florida in honor of the friends he lost and veterans everywhere. He also hoped the adventure would open the door to his future and mend his broken heart.

Ben, Avery's newly unemployed friend, joined him to manage trip logistics, promote Jackson's mission on social media, and enjoy a long vacation. Despite having to keep Ben out of trouble most nights on the road, the start of his journey was working as he'd hoped and blessed him through the first two stops to visit Eleanor and Will's family.

Chapter One

✶ ✶ ✶

Jackson

"What did you think would happen?" Jackson asked, standing over Ben as he sulked on the street curb outside a rowdy Greenville, North Carolina bar.

"I didn't think about anything."

"No shit."

Ben tossed him a smile, evidence of his lack of self-control and the trouble it always attracted dripping down his face onto his shirt. The streetlight reflected off the full set of perfect, white teeth he still possessed… thanks to Jackson. "But she was hot, right?"

With a shrug, he looked around. The empty street suggested they'd stayed out longer than they should have.

"You could have stopped him a little sooner." Ben pointed at his swollen cheek and the stiff paper towel plugging his bloody nose. "This is on you."

"Try again."

"He was twice my size."

"You should have thought of that before touching his *hot* girlfriend."

Ben's dark, bloodshot eyes glared at him as he yanked what sounded like sandpaper out of his nose. "She started it."

"And you sound like a sullen teenager."

He puffed out his disapproval, his fingers flying to his swollen lip with a wince.

"Come on." Jackson pulled him up by the arm.

"Where?"

"The only place you can't get into trouble."

"But things were just gettin' good in there."

"You're welcome to stay." Jackson's stride didn't hesitate as he headed toward the hotel. "But I'm off extraction duty for the rest of the night."

"Fine. I'm coming."

———

Darkness lingered the following morning when Jackson stepped outside to start his run. Hours of tossing and turning had drained him of what little energy he had left, yet he couldn't spend another day doing nothing. He needed exercise and fresh air to soothe his escalating anxiety—courtesy of Ben Stevens.

Cutting his warmup short, he took off down the street. Although he desperately wanted to think of literally anything else, he couldn't get Ben and the bar fight out of his head. It would be nice to have one night where all hell didn't break loose.

The ludicrous situations Ben created—almost always involving a woman—and the boyish charm that leaked out of him like cheap cologne gnawed on Jackson's nerves. Most days, he seemed to be the other side of trouble's magnet, making Jackson fantasize about sending him packing more times than he remembered.

But he never followed through. Ben didn't have malicious or deceptive bone in his body. He just didn't have an off switch or bother thinking through the consequences before acting—a skill Jackson spent eight years fine-tuning in the Marines. They balanced each other out, and in his own awkward way and sometimes without realizing it, Ben also rescued Jackson.

His impulse to cannon ball himself into chaos got Jackson out of the hotel and gave his thoughts another path to track. Spending too much time with his memories in the uneventful solitude created its own disastrous outcome— one that made Ben's antics look like a walk on the beach. And recently, he needed all the distractions he could get.

The first two hundred miles after leaving Richmond accumulated with minimal delays or issues. But over the last two weeks, he had to stop more often, rest for longer, and travel fewer miles each day. Pain slithered back into his daily routine, and he laid awake most nights, terrified it would prevent him from reaching his goals. More pain meant more anxiety, opening the door for memories to creep back in. And Ben's latest angry boyfriend episode hadn't helped his flailing attempts to control it.

Despite being the only voice of reason and not taking a single swing or blow, the interaction with Ben's sparring partner triggered his first migraine in six months. Thankfully, he'd made it back to his hotel room before the freight train slammed against his skull and incapacitated him for hours—an unavoidable reminder that his mission could fail if he didn't stay focused and manage his symptoms.

Sunrays peering over the trees and hitting his face brought Jackson's attention back to the road. He'd made it out of the city, and now traveled down a two-lane with a thickly wooded area lining both sides. Blurry silhouettes of the next town could be seen through the morning fog ahead. While some privacy and shade could still be found, he entered the tree line and located a sturdy branch for his first upper body workout.

He drained one of the water bottles in his backpack and checked his watch. Eleven minutes past seven, and he'd already gone eight miles. Since he had it, he'd take extra time to stretch and hydrate before setting out again.

Eyeing a spot on the branch, he jumped and secured his hands around the smooth bark. Sweat began to bead on his forearms after only fifty pull-ups, the southern humidity already near swelting.

"What are you doing?" a little voice asked from below.

Startled, he dropped to the ground in front of a girl about seven or eight years old, carrying a dirty blue bucket.

She had blonde, messy pigtails and wore a plain white T-shirt two sizes too big with scuffed and muddy cowboy boots.

"Hi, there. I was exercising. What are you doing in here by yourself?"

"Looking for berries and nuts."

He glanced inside her empty bucket. "Didn't find any today?"

"Not yet." She squinted up at him through the dappled sun shining on her freckled face. "Why are you exercising in the forest?"

"When I run, I take breaks to work my muscles. This tree looked strong enough for pull-ups."

"What's pull-ups?"

"I hold on to a branch like this." He demonstrated with his hands in the air. "Then, I pull my body up until my chin is above the branch."

"That sounds easy."

He smiled. "It is until my arms get tired."

"What's that?" A chipped purple fingernail pointed at the silver chain around his neck.

He lifted the tags hanging from it. "They're called dog tags. They help me remember my friends."

"You're not a dog."

"No." He laughed. "You get these when you serve in the military."

"Oh. Does my grandpa have some? He was in the Army."

"I would say he does."

"That's his favorite tree."

Jackson glanced up at the tall tree he'd used, then back at the girl. "He has a favorite tree?"

She walked around it, and he followed, waiting while she turned the bucket upside down and stood on it.

"He made that when he found Grandma." She pointed up again, this time to a heart carved into the trunk with two letters inside.

"Found her?"

"When they fell in love, silly."

"Of course." He slapped a palm to his forehead, making her giggle. "What do the letters stand for?"

"Their names, Olan and Helen." She hopped off the bucket. "Are you married?"

"No."

"Do you want to get married?"

"I'm not sure."

"I guess you have to find someone you love first," she said, her long lashes fluttering while she thought on it.

"It's usually a prerequisite."

"A what?"

"A prerequisite. You should love someone before you marry them. There's an order to these things."

Sadness clouded her eyes before she looked away. "Yeah."

Kneeling, he bent to see her face. "What is it?"

"My mom and dad aren't married."

"People can still be in love and choose not to get married."

"They yell a lot."

"Well, relationships can be hard. It takes a lot of work, and that might be how they communicate. But it doesn't always mean they don't love each other, or you."

"Yeah," she said again, pushing at the dirt with her boot. "Do you yell at people you love?"

He thought back to the times he'd been angry or upset. "No. But I don't yell at anyone. It's not me. Everyone handles their emotions differently."

She raised her gray-blue eyes to him. "I wish you were my daddy."

"Oh, sweetie." Cautiously, he held out his hand and was surprised when she took it. "You don't mean—"

"Callie! Get away from him," a woman screamed, the sound of crushing twigs and dead leaves under her angry steps echoing through the trees.

"Momma."

He stood to greet the frantic mother, and Callie tightened her grip on his hand, heightening his senses.

"What are you doing? You know you're not supposed to wander around the woods, and this is why." The woman threw her hand in his direction, causing her to stumble to the side. Her short black hair fell into her face with the sharp movement as she felt for a nearby tree to steady herself.

"I come in here all the time, and he's nice."

"But I told you to stay out, and didn't they teach you not to talk to strangers in school?"

"I don't know. You don't take me."

His attention snapped to Callie. "You don't go to school?"

"Don't talk to her. Come here, child."

"No. I'm staying."

"Callie." He lowered to a knee and met her panicked gaze. "I *am* a stranger to you. You can't come with me. You have a family who loves you."

She shook her head. "She doesn't. She won't let me see Grandpa or go to school. Please don't leave me."

"Callie Marie, shut your mouth and get over here." When Callie refused again and hid behind him, the woman lunged at her. "Just wait until I get ahold of you."

Contracting muscles shot fire through his veins at the woman's threat. "You lay one hand on her, and I swear…"

"You swear what, tough guy? Are you going to hit a woman? And what were you doing creeping around in here, anyway?" She looked down at Callie, peeking around his leg, then back at him. "Or have you found what you were looking for?"

The woman had slithered closer without his noticing, her eyes glossy and unfocused on his face. As she stood there, challenging him, she swayed and fought gravity like a heavy wind blew against her. She reeked of cheap cigarettes and whiskey.

"You should step back, ma'am," he warned, struggling with how to defuse the situation. "You're scaring your daughter."

"She ain't mine. She's my good-for-nothin' ex's. On second thought—" She took a few unsteady steps backward. "If you want her so bad, you can have her. We'll see how Chris likes finding his perfect little Callie gone when he crawls into my bed again."

She trotted off, and Jackson started after her until he heard Callie crying. "Oh, sweetie. I'm so sorry."

Picking her up, she wrapped her arms and legs around him, exposing how critically thin she was. *Now what?* He couldn't take her back to her house. He'd never be able to live with himself.

"I want my grandpa," she murmured, giving him the answer.

"Does he live near here?"

With her face buried in his neck, she nodded and tightened her grip around him.

Some patient coaxing pulled enough information out of her to start in the right direction. Soon, they came to a one-level, brick house outside the town he saw earlier. She unlatched from him and ran toward it, meeting a man with thinning gray hair in the yard.

He bent down, their embrace desperate and long overdue. "What are you doing here, Callie Bug?"

Unlocking her arms from around his neck, he checked her over, the look on his face breaking Jackson's heart. She meant the world to him, and seeing her upset brought fury and sorrow to the man's eyes.

He could relate.

"Who are you?" her grandfather asked him, but Callie answered, whispering into his ear. Shock brushed across his face before he took hold of Callie's waist and held her at arms-length. His eyes pierced into hers with unspoken questions, which she answered with a nod.

He stood, Callie's hand in his. "What's your name?"

"Jackson Vane, sir."

"Nice to meet you, Jackson. I'm Olan Lewis. Can I interest you in some iced tea or water? It's a hot one today."

"Water would be great."

Olan led Jackson to the small kitchen and prepared two glasses of ice water and a bowl of cereal. "Eat," he instructed Callie.

"Can I watch TV, Grandpa? Momma—" She scrunched her eyes closed and shook her head. "I mean Rachel won't let me watch cartoons when she's there."

"Sure, Buggie. But use the coffee table so it doesn't spill." He placed the bowl in Callie's hands and waited for her to leave before giving his attention to Jackson. "The witch wanted nothing to do with that sweet child but forced her to call her momma anyway. It burns my insides to think of my granddaughter suffering in that disgusting trailer."

Unsure of how to respond, Jackson took a long drink, hoping it cooled his overheated system soon.

"She said you saved her," Olan continued, his mood lighter as he leaned back in the chair.

"I didn't do anything."

"Yes, you did. You kept her safe and from getting beat again. I will forever be grateful to you." Olan studied him. "She had a dream about you."

"What?"

"She dreamed a tall man with long, dark hair would be the one to get her to safety once and for all. That he would be the one to end the cycle."

"Cycle of what?"

"Every time she escapes, she goes to a friend or neighbor's house until Rachel sobers up and comes looking for her. She did that a couple of times here around Christmas. But she's convinced all that is over."

"Why?"

"Like her grandma, God rest her soul, Callie believes dreams have meaning and the power to predict the future."

"That's crazy."

"Is it? She knew you were coming. It's why she wasn't scared of you, and she doesn't trust easy."

"I don't know what to say."

"Do you have children?"

"No. But I recently gained a godson—William."

"That's great. You'll learn a lot about yourself and how infinite your love can be through him. Children can teach us many things if we take the time to listen and observe. Christian, that's my boy, he's always been good at testing my patience, and I had to learn to control my temper. Still working on it." Olan leaned on the table, his sly grin fading slowly. "He's in rehab again, trying to get better so he can provide for Callie. But I predict that when he gets out, he'll be right back where he started soon after. He can't seem to stay away or see Rachel's toxic."

"Does Callie have to go back? Rachel isn't her parent."

"Christian filed to designate her as official guardian before he went into rehab the first time. He was high as a kite when he did it." Olan's eyes rolled. "I think she forced or manipulated him into doing it, so she'd have that hold over him. He loves his daughter, and if she has Callie, she can control him."

"Does he not know how Rachel treats her?" How could Christian leave her there if he did?

"He does, but what can he do?"

"Remove her as guardian," Jackson suggested flatly.

"No judge will listen to an addict who knowingly signed the paperwork. Plus, they think the child is safe. Rachel can play the part, and I have no say in the matter. Believe me, I've tried." With a sigh, Olan leaned back, his arms crossing over his chest. "So, we play the game, over and over, tormenting the poor child."

"But how can they keep her out of school?"

"What?"

"Rachel admitted it. How has that not reached the authorities?"

"They moved back here late last summer, and I haven't seen her much since Christmas break. I doubt anyone here knows she exists. They move around constantly, always skirting the law." He stood and began pacing the small kitchen. "This changes things, Jackson. If I can prove Rachel's unfit…"

"The fact that Callie wanders the woods alone at her age and Rachel—"

"If I call the cops, will you tell them what happened?" Olan interrupted.

"Of course."

"Bless you." He rushed to the ancient, green phone on the wall and dialed 9-1-1. He provided his address and a brief overview of what he'd learned before hanging up. "They're on their way. Callie Bug," he called.

"Yes, Grandpa?"

Surprised, Jackson turned toward her when she rested an arm on his shoulder and absently played with his hair. The tender grin she offered wrapped him around her finger right along with his hair. He wanted to coil around her and protect her forever. Whatever he had to do to keep her from Rachel, he'd do it.

Olan sat in a chair opposite her and took her free hand. "You've told me before that you don't want to live with Rachel. Has that changed?"

Her eyes instantly filled, and Jackson felt her fist tighten around a lock of his hair.

"No, Grandpa. I don't—I can't." She shook her head quickly, sending tears zigzagging over her pink cheeks.

"Okay, sweetheart. Then, I will do everything I can to keep that from happening. And so will Jackson."

She looked from Olan to Jackson and relaxed.

"We'll need your help. You'll have to tell some people everything that's happened. And I mean everything. It won't to be easy."

She nodded. "I can do it."

"I know you can, Buggie. You're so brave." He kissed her forehead and took a deep breath. "Did you finish your cereal?"

"Yes."

"Do you want anything else to eat?"

"I'm full."

"Okay. Go watch your cartoon." Olan motioned toward the living room.

With a nod, she headed that way, then stopped in the doorway. "Grandpa?"

"Yes, sweetie?"

"Can Jackson come, too?"

Melting, Jackson smiled. "I'd love to."

———

The trio watched TV and chatted until a team of officers and social workers arrived. Callie sat in Jackson's lap, both of them recounting what happened after they met. She answered questions about her living conditions and showed the bruises on her back, sending his blood pressure into a nauseating tailspin. When a social worker and officer left during the conversation, he hoped they were heading straight for Rachel.

"Do you really have to?" Callie asked him later when he announced he, too, had to go.

He knelt in front of her and took her hand, the sight of her emotional again pulling at his heartstrings. "I don't want to, but you're safe now. There's no way I would leave if you weren't."

She threw her arms around his neck, and he picked her up.

"I gave my phone number to your grandpa. If you ever get scared or need anything, anything at all, you call me. Okay?"

She nodded but with sad eyes, snapping his heart in two. Reluctantly, he put her down before she convinced him to stay. It wouldn't take much more.

"What happens next?" he asked Olan on the way out.

"When I get official custody…I'm staying positive," Olan added with an unsteady grin. "I'm taking her far away from here. If my son ever gets his life straight, he can come find us."

"Good idea. She deserves to be a happy, carefree kid, and if there's something I can do to help give her that, please say the word."

"You're a good man, Jackson. You will always be a part of our family."

"Thank you. If you're ever in Richmond, I'd love to see you both."

"Richmond, Virginia?" Olan asked, leaning against the doorframe.

"That's the one."

"I have a sister not too far from there. Maybe that's where we'll go."

"That would be great. Keep me informed of what happens here and where you end up."

"Will do. Have a safe trip."

With the people he loved and the new family he'd gained since leaving Richmond on his mind, he took off toward town. Why had he been struggling lately? The journey had been good to him. Better than expected, and his life was full.

Still, by the time he reached the town of Winterville, his heart hurt from missing them all. Pressing a palm against the source of the ache, he stopped at a traffic light to breathe through it, his drive to continue down the road wavering with every erratic beat.

Surrendering, he lowered onto a nearby bench and glanced around. Across the street, a lush yard and cascading Oak trees lining a narrow driveway drew his attention. The park-like property stood out among the commercial buildings and asphalt parking lots on either side. Time seemed to have stopped there two centuries ago, while the rest of the town progressed around it

On the left side of the lot stood a small sign advertising a bed and breakfast. Now that he knew what to look for, slivers of a white structure peeked through the trees in the distance. He shot off the bench and jogged toward it.

The wooded area opened at the end of the drive, revealing a massive historic home with wide plank wood siding painted white to match the towering two-story columns and wrap around porches on both levels. Navy shudders framed every window, and the curved front stairs were constructed with the same red brick as the four towering chimneys above.

His eyes shifted to the perky blossoms planted around the shaped shrubbery, and his chest tightened with thoughts of Eleanor. Her focus would have zeroed in on the flower beds and gardens instead of the stunning mid-19th-century architecture. She'd gush over them for hours with the groundskeeper, sharing secrets and stories and boring Jackson into finding something else to pass the time. The vision lightened his mood as he climbed the steps.

Since the front door sat open behind the screen, he let himself in, stepping into a time warp. The furnishings, fixtures, wallpaper, and wood features from floor to ceiling seemed original to the day the first owners moved in. The grand staircase curved around the ornate crystal chandelier in the center of the foyer, reminding him of the one hanging in his father's home.

Correction; *his* home.

He hadn't gotten used to that life alteration yet.

As he admired the black and white photos on the fireplace mantle in the parlor, a woman with dark gray hair, a plaid dress, and apron joined him. Eleanor's name tickled his tongue with the wave of familiarity she brought into the room.

"Hello there, sweetie," she greeted in an unmistakable southern drawl. "Are you looking for a place to stay for the night?"

"Yes, ma'am. I'll need two rooms if you have them."

"That's wonderful. Of course, of course. Would you like to give the rooms a looksee before payin'?"

"That won't be necessary."

"Suit yourself." She waved for him to follow. "I made some sweet tea and cookies this afternoon. Got a plate of chocolate chip in the kitchen and oatmeal raisin in the oven if you're interested."

"They smell amazing, but I'd like to take a shower first if that's okay."

"Anything you need." She led him to a small office by the back door, soon passing him several forms on a clipboard. While he filled in the information, she did the same for his handwritten bill. He paid with cash since credit cards weren't accepted and listened closely to her instructions. "If you need anything during your stay, just holler."

She narrowed her dark eyes when he smiled. "Did I say something amusin'?"

"A close friend of mine used to tell me to holler if I needed her. She was like a mother to me."

Her frown softened into a motherly grin. "Aww. I can tell you miss her."

"Very much. You remind me of her."

"I'm flattered. I'd love to learn more about your…"

"Eleanor."

"What a lovely name." Her hands clasped together under her chin. "Will you tell me about her at dinner tonight?"

"Nothing would make me happier."

After texting Ben the address, he wandered the gardens to gather details and photos to share with Eleanor. Then, he called Olan to tell him he'd be in town a little while longer. Olan invited him back to the house to spend time with Callie, giving Jackson an idea.

"I'll call you back." Sprinting through the sunflower rows, he took the rear entrance steps two at a time. "Excuse me, ma'am?" he called, embarrassed that he hadn't asked for her name earlier.

"Yes, dearie?" She appeared in the hallway, drying her wet hands on her apron, as Eleanor would.

He smiled at the memory. "Would you mind if two more joined us for dinner? I know a little girl who would love to play on the swings out back."

"Of course. The more the merrier."

"Thank you." He turned to leave, then stopped. "You never told me *your* name."

"Oh. Silly me. It's Hilda."

———

Once in his room, Jackson took a quick shower and changed before visiting the strip mall across the street. Callie had had a rough day, and he wanted to give her something to make her smile.

He returned in time to intercept Ben before he went inside.

"What is this place?" he asked, climbing out of the car.

Jackson glanced back at the flowers and Hilda sweeping the front porch. "Home," he answered absently.

"What?"

"Nothing. Help me grab the suitcases. We have dinner plans."

"Since when do you make plans? Did you happen to find a hot bar on your way here because I saw nothing exciting in this sh—"

"Watch your mouth," he demanded and motioned for Ben to open the trunk.

"Why? Is Scarlett gonna whack me with her fan if I curse?"

"Who?"

"Scarlett O'Hara. *Gone With The Wind*. Old movie. Civil War. Any of this registering?"

"No."

Ben sighed. "God, this place is—"

"A breath of fresh air. That's all you need to say or think." With a warning scowl, he yanked out both suitcases in one motion.

"Are you blind? There's nothing fun to do here."

"Good. That means you'll stay out of trouble."

Chapter Two

⭐ ⭐ ⭐

Jackson

You're still here?" Ben asked when he found Jackson hunched over an untouched plate of food in yet another ordinary hotel restaurant days later. No sweet reminders of home. No connection to what matters. Only strangers and bland food.

"The sun's already up," he joked, but Jackson didn't waste what little energy he had left to respond. "Bad night?"

"Yeah."

"Anything I can do?"

Snatching up his fork, he sighed. "No. Thanks."

"Are you running today?"

"I'm going to try."

"Is it your knees, migraines, or lack of sleep getting to you?" Ben asked, waving to the waiter.

"Yes."

"Got it." After placing an order, he sat opposite Jackson. "I saw a really nice golf course on the way here."

"You play?"

"Not exactly, but it can be a fun drinking game with the right partner. Even better with a couple of hot chicks. What do you say? Might help you feel better," he added with a one-sided brow raise.

"Tempting. But I'll pass."

"More for me." Ben pointed at Jackson's plate. "You better eat that. I can't have Harrison coming after *me* when you pass out on some random highway."

With eyes locked on Ben, he stabbed a bite of sausage and pulled it off the fork with his teeth.

"That's the spirit."

They sat in silence until Jackson slid his empty plate aside and stood. "See you in a few hours."

"Call me when you stop to stretch."

"Why?"

"Just do it."

With a growl, Jackson snatched up his backpack and stalked out of the hotel. He had enough to deal with without Ben hovering around like an annoying mosquito. Reflex had his hand swatting at imaginary insects while he searched through his backpack for earbuds. Getting into a rhythm on the road and sweating out his frustrations solved most of his problems. Music drowned out the rest and added reinforcement.

After turning up the volume on his favorite music app, he took off, forgoing his usual warmup routine.

Ten miles later, he slowed and turned off the music to better navigate the heavy, disruptive traffic and approaching storm. The dark line of clouds over the horizon flashed with lightning that mimicked a firework show, fueling his agitation. If he kept going, his chosen path would take him directly into a storm.

Unwilling to turn back and lose progress, he continued as planned. Maybe he could find shelter before the worst of it touched down. A light drizzle began to fall less than a mile later, dampening his shirt and hair. Steady rain soon followed, and as he reached the city's edge, the clouds unleashed their fury. He'd waited too long, and now he had nowhere to hide.

Sharp raindrops pelted his skin as the wind howled and gusted around him, slowing his pace further. He hadn't been in the right frame of mind when left the hotel, and this was his punishment. As he searched for shelter, he pushed against the storm until he came to a bridge. Ducking underneath, he resigned to wait it out.

Thunder clashed above without warning, and for the first time in a year, a familiar darkness swallowed him alive. Tired, aching, and isolated from everyone who grounded him, his motivation to strive for the light fizzled out like he was a lit match in the rain.

The storm grew closer, louder, in its ruthless battle with the earth. Rain fell in diagonal, silvery sheets, flooding the creek below. Blinding flashes from every direction boomed simultaneously with each crash now—one after another.

Dropping to the ground, he gripped his head and closed his eyes to the punishment. He should never have—

A bolt struck a tree on the other side of the bridge, scorching and slicing it down the middle. He jumped at the cannon-like blast, shielding his face from the flying daggers of wood it sent in his direction. One sliced his arm. More landed on the exposed skin of his thigh and calf. He was defenseless in the center of the battlefield with no protection. There were no rules of engagement, and no opportunities to negotiate with the enemy.

Mother Nature stood over him, her sword raised high in victory. Violent wind swirled around him, and the familiar combination of metal and grit pierced his back. His skin stung on contact, but he felt, heard, and saw nothing after that definitive strike.

———

"Oh, shit, you're bleeding."

"Will?" Jackson struggled to open his eyes. "I can't move."

"Yes, you can." A hand fell onto his shoulder and squeezed. "You're safe, buddy. Open your eyes."

He shook his head.

"Jackson! Open your eyes."

Cold water splashed against his face, washing away the dirt and mud, and his eyes flew open. Confused to see Ben crouching before him, he sat up for a better view.

"What is it? Do you see something?" Ben followed his stunned gaze.

"No." Disappointment landed like a truck load of wet cement on his chest as he slumped back against the bank. "Nothing."

"Come on. Let's get you out of here and stitched up. You took a hell of a beating." He lifted Jackson's arm, braced himself underneath, and hauled him up.

At the car, Ben wrapped a beach towel around Jackson's back and abdomen and handed him the ends. "Hold this and put pressure on it."

He did as he was told, surveying his battered body. Both skin and clothes were ripped and coated with a thick reddish-brown mixture, and every inch of him screamed with a new ferocity.

"Don't worry, buddy. You'll feel better when you're standing on the beach, looking out over the ocean." After a quick search for the nearest hospital, Ben pulled onto the road. "If we ever get there."

Chapter Three

✮ ✮ ✮

Jackson

A fter the storm, Jackson's body began to reject the effort it took to accumulate double-digit miles. He lost at least a week, recuperating longer in dark hotel rooms with little appetite and throbbing joints.

After checking in to their beachfront, two-bedroom condo in Myrtle Beach, South Carolina, he needed a break from it all, including his traveling partner. Less running meant more Ben, more stress, and more remembering.

To get away, he went for a walk and entered the first loud place he came to—a country music-theme restaurant and bar with line dancing and boisterous dancers, stomping in straight lines to crooning vocalists and twangy guitar music. Perfect for drowning out head noise and forgetting.

He took the bar stool no one ever wants—the isolated corner spot—and ordered a drink. Two beers later, he'd successfully established a hearty state of miserable. The combination of hooping country music enthusiasts and thumping speakers exacerbated his symptoms instead of overpowering them as he hoped.

That is until two women claimed stools on the opposite end of the bar, drawing his attention. Both were stunning, unforgettable in different ways. The woman with wavy, dark hair carried herself with an in-your-face conviction. She knew what she wanted and how to get it, unleashing that power on the bartender as she ordered for them both. Witnessing the poor guy succumb to her thick, fluttering eyelashes and sultry posture gave Jackson a chuckle.

The other woman, her opposite in every way, had straight, sand-colored hair that flowed down her back. Her confidence shone like a night light, subtle and alluring, and he couldn't look away. While her friend reminded him of a shot of brandy, she was ice cream on a summer day.

Everything about her called to him, her smile most of all. Because when the full force of it turned in his direction with a laugh, the war raging inside his head went astoundingly silent.

Drawn to her and mesmerized by the effect she had on him, he watched her talk to her friend while she sipped a beer and ate the meal she ordered. Calmness he hadn't felt in years, and certainly not the past several weeks, blanketed him when her twilight-blue eyes met his. Her friend whispered something in her ear, but she didn't look away, seemingly as struck by the gravitational pull between them as he was.

Urgency coiled around his ribcage. He had to meet her. As he prepared his vastly out of practice system for the shock it would soon endure in her proximity, the pair slipped from their stools and rushed to the dance floor.

While she moved with an unassuming grace, he couldn't look away. Each flash of spotlight showcased another angle of her beauty to take his breath away. But to his surprise, she found his gaze and held it whenever the line turned his way. She seemed to question the connection between them less with every moment they shared through the crowd.

The song soon ended, and she returned to the bar alone, giving him a chance to find out why her presence shook loose everything he'd come to understand about himself. As he made his way around the bar, she twisted in her seat to scan the room. He hoped she searched for him. She sank back in her seat and fanned her flushed face with a menu as he approached from behind, her sweet lavender scent smoothing the jagged edges of his nerves.

"Mind if I join you?" he asked.

Her head snapped around at the sound of his voice, offering him an easy smile and the empty seat beside her. "Please."

"I've never done this before, so I hope you can bear with me," he admitted, sliding onto the stool.

"What haven't you done?"

He looked down at his hands, embarrassed by his awkwardness. "Approach a beautiful woman in a bar."

"Oh, really? I thought all men were well versed in the matter."

"You would think so." Grateful for the banter, his heart settled into soft pulses. "I'm Jackson, by the way."

"Nice to meet you. I'm Emily. Are you a local or a tourist?"

"Tourist. You?"

"Same. My friend Genevieve and I have been talking about a vacation for a year and finally did it. What about you? Are you traveling with someone or here alone?"

"Both, really," he answered honestly. "I'm here alone tonight, and I'm traveling with someone."

"Are they not a fan of country music?"

"I'm not sure, but I do know he's a fan of country girls." She laughed, and it was all he wanted to hear for the rest of the night. "Most of the time, Ben's spring break, college boy personality is more than I can take. I needed a break tonight."

"I know what you mean. Genevieve loves this scene— the more noise and people the better. It drives me crazy sometimes. When did you arrive?"

"This morning." Hoping for a long conversation, he motioned for the bartender to bring him a beer. "Can I get you a drink?"

She checked the bottle sitting on the counter in front of her. "I'm okay. Thanks." Her eyes darted over his shoulder before she held up two thumbs and flashed a smile to rival the stars. "Speaking of handfuls. Here comes mine."

He turned to see her friend rushing toward them, her hair and ample curves bouncing with each hasty step. Her green eyes glowed in the neon lights, framing the bar ceiling, and opened wide when she noticed him.

"I'm gone barely ten minutes, and you give away my seat?" she teased and waited for Emily to introduce them.

As they talked, he could tell their bond ran deeper than a familiar, time-lasting friendship. They were like sisters who had endured life's ups and downs together, building something unbreakable. Their differences created a balance and unmatched strength. They were each other's axis point—their true north.

He had the same with each of his three friends, Billy, Josh, and Will. Losing them meant losing his direction. If Eleanor hadn't been there, serving as his guiding light and grounding system, he may not have found his way.

"Sam says there's a hot club around the corner," Genevieve's voice registered her excitement and reclaimed his attention. "Hot bartender," she clarified when Emily's eyes questioned. "Do you want to go?"

He rested both elbows on the bar to give them privacy, grabbed the cold beer the bartender—possibly Sam—set in front of him, and tried not to listen. But since they had to yell over the growing crowd, he couldn't help it.

"Come on. It'll be fun."

He glanced at Emily while she considered the invitation. Wanting more time with her, he silently willed her to stay.

"Well?" Genevieve persisted.

"I'm not sure I'm ready for another loud club just yet. Last night did me in for a while. Go have fun, and I'll join you in a bit."

"Are you sure?"

Emily glanced at him, catching his satisfied grin before he could hide it behind the bottle. "I'm sure. Text me the address when you get there and be safe."

"Alright. You, too."

She gave her friend a quick hug before spinning back into her seat. "Love that girl, but her battery lasts far longer than mine. So, where are you from?"

"Richmond, Virginia."

"Really? I've never been there, but I hear it's nice. What do you do? Are you escaping from work, too?"

"No. Just getting away to clear my head." He hated the vague answer but dampening the conversation with his depressing story would have been worse. Especially when the sunshine in her eyes and the way she looked at him—captivated and compassionate—made him forget about all of it. "What about you?"

"I'm a physical therapist. I've been at my current practice in Savannah for over a year, and it's been a dream… until recently." She took a deep breath instead of elaborating, and he guessed she tucked away something that made her uneasy. "Genevieve started her own public relations firm, and it's booming." She smiled, pride lifting up her beautiful features. "She's celebrating, and I'm doing a little head-clearing myself."

"Did something happen? If you don't mind me asking."

Her eyes darted away on a deep inhale before answering. "It's several things, really. The hardest was losing Joey, a young patient of mine. He had a hard time seeing that his misery wouldn't be permanent if he kept working at it. He took his own life after one of our appointments."

His muscles hardened, catapulting his stomach into his throat—a reflex he'd yet to find a way to control. Someday, he hoped to welcome thoughts of Will, and feel grateful for them, instead of bracing against them. He despised the regret and heart-ripping sadness that always followed.

She placed a hand on his shoulder to comfort him. But she did more than ease his anxiety. She neutralized every battle shredding him from the inside out.

"I'm sorry for your loss," he said, recovering, and took her hand from his shoulder to hold it in his. Her breathing quickened in reaction to his touch, making him want to do it again. "That must have been very difficult."

"Did you also lose someone, too?" she asked softly. "I don't mean to pry, but you seemed to relate."

He nodded without looking up. "My best friend Will two years ago."

On her gasp, he turned to her, the resurging ache dissolving away.

"I'm so sorry. I can't imagine how hard that must have been. I don't know what I'd do if I lost Genevieve."

"Let's hope you never find out."

The words lingered heavy in the air between them, creating an uprising of goosebumps across her arm.

"Would you like to dance?" she asked quickly, lifting the somber mood with her infectious energy.

"Sure."

Threading his fingers with hers, he followed her to the dance floor. The slower music, now a 90's country ballad, had thinned the lines of dancers into a manageable grouping of couples. She selected an empty spot and turned to face him, her direct gaze distorting and blurring the activity around them. If a simple touch of her hand silenced all his suffering, what would holding her do? He didn't know if his body could absorb the shock, but he couldn't continue to stand there, doing nothing and looking like a fool.

Breathing was an excellent place to start. He forced air into his lungs and circled an arm around her waist, the feel of her body jolting every cell in his malfunctioning system back to life. Like switching on a lamp, she reactivated everything dead inside him.

How could a stranger do that? He knew nothing about her, yet contentment flooded his system in her embrace as if they'd been warming each other for years.

Her head dropped to his shoulder, and if several overexuberant dancers hadn't bumped into them, he would have been happy to sway to their own beat for the rest of the night. But they were in the way. The upbeat music had resumed without their noticing, and the group pulsed once again at full capacity.

As the lines shifted away, they escaped to the bar, paid their tabs, then left to reclaim the serenity they'd found outside.

———

From the end of the pier where they'd stopped, the dotted sky above reflected on the ink-black water and cast the moon as a long, pale arrow, pointing directly at them. Jackson leaned on the rail and glanced down at her hand, marveling at how natural it felt in his.

"How long are you staying in Myrtle Beach?" she asked, her mesmerizing gaze stealing his thoughts for a moment.

"I'm not sure yet. What about you?"

"We leave on Tuesday."

That gave him four days to spend with her if she'd have him. "My turn."

"Your turn? Are we playing twenty questions?" She giggled, turning her body to face him. "Alright, go for it."

"What do you like to do for fun?"

"Read. What's your full name?"

"Jackson Gabriel Vane."

"Nice. Where do—"

Bringing her hand to his lips, he silenced the question she'd planned to ask, loving how her lashes fluttered in response. "It's not your turn."

"Sorry."

Her pulse tripped under his fingertips, showcasing how the new intimate touch affected her. Lingering there a little too long, his bloodless brain could only assemble one simple question. "What's your favorite color?"

"Blue. The same ocean blue as your eyes."

The sultry way her eyes fixed on him started a new war to fight. Give in to desire or be the gentleman Eleanor raised him to be. That line wouldn't be so muddled if their bodies hadn't fused together—that inescapable gravitational pull between them dialed up to maximum. He hadn't noticed moving closer until her slightly breathless tone activated parts of him he'd forgotten about. For the first time, waving an enormous white flag like cheerleaders at college football games after a touchdown had his body screaming for him to go for two.

"Where…uh…is the farthest you've traveled?" she asked in a thick whisper, telling him she felt it, too.

"Thailand."

"Your turn," she encouraged when he continued to drink her in.

"Right." He brushed away the strands of hair a breeze tossed into her face and let his eyes wander over her. The light dusting of freckles on her nose, the feel of her silky hair, and the soft curve of her bottom lip. She licked her lips and caught the pink, glossy skin between her teeth, sending his need to kiss more than her hand spiraling. "Can I see you tomorrow?"

"I thought you'd never—Oh, no." She dug into the small purse draped over her shoulder. "What time is it?"

He twisted his wrist to check his watch. "Wow. Almost one o'clock."

"I should go check on G."

"Okay."

Reluctantly, they strolled up the pier toward the address Genevieve texted.

"I have another question," she said.

"Nope. That's a violation."

"What is?"

"You never answered my last question, so until you do…"

She smiled and bumped him off stride with her shoulder. "I would love for you to see me tomorrow."

"Good. Now, you can ask your question."

"Thank goodness," she teased. "Such a stickler for the rules, you are."

"Following the rules has been engrained into my DNA."

"Let me guess… you went to a military school or were in the military."

"Served in the Marines for eight years."

"Did you do any tours overseas?"

"Two." With considerable effort, he suppressed the ache that wound around his heart. "Almost three."

"Did you not like it?"

Surprised by the question, his gaze shot to hers. He thought he'd been successful in hiding his reflex response.

"I'm sorry. I didn't mean to—"

"You didn't do anything," he said to set her mind at ease, then looked ahead. "Mind if we sit for a minute?"

They claimed a bench near the entrance to the pier. While he gathered his thoughts, staring blankly at their hands still linked together and resting on his thigh, she studied him.

"Everything okay?"

"When you asked if I liked being in the military, I know I made you think I didn't. It was a gut reaction for a different reason." He lifted his eyes to hers and wished he hadn't dulled them with worry. "Being a Marine was all I ever wanted. Well, that and to see the world." He smiled when she did, all anxiety and tension fading away with the tranquility that one small sentiment poured into him. "What?"

"I've always wanted to travel, and Thailand is top on my list. Maybe you can tell me about it sometime."

He nodded and raised her hand to his lips again, suddenly willing to tell her everything.

"I'm sorry for interrupting." The sound of her voice drew his gaze to her lips. "Please go on."

"Well," he began, trying to remember where he'd left off. The hint of desire in her eyes made thinking near impossible. With a forced inhale, he rallied together enough details to continue. "The military was supposed to be my lifelong career. I loved it."

"Did something happen?"

"Our convoy was ambushed in enemy territory. My best friend and I were the only survivors. He saved my life."

"Will?"

"Yes. He tried to save two more, but they didn't make it."

"I can't imagine how terrifying that must have been. Did he have PTSD afterward?"

"Yes."

"And you, too, I imagine." His silence confirmed it. "How badly were you injured?"

He looked away, his long recovery and Will on his mind.

"We don't have to talk about this," she soothed, noticing his hesitation, and draped an arm over his shoulders. Tucking a leg under her, she scooted closer.

"Thanks. It's a long and miserable story, and we've had such a good time." His thumb grazed over her soft knuckles. Strange how their hands hadn't parted since he took hers at the bar. Yet, it didn't feel strange at all. It felt right. "I don't want that to be the last thing we talk about tonight."

"Another time, then." She smiled and rested her chin on his shoulder. "Does that mean you're not coming with me to the club?"

Everything in him wanted to. "I should get back and make sure Ben is alive and not in jail."

Glancing over his shoulder, passion snapped into the air. If he shifted slightly, his lips would be on hers.

To keep himself in gentleman territory, he stood and pulled her to her feet. He tucked her hair around her ear, letting his fingers slide down to the end, his eyes following. "Thank you."

"For what?" she asked with a curious smile.

"For listening and being here."

"It feels like this is where I'm supposed to be."

The surprising confession, the silky tone coating the words, and the meaning behind it sent a jolt through his chest. "Yes, it does."

"How?"

"I don't know. Does it matter?"

"No."

There they stayed on the edge of a crowded sidewalk, clinging to each other, unable to break the connection. Emotion buzzed under his skin, bouncing back and forth between them like a current through live wires with her as the power source.

Weary of fighting with himself, his head tilted closer in search of reservations. Conviction flickered in her eyes and called for him to do anything except hold back. Her lips parted in anticipation as her breathing stalled. Feeling nothing but her warmth and a new river of desire coursing through him, his lips hovered feather-light over hers as a car screeched to a stop nearby, the driver holding down the horn.

Instinct jerked him upright as terror shot through him like a flaming arrow. He searched for the threat but found nothing out of sorts… except him.

"Maybe we should keep moving," she said gently, but he couldn't make his body obey while his brain still strained to process reality verses memory.

It took meeting her empathetic gaze to set the final pieces back into place. "Okay."

Falling in step together toward the club, his arm banded around her waist like a clutch. He hoped he hadn't frightened her. That she hadn't noticed his panic—at least not to the level he felt it.

"I think this is it," she said when they came to a large metal building painted a muted black and neon green. A loud noise masquerading as music boomed through the open door. "It's not my idea of fun, but she loves it." Staring at her destination, she sighed before turning back to him. "See you tomorrow?"

The sparkle in her eyes nearly crippled him, and he had to stop himself from picking up where they left off before the past slapped him in the face. "Looking forward to it. How about eleven at the pier?"

"Deal. Be safe walking back."

He watched her rush across the street and glance back from the doorway. The second she disappeared inside, he snapped. The string that had been holding him together yanked away, spinning his thoughts and emotions like a top.

Breathless and unsteady from the rush, he dropped to the curb.

Looking up at the night sky, he thought of Will. "This was all your doing, wasn't it?" The stars seemed to flicker in response, giving him an amused chuckle. "Using your room-brightening talents in heaven, I see. Well, thanks for saving me again, buddy. You've outdone yourself with Emily."

With his heart and mind back to normal again, he stood on wobbly knees and headed toward the hotel.

Chapter Four

✩ ✩ ✩

Emily

I't's about time you showed up," Genevieve yelled over the music. "Where have you been?"

The dark, throbbing club with its pulsating lights and screaming inhabitants felt like a different world from the fairytale Emily left outside. "We took a walk."

"Ah. Is he as wonderful as he is hot?" Her smile widened when Emily nodded. "He didn't come with you?"

"No."

"But you got his number, right?"

"Actually, I forgot."

"How are you—"

"We made plans to meet tomorrow."

"That's my girl. Let's get you a drink and rejoice in how clever I am." She motioned for the waitress. "I told you something special would happen tonight."

"Yes. You're the smartest of them all."

By the time the waitress delivered another round of drinks, Emily sat alone at the table while Genevieve danced. Happy to avoid the rowdy mob of sweaty bodies, she took a moment to reset from the shock to the system that was Jackson Vane.

She watched Genevieve and Sam move to the beat while several other men circled and salivated nearby like hungry wolves on the prowl. While she found the usual spectacle entertaining, it didn't prevent her thoughts from wandering back to her almost kiss with Jackson.

The world she'd forgotten existed in his arms interrupted the moment, and she wished he could have stayed. What she wouldn't give for another chance to peer into his eyes and feel the magnificent way her skin shimmered under his touch. The sensation still lingered but not as potent.

As if granting her wish, he appeared across the room, but only in flashes whenever spotlights grazed the crowd— her brain torturing her with visions of her heart's newest and most intense desire.

Real or not, his eyes zeroed in on her. His long strides carried him with determination and urgency quickly to her.

"Jackson?"

She jumped off the stool as his hands cupped her face, his lips proving he was most definitely and intensely real. She expected fireworks to accompany his kiss, but not like this. Electric shockwaves, carrying every hopeless romantic sensation she'd convinced herself wasn't possible, rattled through her body. Her head floated in a dream while soft, possessive hands held the rest of her in place.

Tilting for another angle to explore, she didn't recognize the person now grasping handfuls of his hair for balance. With that one compelling kiss, she stood on the edge of life finally ready to jump. She no longer feared letting go or the unknowns that always held her back.

Soaking in every ounce of this beautiful man, she leaned forward and fell head-first into her fantasy.

———

Jackson

His mind went blank the moment he touched her. Every doubt that tortured him on the way there vanished with the brush of her lips. For the first time in years, he could feel again. He wasn't empty inside after all. He'd only been waiting for her.

Somewhere between seeing her across the bar that night and feeling her melt into him, she claimed the heart now colliding recklessly with his ribcage. Drawing back, he couldn't hide how she'd affected him.

"Am I dreaming?" she asked, breathless and clutching the cut of his biceps for support.

"If you are, so am I." His forehead rested against hers as he wrangled the web of feelings that came with her kiss. They were making a spectacle, but he couldn't stop himself from getting swept away by the magnitude of this moment.

Distracted with the feel of her skin tingling under his fingertips, she surprised him by rising onto her toes. Her lips collided with his through the movement, and he tried not demand too much. Tried not to consume everything she offered like a starving animal. But her body shuddered, her lips gave without request, and her roaming hands disintegrated his control.

"I'm not usually this bold," she said, separating from him before he could locate his bearings. Her head fell back to meet his gaze. "Did you already find Ben?"

With their bodies still compelled together, he appreciated the diversion to a safer topic. It was unlike him to get carried away, especially surrounded by a sea of strangers and unfamiliar territory. He needed to summon his training and get a grip. "No. I couldn't leave."

"I'm so glad you didn't. Stay with me, Jackson."

Four little words. That was all it took to set him back ten-fold. In answer, he held her hands to his lips—the intimate gesture just as electric as a kiss.

After settling onto the tall stools at their table, Genevieve returned, both out of breath and flushed. The DJ had taken a break, reducing the music to a tolerable level.

"What are you doing here?" Genevieve asked him.

"Change of plans."

"I see." She winked at Emily. "I've had enough of this place. Ready to get out of here and try something new?"

"What about Sam?"

"He had to take his friend home. He'll meet us where we land. Anywhere you'd like to go?"

Emily turned to him. "You needed to check on Ben, right?"

"I should."

"Want to go together?"

"Sure." He'd do anything with her by his side, he thought while texting Ben to get his location. His immediate response drew out a rare chuckle. "Time to close the loop."

After a short walk, the trio found themselves back inside the country bar. The crowd, twice the size as before, pulse with the music now set to concert level.

"I'll come find you," Genevieve promised and rushed to the dance floor.

Expecting to find Ben at the bar, he guided Emily in that direction. "There he is." He pointed through the crowd to the booths on the far side, where Ben had a woman cradled under each arm.

"Jackson! What are you doing here?" he asked as they emerged from the cluster of people, waiting for drinks.

"Checking in. Everything all right?"

"What do you think?" He huddled the girls closer, and Jackson rolled his eyes. "How about you? I see you're shockingly not alone."

He introduced Emily, and Ben uncoiled an arm to shake her hand, holding on for a bit to study her, his eyes alive with both pride and suspicion.

One of the girls slid out of the booth, eyeing Jackson from head to toe with a sultry look as she rose. "Hey! Where are you going?" Ben called after her, then jerked his shoulders. "Where'd you two meet?"

"Funny story…we met here," Emily answered.

"Here? I didn't see you. I've been here for hours."

"It was earlier. We went—"

"There you are." Genevieve interrupted stopped behind Emily, placing a hand on her shoulder. She used the same hand to toss her hair back after the sudden motion sent it flowing over her shoulder. "I'm getting a drink. You want anything?"

Jackson's eyes took another, deeper roll when Ben's jaw dropped open, and his arm not-so-slyly unraveled from around the shoulders of the last woman in the booth.

"No, thanks." Emily turned to Ben. "This is my friend, Genevieve. Genevieve, this is Ben."

And just like that, all his charm bled from his body, taking with it his ability to speak. *Classic Ben*, Jackson thought and hoped no one else noticed his gawking.

Unfazed, Genevieve tossed up a wave before pivoting toward the bar.

"Wait a minute," Ben managed. "Who was that?"

"My best friend, Genevieve." Emily pinched her lips to suppress a laugh when the girl sitting next to Ben puffed her bangs with an audible sigh and pushed him out of the booth. Clearly, weary of being ignored.

Emily and Jackson moved aside as Ben tumbled out of the booth, allowing her room to storm off in dramatic fashion.

"I could use a beer," Ben said absently, slapping Jackson on the arm as he passed.

Shaking his head, he held up the full beer bottle Ben left on the table, making Emily laugh. "Think you should warn her?"

"Absolutely not. I just wish I had a better view of the show."

Claiming the vacated booth, they sat close on the same side. He pulled her lips to his before saying a word, amazed by how at ease he felt with her already—affectionate and satisfied, yet always needing more.

"That was fun," Ben complained as he dropped into the booth empty-handed.

"What's the matter? Was she not interested in the Ben Stevens charm?" Jackson rested an arm on the back of the booth behind Emily. "She did have plans to meet someone here."

"No shit. He just showed up."

"Sorry, Ben. She can be a little ruthless sometimes," she empathized, unnecessarily, Jackson mused. Ben got what was coming to him. "Hope she wasn't too rude."

"I can take it, and I don't give up that easily." He leaned back, then straightened again when Genevieve appeared beside the booth.

"Hey, Em. We're going to get out of here. Don't wait up." She winked over her shoulder before disappearing into the crowd with Sam following close behind.

"There's always tomorrow," Emily told Ben. "They never last long."

For the next twenty minutes, Jackson and Emily attempted to lift his spirits with casual conversation, but he continued to sulk. When Emily excused herself for a visit to the ladies' room, he ambushed Jackson. "What the hell, man?"

"What?" He'd been expecting this.

"You know what. You didn't look at one woman this entire trip, no matter who I dangled in front of you. The one time you go out by yourself, you come back with *her*." He tossed his hand in the direction Emily went, then slumped back in against the booth.

Jackson bit back a grin. "What's your problem?"

"You've been a shitty wingman. That's my problem. And when you finally do what I knew you could, I'm not there. I could have been the one with her friend right now."

There it is. Rejection was a hard pill to swallow. "Doesn't matter. You wouldn't have had a chance, anyway."

"Oh, no? Fuck you."

"What'd I miss?" Emily asked, taking in the scene. Ben's brooding had worsened, and the guilty grin on Jackson's face surely told her he played a part.

"Not a thing," Jackson answered with a yawn.

"Are we keeping you up?"

Rolling his eyes, Ben grabbed the beer he'd abandoned earlier. "He's not used to staying out this late."

"Really? I pictured you two out living it up every night."

"I wish," he grumbled. "He acts like an old man— usually in bed by eleven. It's a total buzz kill."

"Sounds like my speed." She turned to flash Jackson a smile. "I don't like staying out late either."

"Then you two are made for each other."

Jackson held her gaze, knowing Ben was right. He could feel it in his bones.

"Well, if you're ready for some peace and quiet, I could use an escort back to the condo," she said, her brow popping up with suggestion.

Desire flared inside him. "It *is* getting late."

Together, they scooted out of the booth, ignoring Ben's protests.

"Nice meeting you, Ben," she called as Jackson pulled her away.

———

Standing outside her condo, he held her as he searched for a way to let go. He went to the club earlier, not only because he longed for her but because the war in his head resumed the instant he left. The farther he walked, the louder his symptoms became. Her absence, coupled with the raging war, nearly broke him, and he wasn't looking forward to doing it again.

With a sigh, she drew back to look up at him. "Eleven o'clock sharp."

"Yes, ma'am." He held her hand to his lips, and forced a step back, then another and another until she disappeared inside.

Eight hours. He'd endure anything for eight hours if it meant seeing her again.

Chapter Five

★ ★ ★

Jackson

Jackson tossed and turned the remainder of the night. He'd racked up enough sleepless nights during the journey for it not to cause alarm, but this one felt different. As his head hit the pillow, war raged at a new level, all because he had a little taste of freedom, and it was gone.

For a few short hours, he had a reprieve from the pain, freeing him to feel again—desire, longing, passion, affection. Sensations he'd given up on ever genuinely feeling again.

Until now.

The throbbing reduced to a manageable level by mid-morning, allowing for just enough time to get ready and walk to the pier. His misery would soon be over.

"Going somewhere?" Ben asked when he saw Jackson leaving the hall bathroom after a shower, wearing khaki shorts instead of his usual workout gear.

He kept watch by the door as Jackson picked through his suitcase for a shirt. "You know what?" he asked, continuing when Jackson ignored him—an annoying habit he picked up over the last month. The man could never read a room. "In all the weeks we've been at this, you've never swayed from your routine. You get up before the crack of dawn, eat on a tight schedule, and go to bed at the same time most nights." With a smirk, he paused when Jackson scowled at him through the mirror before slipping on a shirt. "She must be special."

He grabbed his wallet from the dresser, the anticipation of seeing Emily again growing with every second he wasted with Ben.

"How about the four of us get together tonight?" Ben suggested, finally getting to the reason for the one-sided conversation.

"Maybe. You have competition, remember?"

"Whatever. A bartender is no match for this unemployed hunk of meat. I'll have her melting in my hands by the end of the night."

"End of the night? Not the usual confidence with this one?"

"You know the saying… under promise and over deliver."

Jackson stalked by him. "I'm leaving."

"Good. It's about time you got some." Ben mirrored his hurried pace down the hall. "But don't get her pregnant," he added with a laugh before the door slammed shut.

————

He arrived first at the pier and waited for Emily at the end where they talked the night before. Street artists, vendors, and joyful families packed the area, the air brimming with happy expectation. He wanted to feel the same, but the night had been long and miserable.

Then, with her in his sights, it all drifted away as if the eight-hour torture session never happened. Pushing from the rail, he made his way through the dense crowd to meet her.

She smiled and took his hand as if it was the natural thing to do. "Looking for me?"

My entire life, he thought before checking himself. "Of course."

"What do you want to do today?" she asked.

"Ever ridden one before?" He tilted his head toward the Ferris wheel behind her, making her glance over her shoulder.

"It's been a while, and none that big. Let's do it."

Navigating to the ticket booth, they found the line of expectant riders and settled in to wait.

"Get any sleep last night?" Her flirty smile made it near impossible to maintain a gentlemanly, first-date distance. Not to mention she looked even more stunning with the sunlight on her face—if that were possible.

"Not one second. You?"

"None."

They moved forward a spot.

"How was Ben this morning?"

"He's still upset about Genevieve's rejection and wants us all to get together tonight, so he can try again."

"I think that can be arranged. I like him."

"He's going to make a fool of himself," he declared, hoping he won't have anything to clean up after she dismantled him. "He's not used to women like her."

"Oh, yeah? What type of woman is he used to?"

"You saw the two he was with when we found him. What do you think?"

She couldn't hold back a laugh, the melodic sound floating with the breeze. "He has no idea what he's in for. She's going to eat him for dessert."

"I'd like to see that, actually."

"Then, it's a date."

After purchasing tickets, they followed the signs to a boarding area, soon climbing inside a glass-enclosed gondola on the Ferris wheel. Still holding hands, they sat together on the same side, facing the ocean.

"I can't wait to see the beach view from the top," she mentioned, her voice quivering slightly with nerves. They sat close in the intimate space like they've been doing it for years, yet the air simmered with excitement at discovering something new.

As the wheel took them higher on the first loop, her delight with the 360-degree views took over, and she lost herself in the thrill. She pointed at interesting scenes off in the distance, and he followed her gaze each time, her enthusiasm fueling his own.

On the third go-round, she settled back in her seat to enjoy the ride. "So, Jackson Vane, what do you do in Richmond?"

He looked out over the beach and attempted to assemble a description of his current situation that wouldn't make him sound like an impulsive lunatic. "Well, that's complicated."

"No problem. I'd like to know… if you're comfortable telling me, of course."

"I don't mind. It's just not easy to explain."

Bending a leg under her, she turned to face him, batting her eyelashes, and making him laugh.

"Alright. I told you about my disrupted military career and being discharged because of my injuries. They were too severe and the recovery too extensive. My doctors weren't sure I'd ever walk again."

"You proved them wrong. How long did it take?"

"Two years. But without the Marines, I have no idea what I want to do with my life."

His honesty touched her, and empathy shown in her eyes. "Do you mind if I ask about your injuries?"

"Of course not. You can ask me anything." He told her about the damage to his legs and surgeries and answered her questions. "I needed a wheelchair for a while, and had a long, painful recovery to get to where I am now, physically and mentally."

"You must have been so lost."

Tears glistened in her eyes, and he wondered what she was thinking. As a physical therapist, she understood how difficult it can be to learn to walk again, and how that can affect a person mentally with or without trauma.

"How did you get through it? You must have a large support network at home."

"Just Eleanor, really." She helped him through the worst days of his life.

When her eyes questioned, he continued. "Eleanor is a close family friend. She's been on my side my entire life, and I'm not sure I would have survived without her."

"She sounds like an amazing woman who loves you very much."

"She is, and she does. The feeling's mutual," he said with a shy smile and brushed the sand on the floor with his shoe.

The Ferris wheel began to slow, stopping at intervals to let passengers on and off.

"Are you here looking for a job?"

"No. We're here as part of a larger trip."

"Oh. So, you and Ben are traveling around?"

"Kind of."

She scrunched her face. "You're being very mysterious."

An attendant opening the door to their compartment interrupted the explanation he geared up to deliver. Exiting the platform, they meandered through the exit ropes until reaching the pier, where he pulled her in for a kiss. "I've been wanting to do that since you got here."

"And I've wanted you to do that since I got here." Her lashes fluttered open as her body molded into his. "What were we talking about?"

He laughed. "You accused me of being mysterious."

"Oh, yeah. You're making me pry information out of you."

"Sorry. How about we grab lunch, and I'll tell you all about it?"

"Deal."

They walked down the strip and picked a quaint little bistro with local flair. After ordering, Emily propped her elbow on the table, the commotion of the open dining room barely registering.

"The time has come, mystery man. Tell me about your trip."

"Okay. I'm just going to get it out. Then, we can work backward from there."

"Now, I'm really curious."

He took a calming breath when his body tensed, remembering the shocked reactions from the others he'd told along the way. "I'm running to Orlando."

"That's amazing." She sat up, unable to conceal her enthusiasm. "Please tell me more, or should I ask the thousand questions racing through my mind?"

"Is that a pun?"

"Maybe."

Grateful she wasn't treating him as if he belonged in an asylum, he relaxed. "I'll try to explain, and you can ask any questions that remain."

He told her about losing his friends—Billy and Josh— in the explosion and his own struggles with PTSD. "I needed to do something to honor them and veterans who struggled as Will and I did. To pay Will back for saving my life, I'd hoped this journey would help me find my future path and ways to make a difference. I can't sit around doing nothing, wasting this second chance. There has to be a purpose for me—a reason why I was spared. I just haven't found it yet."

"Oh, Jackson."

"Running has always been my outlet. A way to think, reconnect to what's important, and heal. I thought taking this trip would be the answer, and it worked for the first few weeks. I'd never felt better, but that all changed recently."

"Why do you think that is?"

"I'm not sure. A test, maybe, to prepare me for what's next. It hasn't been easy, and the further I go, the more my symptoms return. But you know what?"

Her eyes brightened, and she leaned forward, anxious to hear what had moved him so profoundly. "What?"

"When I saw you and every minute we're together, all I'm dealing with vanishes." He still had no idea how, but her presence did that for him and more.

She reached a hand across the table, and he took it.

"I don't know what to say."

"You don't have to say anything. I just wanted you to know."

Her breathing quickened, matching his pulse, while she soaked in the meaning behind his words. "Myrtle Beach seems a little out of the way between Richmond and Orlando. Did you have a reason to come here?"

"This is the last of my three planned stops. First was Eleanor in a little town south of Richmond, then Will's parents in North Carolina. I met his girlfriend for the first time there."

"No wonder you were feeling so good in the beginning."

"Exactly. The guys and I had always wanted to come here but never did." She squeezed his hand, keeping the ache from creeping back in. "Getting to Orlando from here is a mystery."

She smiled at his joke, quick and adorable. "One more to add to the Jackson Vane story. When did you leave Richmond?" she asked, sitting back as the waiter arrived to drop off their plates.

"April first."

"Wow. You've been at this for over a month. Aren't you tired?"

"That's why we're staying a little longer than we do in most places. I need to repair. Plus…" He grinned over his fork. "I found another reason to stay."

"When are you leaving?"

"Whenever you do."

A gleam in her eye gave him a glimpse of her satisfaction with his decision, and he basked in it. "Why Orlando?" she asked.

"I needed a destination far enough away to be a challenge. Since the four of us went there several times when we were young—our first taste of adventure—it seemed like the perfect finale."

"I bet you were a handful together."

"You could say that."

"How does it all work? Running, Ben, days off, all of it." She stabbed a carrot with her fork and nibbled. "I'm fascinated."

"I usually leave early in the morning before Ben comes out of his drunken coma." He paused when she laughed, his new favorite sound, then recounted a typical day of running, meeting for meals, hotels, luggage exchanges, and resting. "It's a lot of coordination, and surprisingly, he hasn't let me down."

"That's surprising?"

"Ben and I weren't friends before this. We went to high school together, but I didn't know him very well. His joining me happened last minute." He thought of his conversation with Harrison the night before he left and how he'd been right to worry. The journey to Orlando would have been infinitely harder on his own, especially during the rough patches. He could see that now. "I thought that I needed to do this alone."

"I'm glad you didn't."

"But it doesn't change the fact that Ben is unbearable at times. We're complete opposites."

"Yeah, you are. Though, I'd be willing to bet there's more to him than he's shown."

"I've seen glimpses. They've just been too rare to put my money on yet."

Picking up her wrap, she giggled. "What is he doing to drive you crazy?"

"That's quite the list. I'm not sure we have time." He lifted his wrist to pretend to check the time.

"Funny."

"Let me count the ways," he began, loving the way her eyes sparkled in amusement. "He goes out every night. I don't know how he does it. I think he's making up for lost time."

"Lost time from what?"

"In high school, he was a scrawny, awkward kid and always a mess. I think he felt ignored by most everyone. Since then, he's been working out, taking care of himself, and forming an unhealthy addiction to women."

"Ahh. So, he's showing the world what they missed out on all those years."

"Exactly. Although, I shouldn't complain. All the trouble he finds gets me out of the hotel and out of my head."

"What do you mean? Aren't you his trusty wingman?"

Jackson nearly choked on the chicken he was chewing and coughed. "Never," he managed after a sip of water. "In fact, Ben brought that up last night when you left the table."

"What? All the women you two have picked up along the way?" She grinned through a bite, a little too proud in her teasing.

"Not even close. He complained because the one time he wasn't there, I found you."

"I noticed he was upset, but I don't understand."

"In his words, I'm a shitty wingman. I haven't been with any women on this trip—talked to or otherwise. No matter how bad he wanted me to."

"Why would he care if you did? Doesn't look like he needs a wingman."

"He thinks he does to pick up women like Genevieve. The others became insignificant at the first sight of her."

"What else is new? I should have welcomed him to the club."

"What?"

"Metaphorically speaking. His reaction happens to all men."

"Not all," he corrected.

"Right. Thank goodness for that. But I still don't understand why he's upset with you about last night."

"He's convinced he would have found more women of Genevieve's caliber along the way if I hadn't been so disinterested."

"Disinterested? Wouldn't a handsome, single man like yourself be flirting and living it up on an adventure like yours? You're kind of a magnet."

"You think so?"

She leaned forward again, and whispered, "Big time," then returned to her meal. "So, why did you disappoint all those women? I'm sure there were many begging for your attention."

"I wouldn't go that far. Healing and working toward the goal were all I cared about. The last thing I wanted was to be with or talk to anyone."

"You talked to me."

"You're different."

"Why?"

"I don't know. You just are."

His mind went blank at the confession. She was special, and he wanted no one else. The finality of that realization made his heart hammer in his chest. The server stopping by to refill their glasses provided the disruption he needed to gather himself and not sound like a blubbering fool with his next words.

After finishing their meals and paying the bill, he suggested a walk on the beach.

"What are you thinking about?" he asked a while later. She'd been quiet since leaving the restaurant. Now, she sat beside him, lost in thought with her knees up and feet buried in the sand.

She turned to face him. "You, and how much I want you to kiss me."

And just like that, his survival depended on satisfying her command. With a hand on her cheek, he drew her close. The first touch of her lips made the waves recede into the ocean, the people on the beach disappear, and the sun's rays dance around them in radiant and colorful patterns. For a moment, there was only her.

When he could summon the resolve to release her, she took a long, steadying breath. "Ready to head back? I need to get all this sand off me before dinner."

Consumed with her, he ran a hand lightly down her leg to brush the sand off her skin, his eyes following. "You're so beautiful."

"Jackson," she said on an exhale before he kissed her again.

Urgency pulsed through him, and she responded, giving more than she allowed herself to take. But he'd soon change that. She deserved the world, and he'd make sure she had it.

———

Emily

At the condo, Emily searched for Genevieve, finding her asleep on a lounge chair beside the pool. Four empty plastic cups littered the deck around her.

"Lush," she accused jokingly, and quietly seized an empty cup. After filling it with pool water, she suppressed a laugh with her free hand as she tilted the cup above Genevieve's abdomen.

"Don't even think about it," she warned, her eyes still closed.

"I have no idea what you're talking about." Tucking the evidence behind her back, Emily emptied the contents before sitting on the adjacent chair.

"Yeah, right. Where have you been? I had to start the party without you."

"Looks like you started and ended it without me."

"Ha, ha." Reaching for the bottled water in her bag, Genevieve opened it and gulped down half. "My throat feels like I've run a marathon."

"You probably have all these drinks to thank for that." She kicked the closest empty cup and watched it roll under Genevieve's chair.

"But they were so yummy."

"Glad you've had a nap. We have plans tonight."

"You want to go out tonight? I figured by now you'd be begging for a little boring and blah." Genevieve tilted her head and grinned.

"Not tonight. We have a double date. I guess yours doesn't have to be a date, but two gorgeous men are joining us for dinner tonight."

"Oh." She downed the rest of the water. "Does that mean your date went well?"

"Better."

"So, you get Steamy Eyes, and I have to put up with…what's his name again?"

"Ben. And don't be like that," she scolded when Genevieve frowned. "He likes you."

"I barely spoke to him."

"Since when do you have to speak for men to fall over themselves for you."

"True." She flashed a proud grin. "But you know what I like, and he's obviously not that."

"You can't know that already. Apparently, he's quite the ladies' man."

"That's my point. What ladies' man," she asked, motioning quotation marks with her fingers, "actually knows what he's doing? They're usually obnoxious newbies." When Emily glared at her, she relented and tossed up her hands. "Don't worry, I'll be on my best behavior."

"Somehow, I doubt that." Emily's leg sprang into a nervous bounce. "I really like him, G."

"I know, and I'm happy for you. Come on. Let's go get you ready to knock his socks off, and you can tell me about your hot date."

She patted Emily on the knee before gathering her bag and standing. But on the way up, she lost her balance, tumbling back into the nearby fence.

"Are you okay?" Jumping over the chair, she grabbed hold of the arm Genevieve wasn't using to hug a fence post.

"Yeah." With a deep breath, she straightened and attempted to focus on Emily's face. "Got a little dizzy. Too much sun, I guess."

"Or too much alcohol."

"Not possible." She allowed Emily to take her hand and lead her toward the gate. "You know I don't get drunk."

"No. Not since sophomore year of college when you puked all over… What was his name? It was something unusual."

"Alessandre."

"Yes. Alessandre with his stringy black hair and ponytail."

"His name means 'warrior.' You can't be a warrior without a ponytail."

"Agreed." She patted the arm Genevieve draped around hers. "But I believe he was also the only man to ever turn you down."

"Ha! The bastard. But I don't blame him. I had covered us both in strawberry margarita vomit." Laughing at the memory, her energy surged. "There," she added with a deep breath as the elevator door chimed and opened, "all better."

While they got ready for dinner, Emily recounted her date and Jackson's past, what he'd told her at least. He'd held back some of his story, but at least he felt safe enough with her to start. Then, she explained his trip.

"Where does Ladies' Man fit into all this?" Genevieve asked, holding up a blouse and tossing it aside.

"He's helping with logistics. Jackson said they got together right before he left."

"Just so we're clear. I'm only going because you asked." She pulled on a tank top and wiggled the tight fabric into place, straining the fibers across her breasts. "And I'm starving."

"Understood, but he doesn't have a chance with you in that outfit."

Genevieve glanced down at the mile of cleavage showing and shrugged. She watched Emily turn side to side, checking her own outfit in the mirror. On the third spin, her short fuse sent her patience up in smoke. "You look beautiful. Let's go."

Chapter Six

☆ ☆ ☆

Jackson

Uncharacteristically fidgety, Jackson's pulse skipped inside him as he scanned the restaurant from the bar.

The popular seafood restaurant overlooking the pier had an extensive waiting list that night. With every table in the multi-level space taken, the lobby, bar, and sidewalk outside had been full of patient customers since they arrived an hour early—not to secure a table or prominent spot on the list, but because Ben couldn't sit still in the hotel for more than two minutes at a time. His excitement to get the evening started wore on Jackson's nerves until waiting in a loud, confined space had more appeal than their cozy living room.

When the door opened, allowing a stream of sunshine into the restaurant, his eyes cut immediately to Emily as she and Genevieve entered. Ben followed his gaze, his next random comment cut short by his dangling jaw.

"You're drooling," he informed Ben, pushing from his stool to reach an arm around Emily's waist and peck her cheek.

She smelled of the flowers he now wished he'd brought and looked even better in the short lavender sundress. She wore more makeup than she had earlier in the day, highlighting her eyes and lips.

"Long time no see," she joked. "You guys remember, Genevieve."

"Of course. Nice to see you again," Jackson greeted, then turned to Ben to find his stunned expression hadn't changed.

"Hi." Genevieve reached out a hand, but instead of shaking it, Ben raised it to his lips and kissed the top.

She shot Emily an *I'm-going-to-kill-you* look, which to her dismay, was ignored. Jackson held back a chuckle as the scene unfolded before him.

You owe me, Emily mouthed back before leaning closer to whisper in his ear. "He's digging himself into a hole."

"This is nothing. Just wait until he's had a few more drinks."

As he said it, a flash of sympathy smacked Jackson across the chest. If Ben couldn't wrangle himself, the alcohol he would soon guzzle like a fire hose would send him crashing and burning at Genevieve's feet. Then again, a hard lesson in humility would do him some good.

Crash away, my friend, he thought, all sympathy forgotten. Ben looked over his shoulder and flashed a big, goofy smile, and Jackson tipped his beer in salute. *Yep, crash and burn.*

———

Emily

While they ate, Ben's lively personality commanded the conversation. His stories, while entertaining and sometimes charming, couldn't hold Emily's attention. She kept getting consumed by Jackson's gaze or the feel of his hand on her leg. But when story time switched to their journey to Myrtle Beach, she tuned back in.

"I heard you take photos of his trip. Can I see them?" She glanced over her shoulder at Jackson for permission.

"My life is an open book thanks to him." He waved for Ben to show her the social media page.

"Start at the end and scroll up for the progression."

She accepted the phone and started at the first photo of Jackson at Will's grave as Ben instructed. Her heart hurt as she read the caption.

"Jackson, you take my breath away." She continued scrolling and reading until she came to a photo of him standing outside a diner with a young woman. "Who's this?"

"You should ask Ben that question."

She turned to him and held up the phone.

When all color left his face and he struggled to explain, Jackson came to the rescue. "That's Julie. She was our waitress at a diner we found on the first day and taken with Ben's irresistible charm."

"I don't know. She looks quite taken with you in this picture," Emily teased.

"That's just Ben's artistry coming through."

Pinching her lips in amusement, she nodded before continuing through the photos that followed. "You've met a lot of people over the last month."

"I didn't set out to."

"Who are they?"

"Veterans and families of veterans. They seem to come across my path wherever I stop, and each has left a mark on me."

"I can tell," she said, noticing how his eyes softened as he glanced at the photos. "This one is so touching." She pointed to a photo of Jackson sitting at a tiny table with an older man in a diner. His clothes were frayed along the seams, and the faded navy cap he wore had 'VETERAN' embroidered across the front. Jackson's hand rested on his bony shoulder as the man hunched over a plate of food. "Who was he?"

"We saw him eating alone when we stopped for lunch one day. That was in North Carolina, I believe. I tried to get him to talk to me, but I don't think he could. Our waiter said he came in a few times a week, doesn't eat much, but takes the leftovers to share with others wherever he lives."

"That's so sad and sweet at the same time."

"I thought so too and wanted to help."

"What did you do?"

"I put some money on a tab for him at the restaurant. He should be able to feed himself and his friends without having to sacrifice for a while."

Shaking her head in awe of his compassion, she turned the phone around to show him another photo. In it, Jackson hugged a little girl, her arms wrapped tight around his neck, in a flower garden. "I think this one is my favorite."

"Mine too."

"Who is she?"

"Her name is Callie. We crossed paths on a difficult day for both of us, and she stole my heart. We ate dinner with her and her grandpa later that night, and she wouldn't leave my side."

"Are you saying I have competition?"

"Sorry." He mouth tilted up on one side. "But don't worry, there's enough of me to go around."

"Alright, I guess I can share you with this cutie. What happened to make it a tough day?"

He told her about coming across Callie in the woods beside the highway and why he took her to Olan. He didn't want to think about their sad goodbye but mentioned how hard it had been to watch her cry and reach for him as her grandpa carried her to the car.

"Sounds gut-wrenching."

"It was. Olan called a couple days ago to tell me he got full custody. She's safe now." His smile of relief and care for the little girl warmed her to the core. "They plan to move to Virginia soon."

"Oh, how wonderful. She's going to be so excited to have you—"

"Are we going to sit here all day, or can we go do something fun?" Ben interrupted, officially tired of small talk.

"Great question." Genevieve raised her eyebrows for a little added encouragement. "It's time to take this show on the road."

"Fine. Up for it?" she asked Jackson and returned Ben's phone.

"If you are."

She wasn't sure if she was ready for what Genevieve and Ben had in mind, but she needed more time. If they went somewhere the other two could be happy, maybe she and Jackson could sneak away for some quiet time. That was what she was up for.

———

Ben

"Will you two give it a rest and keep up?" Ben called to their friends, who had stopped for a kiss several yards back. Frustrated with Jackson's new distracted side, he mentioned it to Genevieve. "He's acted like a damn monk since we left."

"Really?" she asked, giving him her full attention. She was eager for a glimpse into Jackson's life, and he was happy to oblige so long as those sexy, dark eyes stayed on him. "He hasn't been sleeping around on this trip?"

"Shit, no. I've tried to get him to loosen up and at least talk to a woman. He's had plenty of opportunities, believe me, but he always refuses with that titanium resolve of his. It's infuriating. I was beginning to think his dick didn't work."

"Not funny. Emily's the same way. She's had a few guys make passes at her, but she never acts on it or encourages it. Seeing them like this is a little strange for me, too." She glanced over her shoulder at the happy couple in their own world, hands linked, and eyes locked in a sappy romance movie way.

"Want to try this place?" he asked, rubbing his hands together with excitement as a dance club with a long line of people out front came into view. "Must be decent."

She scanned the line of hopefuls waiting to get in. "Sure."

They joined the line, and Jackson and Emily did the same further back, still oblivious to reality happening around them.

"What do you normally do when Jackson's running?" she asked, her tone laced with agitation, not genuine interest. He'd change that soon enough.

Playing along, he answered, "I keep track of him, take pictures, and check in when he stops for too long. He's had a couple episodes on the road, so I'm a little paranoid. Other than that, I try to find something fun to do along his path on his good days. I went bungee jumping last week. That was fun."

Exploring had become a new habit he hoped to continue after their trip ended, but he'd need a job to support it.

Jackson had been gracious enough to let him use the credit card for his little adventures, but that wouldn't last forever. "I hope to find a place to go skydiving one day. What about you? What do you do for fun?"

"Not that. I much rather have air conditioning and my feet planted firmly on the ground."

"I bet you're more adventurous than you're letting on," he said with a wink.

Her gorgeous full lips opened to spout out a rebuttal, but someone calling her name from up the line cut her off.

Rising on her toes, she looked over the line of heads. "Hi… Sam." She waved and forced a smile before dropping to her heels with an exasperated sigh.

"The bartender?" He failed miserably at trying not to sound like a whiney teenager.

"Shit. He's coming." She turned her gaze to Ben. "Listen Whatever I do next, it means nothing. Got it?"

"What are you talking about?"

"Shhh!"

"I can't believe you are here," Sam said when he reached their location, anticipation written all over the lucky bastard's face. He looked Ben over, then gave Genevieve his attention. "I was hoping to see you again."

"This is so awkward."

Her tone dripped with sweetness, catching Ben off guard, and his eyes dropped to the source of electricity now searing up his arm. She'd taken his hand.

"My ex-boyfriend followed me here, and we got back together today." She brought Ben's hand to her lips and smiled adoringly at him.

Damn, she's good. Understanding her, his eyes widened with his smile.

"I see."

As Sam lingered, Ben pecked her cheek for added effect, thinking it would send the guy packing. But the second his lips touched her skin, it was like he'd taken a baseball bat to the head. Dizzy for more, he couldn't think clearly.

She may have started this little manipulation, but he would be the one to finish it. Bending down, he whispered in her ear. "This means nothing."

To question, her head turned toward him as his lips collided with hers, instantly shooting off a flare of surrender. This gorgeous woman, with a body to make every fantasy look like daydreams, had his brain conjuring up a hurricane of unspeakable ideas. All the things he'd like to do with these plump lips and endless curves in his hands.

Leaning her back, his tongue slid around hers for one last taste. Her body responded with a shiver, and he figured he'd be better off leaving her wanting…for now.

"I'm so glad to have you back, sweetheart," he said and tapped her nose with a finger.

She checked over his shoulder to ensure Sam had left before setting her fuming eyes on him. Based on her reactions to him earlier that night, it right on cue. "I've known you for just over an hour, and I hate you already."

Reading her like a sexy book, he flexed in time for her palm to slap across his bicep.

"Now, let me go."

The fire in her eyes may have been enough to turn him on, but feeling her squirm in his arms, the full expanse of her breasts pressing against his body, did things to his system he couldn't explain.

"You started it," he informed her lamely and set her upright.

"I didn't ask you to kiss me."

"It got rid of him, didn't it? That's what you wanted. The way I see it, you should be thanking me for both."

"Both?"

"I got rid of that douchebag *and* got your motor running."

"You did no such thing." Her blazing indignation lit his ego like a hot air balloon.

"Oh, yeah? Why did you tremble and kiss me back?"

"First of all, I tremble for no man. As for the kiss, I simply played the part of doting girlfriend." Her face curdled at the mention like she might puke just thinking about it. He would have taken offense had she not been lying.

"I know you're lying. Frankly, I thought you'd be better at it."

Her head snapped toward him, insulted by his challenge. "Better at what?"

"You'd never win at poker. I can tell when a woman is turned on, and you most certainly trembled for me."

Her jaw dropped open, and he braced for a snappy comment. "Shut up," she ordered lamely, spinning to face forward and crossing her arms in defiance. "You can wipe that smug look off your face now."

"Not a chance."

A few more paces later, they made it inside and waited near the door for Jackson and Emily.

"I could use a drink," he said to break the silence. She'd been snubbing him since their lips came together, brooding over how much she liked it despite her best efforts not to.

A major win for Team Ben.

———

Genevieve

"They're in," she blurted out and grabbed Emily by the arm. "Come with me."

"Why? What's wrong?"

She waited until reaching the bar and ordering two shots before answering. "I need you to help me disappear."

"Disappear? Why?"

Snatching up the tiny glasses set on the counter, she handed one to Emily. She emptied hers, then slapped her credit card on the bar with an order for a refill.

"Did something happen?"

"Ben kissed me." She grimaced and looked around to ensure he hadn't slithered his way into listening range without her noticing. "And I liked it. But I need to get away, so it doesn't happen again."

"Wait a minute. Slow down. You're saying that Ben kissed you—I'll need details on that—but you want to avoid him because you enjoyed it? G, you're not making any sense."

"He's not my type, and I don't want to be tied to him all night, giving him false hope."

"Or maybe being with someone *not* your type is a good thing."

She appreciated Emily's concern, but sometimes she worried and droned on too much about Genevieve's choices in men. Sure, she had interesting taste, but all the so-called *good* guys bored her to tears and usually wanted more than she could give.

"I've never seen you run," Emily continued. "Especially from someone as harmless as Ben. If he makes a pass you don't want, treat him like you do everyone else."

"What if it makes things uncomfortable? I see the way you look at Jackson. I won't be the one to cause a rift." She downed the second shot when it arrived.

"I appreciate that, but I think Ben can take it, and Jackson understands. Please don't go. Let's have some fun tonight."

"If you insist. But he'll get no special treatment tonight."

"Fine by me."

Since Emily ignored her shot, Genevieve tossed it back and pushed the empty glass down the bar. She needed it to help her forget the feel of Ben's hands. For a novice flirt, he certainly knew how to use them.

"Let's get this over with." She signed the bill then followed Emily to the high-top table Jackson and Ben had claimed.

"Who's ready to dance?" Ben asked, rubbing those capable hands together.

To ensure her body didn't betray her again and to avoid eye contact—a motion every guy took as encouragement—she spun to scan her possibilities on the dance floor. Ben may be easy to look at with his dirty-blond hair, dark eyes, and quick smile—complete with dimples impossible to ignore—but undisciplined schoolboys were not a turn on. And never would be.

———

Emily

As expected, Genevieve soon dragged Emily into the sweaty mob on the dance floor. Dinner, dancing, and drinks—G's favorite combination.

"Where's Ben?" she asked Jackson after escaping one song later and found him alone.

"Who knows. Where's Genevieve?"

"Someone with far less estrogen offered to take my spot."

"Does that happen a lot when you two go out?"

"Yes. She loves to dance to this alleged music, but I can only take so much. It's deafening and exhausting. Plus, she's usually surrounded by a pack of salivating men after a couple songs. So, I guard the table and watch the show from a safe distance. The competition for her attention is usually quite entertaining." She smiled before taking a drink of the beer he'd ordered for her.

"I find it hard to believe that you haven't had a line just as long."

"Scouts honor. I wouldn't lie to you. Ask G," she challenged and leaned her elbow on the table to face him. "We have a running joke that I must have a look or vibe that turns men off."

He puffed out his disagreement, and her heart swooned. "I don't know what they're looking at. When I saw you, I had the opposite reaction." He pushed her hair off her shoulder and ran a hand slowly down her bare arm, leaving a trail of goosebumps in its wake.

Watching him, she waited until he raised his eyes to her again. "Who are you, Jackson Vane? You can't be real."

"I could say the same about you," he countered and lowered his head for another kiss. He lingered lightly on her lips, trying to take things slow, but passion sparked when she deepened the kiss—her control like a loose string in the wind around him.

"What about you?" It was the first question that came to her clouded mind when he released her. "What do you do when you're not bailing Ben out of his predicaments?"

"Same as you. I sit alone while he searches for the next victim."

A laugh burst from her throat, and the look he gave her as a result tossed gasoline on the spark they ignited moments ago. Hooking the tie around her waist with a finger, he pulled her close. Her lips, a magnet for his, parted instantly. Reason abandoned her as her hands tangled in his hair. She'd never felt this free to express herself before, or this needy to be devoured. But not by anyone…only him.

"Looks like it's time for you two to get a room," Genevieve joked, returning to the table with a wide grin.

Once separated from Jackson, Emily attempted to focus on the activity around her, but her head drifted like a feather in the wind. With considerable effort, her eyes landed on the tall, muscular man with a shaved head standing behind Genevieve. He must be the winner of the dance competition.

"This is Dwayne," she told them, but Emily barely listened.

Jackson's hand trailed up and down her back, his body still pressed against hers—a recipe for rendering her thoughts and ability to speak null and void.

"Hey, Genevieve. I've been looking all over for—" Ben stopped when he saw the group's new addition. He looked from Genevieve to the man with an arrogant arm wrapped around her shoulders.

"Dwayne, this is Ben, Jackson's friend," she explained, unconcerned with the dumbfounded look he gave her. The ridiculous scene could have been written into a ninety's sit-com. "We came to get a drink. It's hot out there."

Here we go, Emily thought and shook her head when Genevieve's hand sprang into motion, fanning her flushed face. She'd used the move often over the years, and it never failed to award her a fresh drink, courtesy of the current suitor.

This time, both Ben and Dwayne called for the first waiter they saw, kicking off the contest for her affection. Once she'd finished her drink, she announced the winner.

"Ready to get back out there, handsome?" she asked Dwayne before sauntering off with him riding her stardust like a magic carpet.

Ben leaned on the table. "Can you believe that? She acted like I wasn't standing right here."

"Sorry, Ben. She lives in her own world," Emily consoled. "You're a handsome guy. I'm sure there are others here that would—"

"That's right. Why am I wasting time with you two? There are plenty of women here who would like a piece of this." He tapped his chest with his palm and danced off toward the crowd.

"Poor girl," she laughed, feeling sorry for the next woman to catch Ben's eye.

Chapter Seven

☆ ☆ ☆

Jackson

Over an hour had passed since their friends disappeared to enjoy the club. When a booth opened up near the bar, he and Emily claimed it, happy to have some private alone time.

"Have anything planned for tomorrow, soldier? Whoa. What's that look for?" she asked when his face crunched into a hard frown.

"Nothing. Sorry. Tomorrow, I was thinking—"

"I don't think so, buddy," she leaned back for a better view. "What did I say that was so bad?"

He paused, wondering if he should tell her. "It's silly."

"Wretched is more like it based on your reaction."

"Again, sorry about that. It's just... Marines aren't soldiers."

"They're not?"

"No. That's an Army thing."

"Interesting. And that matters?"

He stared down his nose at her.

"Alright." Her hands flew up with a wide grin. "It matters. Got it. I'll ask again, correctly, this time. What's on the agenda for tomorrow… Marine?"

"Well—"

"I can't. It just doesn't have the same affection. You might just have to suck it up and let me call you soldier. It's endearing."

"Not when you're a Marine."

"Even when I say it?" She leaned in and waited for a kiss.

When she looked at him like that, he would relent to whatever she asked. "You could call me anything, and I wouldn't care."

"Soldier will do."

"Fine." He leaned back in the booth with a loud exhale.

"Third time's a charm. So, soldier…" She stifled a giggle.

"That's going to take some getting used to."

"Plans. Tomorrow. Go."

"Being with you, if you'll have me."

"I was hoping you'd say that." She went to settle against him but stopped when she caught him smiling at something behind her. "What?"

"Looks like our friends are about to make a scene."

When Jackson motioned toward the bar, she turned around in time to see Genevieve resting her elbows on the counter and Ben approaching behind her. He seemed to be plotting, looking both anxious and giddy about what he was about to do.

"Oh, Ben," Emily empathized from afar and leaned back against Jackson to watch the spectacle in his arms. "Should we intervene and protect the wayward lover's heart?"

"Absolutely not. It's time he gets what's coming to him."

"I thought it would be fun to watch her dismiss him, but I don't think I have the stomach for it. This could be gut-wrenching, and we were having such a good time." She laughed about it until Ben moved closer, his eyes on Genevieve's waist.

"Nope. I can't do it." Grimacing, she twisted around to face Jackson. "Anyway, I much rather look at you."

———

Genevieve

"Just a water for now, please," Genevieve informed the bartender. While waiting, she gathered up her hair and tied it in a loose bun on top of her head.

She'd taken a break from dancing to cool down, fully expecting Dwayne to follow and take advantage of this opportunity. Why hadn't he kissed her yet? She couldn't possibly have given him louder signals—other than saying *kiss me, you fool* to his face.

The bartender placed a cup of ice water on the counter in front of her with a wink. But she'd had her fill of bartenders on this trip and offered him no encouragement. Instead, she raised the cup to drink as two masculine hands slid around her waist. She smiled but didn't turn around.

"It's about time," she purred.

His hard body pressed against her back with every glorious muscle on high alert. *Finally*, she thought when his lips found her neck. She considered stalling, making him work for her response, but he felt too good. With eyes closed, she leaned her head back on his shoulder, allowing him more space to explore. But she lost all patience when his lips found the sensitive dip behind her ear. She no longer wanted to play games or be teased with slow caresses on the safe spaces of her body.

Spinning her around, those magical hands framed her face, bringing their lips together. The kiss, urgent and hot, had every biological function rejoicing in a way she'd never experienced. His hands, now traveling down her sides, quickened her pulse and sped up time. The noises of the club melded into a gentle hum. The dark fog of desire glided around her like an electric blanket. Then, something about the way his tongue twisted around hers…

Oh, my God!

She yanked herself free, hating how much she regretted it. "What in the hell are you doing?"

"Satisfying you, from what I can tell," Ben smirked, too pleased to have flustered her again, even if she'd believed him to be someone else. "And I'd like to get back to it if you'd get out of that gorgeous head of yours."

"I didn't know it was you."

"Your body didn't seem to mind. In fact, just the opposite."

He took a step closer, and she sucked in a breath. She desperately wanted him to put those hands on her again, yet she silently begged for him not to torture her with them.

"What do you want me to do, Genevieve?"

He leaned closer, placing a hand on the bar behind her, watching her as he brushed a light kiss to her cheek. Air seeped out of her lungs when his shockingly talented lips found her jawline.

"Say the word, and I'll leave," he whispered against her mouth.

He made her want to do things she never did, like beg. How could that be when she also wanted to punch him in the face? Where was her resolve? How could he dissolve everything she'd ever been with one kiss? Her body and mind had abandoned her when she needed protection the most. "I…" She swallowed hard. "I just… screw it."

Conceding, she threw her arms around his neck and took what they both craved. She wasn't thrilled about it, but the need streaming through her flooded her ability to think about anything else. He shouldn't feel this way, like warm sunshine, an ocean breeze, home.

Like what? The unsavory—and impossible—revelation put the bizarre situation back into perspective. This out of body experience could be rectified and forgotten about with a little reality check. She placed a hand on his chest and pushed back, his heart pounding as fast as she gulped for air.

"Ben." She had so much to say, yet nothing rose from the pile of dust her brain became with that kiss.

"Don't overthink it, Genevieve. You make me feel things I didn't know were possible."

All she could do was shake her head and look away. His eyes, fixated on hers, seemed to have the key to her soul.

A nearby commotion yanked his attention away. He stumbled into the growing crowd around the bar before either of them realized what happened.

"I should have known you'd be a nuisance," Dwayne accused. "Can't you take a hint? She doesn't want you."

Ben smiled, igniting Dwayne's fury. "I'd be willing to bet you're wrong about that."

"Oh really? She's dismissed your ass multiple times already, but you still creep around, watching her like a punk."

"Why wouldn't I? She's stunning." He grinned when her gaze snapped to his. "And I doubt I was the only one. She's free to do as she pleases, including dismissing you for me now."

"Guys," she attempted to defuse a situation sure to ruin her good mood. "I can make this real easy. You're both dismissed. I've had enough."

After riding a brutal wave of emotions she'd yet to comprehend, her patience for their exhausting standoff crashed the second it started. And speaking of exhausting, she refused to go on fighting with herself over a man. Ben wasn't her type. Neither he nor Dwayne meant anything to her.

Over it all, she snatched the cup of water she'd yet to drink from the counter and headed toward Jackson and Emily. But as she passed Dwayne, he grabbed hold of her arm.

"Don't leave. I thought we were having a good time," he whispered.

"Not anymore. If you don't mind." She glanced down at his hand burning hot on her skin.

"I do—"

"Hey, asshole," Ben called over the noise. "She said to let go."

"This conversation doesn't involve you."

"You two can go on arguing if you want." She sighed. "But leave me out of it."

"Impossible," Dwayne informed her.

"Excuse me?"

"If you hadn't teased me and sucked face with him, this wouldn't have happened."

"I will give you one more chance to take your hands off me."

"Or what?"

Irritated, she yanked her arm, but his grip tightened with the movement. The flimsy plastic cup she carried collapsed in her angry grasp, spilling ice-cold water down the front of her shirt. He released her as laughter took over his body, and that's when everything she believed she knew about herself and her little world, crumbled like the cup.

She'd never been laughed at before, and what she felt in response wasn't her usual disregard. Her heart didn't act like the fucking tank she built it to be. She felt insignificant, small, mortified like the idiot Dwayne saw her to be.

And as if that wasn't enough to send her over the edge, Ben rushed to her aid, blotting water from her arms and chest with his shirt. She would have preferred he slapped her instead—*that* she knew how to handle.

She opened her mouth to protest and tell him to piss off, but his thumb wiped the drops from her cheeks. The gesture shouldn't have soothed her, and the commotion of the scene around them shouldn't have faded away. His soft brown eyes, the ones she'd been trying unsuccessfully to avoid, watched her closely, sending her system into a tailspin. Because what she saw in them rarely came from others when they looked at her—compassion, understanding, tenderness.

He closed the distance between them, and with a gentleness she hadn't realized she needed, his hand cupped the back of her neck and brought her forehead to his lips. Since when did she melt for sweet, protective gestures? Since when does she melt for anything?

She didn't, she reminded herself, bringing everything into focus again. "Ben, I'm fine," she blurted out, tilting her head away from him. "It's just water."

"And he's a moron," he said loud enough for Dwayne to hear.

"What did you call me?" Dwayne shoved him from behind, knocking him past Genevieve and into a couple sitting at the bar.

With his temper boiling over, Ben whipped around, ready to fight, until a black pistol pointed in his direction.

———

Emily

"Did you hear that?" Emily asked Jackson. "Sounded like a scream."

When the music cut off, he climbed over her and rushed toward the bar. She followed and paralyzing fear took control of her system when the frightful scene emerged ahead. She wanted to be brave and save her best friend and Ben. But what could she possibly do to stop an angry bull of man with a deadly weapon?

"Let's talk about this," Ben urged, hooking an arm around Genevieve to keep her behind him.

Where in the hell are the bouncers? Emily thought as Ben continued to talk down his assailant. *Where did Jackson go?*

"Is it her you want?"

"Ben!" Genevieve scolded under her breath. "What are you doing?"

He held up his hands, causing her to tighten her grip on his shirt. "Put the gun away, and you can have her."

"What are you up to?" Dwayne asked, distracted by the turn of events, and that's when Jackson pounced from the shadows.

In three swift moves Dwayne never saw coming, he was pinned to the ground with the gun tucked safely in Jackson's back pocket.

With the threat under control, Emily's legs came back to life. She forced her way through the crowd and pulled a shaking and soaking wet Genevieve into her arms.

"What happened?" she asked after leading Genevieve to the booth while Ben and Jackson dealt with management.

"He's crazy," she answered and wiped her nose with a cocktail napkin.

"Who is?"

"Dwayne. We were having a good time. He hadn't kissed me yet, but it was coming." Slowly, she recounted what happened at the bar before the incident evolved into a party of three. "For a reason I'll never understand, I couldn't turn him away. I wanted him to kiss me. But then Dwayne showed up, picked a fight, and got out his dumbass gun. It's all so stupid."

"Oh, G." Emily knew her sexuality would get her into trouble, but that lecture would have to wait. She held her friend close, grateful to have her back safe.

The music and hustle of the club had resumed its normal chaos by the time Jackson and Ben rejoined them.

"We should go," she suggested.

Once outside, Genevieve turned to Jackson. "I'll never be able to properly thank you for what you did. Please know I appreciate it."

"It's no big deal. I'm used to bailing out this idiot." He tossed his thumb at Ben and grinned.

The motion drew her attention in his direction. "I didn't mean to put you in danger," she said and allowed him to wrap her in a hug.

"You didn't do anything. I provoked him."

"Can we walk you back to your place?" Jackson asked Emily, giving their friends space to talk.

She nodded, and together, the group headed toward the condo.

As they walked in silence, Jackson glanced over his shoulder, and she did the same. Ben and Genevieve followed closely behind, his arm still wrapped around her as they walked in stride.

"I have an idea of what we can do tomorrow."

"Oh yeah?" She looked up at him and marveled. "I'm all ears."

"I'd like to spend all day on the beach with you. No clubs, no complications, no drama."

"Sounds like heaven. What about them?" She tilted her head toward the other two.

"They can join us or not. I don't care so long as you're by my side."

"That's my favorite place to be these days."

Chapter Eight

★ ★ ★

Emily

The sun was high in the sky before Genevieve rolled out of bed and located Emily reading on the balcony

"Good morning, sunshine," she greeted with a touch of sarcasm as Genevieve dropped into the empty chair, sleepy-eyed and irritable. Her wild hair, unbrushed since she fell into bed last night, contrasted the perky, plaid pajamas she wore.

She growled over her steaming coffee mug before taking a sip. "You're frustratingly cheerful today."

"It's a beautiful day, and I'm excited to see Jackson again. Will you be joining us at the beach later?"

"And be a third wheel while you two have sex with your eyes all day? No thanks. What the hell, Em?"

"You've seen him."

"Yeah, I know," she surrendered. "I don't blame you."

"The way he looks at me with those Caribbean-blue eyes and the things he says. G, I'm in trouble. I've never met anyone like him."

"Why does it sound like you're about to be all negative about it?"

She picked at a loose string on her shorts and thought through her unease. "I believe everything he says, I do. But why me? He obviously could have anyone."

"He wants you because you're just as special as he is. I'd argue more so." She mustered up a grin and placed a hand on Emily's knee for emphasis. "Don't think. Do what feels right."

"Thank you." Emily let the advice sink in. "One thing's for sure, he certainly feels very right."

"That's my girl." With a pat on Emily's leg, she sat back in the chair to sip her coffee.

"How are you feeling?"

Looking out over the distant ocean through the balcony railing, Genevieve seemed to contemplate her answer. "I don't know."

"Do you want to talk about it?"

"Maybe later."

"Alright. Why don't you come with us? A little fresh air and easy fun might help you feel better." When it garnered no reaction, she tried a different tactic. "I imagine Ben will be there."

Genevieve puffed and dismissed the news with a wave of her perfectly manicured hand. "I can't go there."

"Why?"

"I don't date, you know this, and after what happened…"

"You don't have to date him. Start with being nice and see what happens. It was sweet how he supported you."

"That's the problem."

"What is?"

"He's sweet and attentive and thoughtful." Grimacing as if a bug had landed in her coffee, she stared into the mug. Her disapproval over Ben's treatment written in the thin lines between her eyes and the purse of her lips.

"And? Maybe having someone who cares about being more than your bedmate is exactly what you need." She caught a glimpse of Genevieve's eyes rolling before she covered them with sunglasses.

"You find your dream guy, and suddenly you're an expert on what man I need." Avoiding Emily's disapproving glare, she set down the mug. "For your information, I'm not rejecting him because I don't want a relationship, which I don't. I told you, he's not my type."

"So you said…repeatedly like you're trying to convinced more than just me."

"I have to repeat it because you won't listen."

Ignoring the comment, Emily continued to make her point. "He's not the messy trouble everyone thinks he is. It's an act. That kind, attentive side he showed you afterwards, that's the real Ben."

"Doesn't matter. I'm not interested."

"I'm just saying, he's a good guy, and you seem to give him special treatment whether you want to or not. Maybe he deserves a chance." She rose and squeezed Genevieve's shoulder. "I need to get ready."

Before opening the balcony door, she glanced back at her friend. It broke her heart to see Genevieve missing her standard glow.

In her room, Emily wiggled into the red bathing suit she bought for the trip. The thin straps tied low on her hips and around her back, exposing more skin than she liked to show on a date. But with Jackson, she craved his touch. Wanted his hands on her skin. Other than a few safe places on her body, he'd yet to venture elsewhere. If the skimpy suit did its job that day, he won't be able to force distance between them—as he did whenever their connection heated up.

Blushing, she hoped the sun wouldn't be the only thing dialing up the heat that day.

———

Jackson

"Hello, handsome," Emily greeted seconds after he knocked.

The first sight of her with the bright sunlight from the balcony glass doors spotlighting her from behind set him free from the misery of another painful and sleepless night. "Hello, yourself."

Lost in the peace she gifted him, he found more in her embrace. He wrapped an arm around her waist and tucked her close for a kiss. Through the thin coverall she wore, he felt her bare skin and looked forward to seeing it glistening in the sun and saltwater.

Then, her arching back and low moan response disintegrated the innocent thought and turned him ravenous. Hungry for her, he dropped the bag he'd carried in, reached for the wall behind her, and backed her against it. The door slamming shut didn't register. He hadn't cared to check to see if they were alone. He could only follow his primal need for her and succumb to how her fingertips skimming over skin inside his shirt made his mind go numb.

His instincts to give and feel and consume intensified as she curled a leg around him, begging for more. He could have her, right there in that moment, but she deserved better. Despite how much he wanted to let go of the person he'd always been and let her carry him away, he held on.

Breathless from the energy surge and the effort it took to tear himself from her, he took a moment to recover.

Her lazy eyes refocused on him. "That's a greeting I could get used to," she said on a sigh and moved a hand to his cheek. "If you can't tell, I'm happy to see you."

Turning his face, he warmed her palm with his lips. "Me, too."

"Can I get you anything? Beer, water, wine, snack?" She led him by the hand to the tiny galley kitchen.

"Sure. Whatever you're having."

She removed the cork from the wine bottle sitting on the counter and filled two glasses. "Did Ben come with you?"

"Yes, but he's waiting downstairs to see if Genevieve is joining us. If not, he'll leave with tail tucked."

"I don't know what she'll do since she left without telling me." She swirled the maroon contents of her glass, staring blankly through it, before setting it down. "I might have said something she didn't want to hear this morning."

Not knowing how to respond, he sat on a nearby bar stool to listen.

"I'm worried about her. She's still processing what happened last night and probably shouldn't be alone." Rounding the counter, she stood between his legs and rested both arms on his shoulders. "But then again, I would be fine with some alone time today."

"I like the sound of that."

"There's still a lot I'd like to discover about you, Jackson Vane."

With her just inches away, he drowned in her beauty as a hand slid up the back of her thigh. Her skin responded and she leaned in, her eyes focused on his lips. It would be near impossible to resist her again. Her breath skated over his skin as she waited for him.

"At it already, I see," Genevieve said, letting the door slam shut behind her. She dumped a box of wine and several grocery bags onto the kitchen counter without a care for the contents inside.

Emily cursed the interruption under her breath, straightening to take in the hurricane her friend seemed to be in that moment. She took his hand and spun around to lean back against him "What's all this?"

"I thought we could use some libations and snacks for the beach. Don't mind me. I'm not here."

"Yeah, right."

While she opened and closed cabinet doors, looking for who knows what, Emily laid her head back on his shoulder.

"Where's Loose Lips?" Genevieve asked him, setting the blender on the counter. "Is he coming?"

"I believe he is." He grimaced as she poured vodka into the blender, leaving little room for the remaining ingredients. Somehow, she squeezed in a frozen mixture and ice before closing the lid and sending it swirling.

"Want some?" she asked Emily, hitting the off switch.

"No way. I saw the lethal portion of alcohol you poured in there. I'll stick with wine."

"Lightweight." After transferring the contents into a massive thermos she'd bought at the store, she took a test sip and shrugged. "I'll be ready to go in five," she promised and headed down the hall to change.

"Finally." Spinning, Emily crushed her mouth to his. She may have accepted his skimming the surface of their connection earlier, but he felt her urgent passion and knew she'd want zero inhibitions with this kiss.

Her fingers buried in his hair as she pressed against him. The more she dared him to touch and take, the more he struggled to breathe. His hands ran up her sides, under the cover she wore, and his fingers tangled in the tiny strings of her bikini. Repositioning, she bit his bottom lip, and all the blood drained from his head.

With a tight grip on her hips, his arms straightened to separate them. She tested his limits and destroyed his resolve every time she demanded more. Trying to focus through the haze, his eyes found her lips, still plump and wet from his kiss. He missed them already.

"If you do that again," he said, near breathless, "I can't be responsible for what happens next."

"Oh yeah?" With her fingers still locked around his neck, she pulled herself back into his arms. "Good to know."

––––––

Emily

At the beach, the group floated in the waves, played games, and lounged on the sand. Ben and Genevieve were cordial, even flirty at times, and he did everything he could to make her comfortable. After emptying the thermos and wine box, they retreated to the pool to enjoy the swim-up bar together.

As Emily lounged next to Jackson under a large beach umbrella, she realized that day couldn't have been any better and she was beyond happy. Genevieve seemed to be trying with Ben, and she had the man of her dreams locked in an embrace on the beach like a couple on the cover of a steamy romance novel.

But the joy in that perfect moment, didn't outshine the worry when her thoughts drifted to the weeks ahead. Although she tried not to, she wondered what would happen next between them. She had to work, and he had a goal to accomplish. After that, they would be over five hundred miles apart in different states, living separate lives.

Could their new relationship survive long distance? Did he plan to return to Virginia permanently when his journey ended. If so, was he happy there? She had no doubts about continuing their relationship after they left Myrtle Beach, but what did he want? Did he know yet? They'd only been together two days, after all.

"What are you thinking about?" he asked, noticing her tensing with worry. A florescent marquis message might as well appear on forehead with how pitiful she masked her emotions.

She rolled onto her side to face him and propped her head up with a hand. "How I don't want this to end."

"I feel the same."

She smiled at the admission. "When you get to Georgia, do you think your path will bring you near Savannah?"

"It will now."

"Really?"

"My path goes wherever I lead it."

"Oh, I'm so excited." Unbridled, she threw her arms around his neck, the force of it pushing him onto his back. He shifted her on top of him, and her wide smile gave away her pleasure over the new vantage point. He couldn't put distance between them when she pinned him to the sand. "How long do you think it will take to get there?"

"Not sure. My body hasn't exactly been playing along lately. Maybe a couple weeks."

"I can handle the wait if there's a promise of having you all to myself at the end."

His thumb brushed at the sand on her cheek, the dreamy look in his eye melting every concern as if they never existed. "You're making it infinitely harder to want to finish this trip to Orlando."

He wasn't joking, she realized. "It's going to feel like forever before we see each other again, but you must keep going, Jackson. What you're doing is too special, too important, and I'm so proud of you. I'm proud to know you and be the one in your arms. And I'll be counting the minutes until you're back in mine."

"It's my favorite place to be," he said, repeating the words she said to him the night before.

"Well, when you're done with your trip, my arms will be impatiently waiting for you. And if you don't watch it, they may never let go again."

Overwhelmed with emotion, his hands framed her face and drew her lips to his. He tasted of salt and honey, heat and tenderness. He took his time, letting the moment guide him, and she didn't rush him. They had all day to explore each other, and hopefully, all night, too. Her body shuddered under his touch as her hips swayed over him, overwhelmed by the feel of his firm body under hers.

He rolled her onto the towel beside him for a deeper kiss that had forever flashing through her mind. Since he took her hand at the country bar that first night, she knew her life would never be the same. Whatever she had to do, however long she had to wait, she'd do it all again to feel this way and be with him always.

Winded, he rested his forehead against hers before they went too far to turn back. "You drive me crazy."

"Ditto," she exhaled, snuggling against him with her eyes closed. "Can we stay here for the next two days?"

"If the others come back, we can pretend we've fallen asleep. Maybe they'll leave us be."

She hummed in agreement, enjoying the tiny circles his fingertips traced on her back. "But what about the sand fleas?"

"Let 'em try. They'll have to fight me if they want a bite of you. You're mine."

"Yes, I am." Realizing she'd spoken out loud, her eyes flew open, expecting to see retreat staring back at her.

Instead, he brushed a thumb lightly over her cheek, touched by her affirmation. Her heart took off, soaring with appreciation for this man. This beautiful, kind, compassionate, unforgettable man who didn't run from his feelings. He cherished her and made her feel like the only woman in the world—the only woman in his world—and that was all that mattered.

"I know it's absurd," he began, his tone melodic and definite. "But I can't help how I feel. I'm falling for you."

"Welcome to the club, soldier."

Chapter Nine

☆ ☆ ☆

Jackson

Later, after the sun fell behind the condos, casting domino-like shadows over the beach, Ben called for them from a distance away.

Jackson sighed. "What could he possibly want?" Without opening his eyes, he tightened his arm around Emily. "Maybe he'll go away if we ignore him."

"Mmm. Let's hope so."

But when he yelled for them again, closer this time, the frightened inflections in his voice had them sitting up and searching the beach.

"What's wrong?" he asked after Ben stumbled to a halt next to their umbrella, his hands on his knees while he struggled to catch his breath through the panic.

"Where's G?" Emily asked, worry creeping into her voice.

"They took her," he puffed out between gulps of air. "The ambulance."

"Oh, my God."

As terror consumed her body, gluing her to the blanket, Jackson gathered up their belongings. "Did you get where they are taking her?"

"South Strand Hospital."

"Come on. I'll drive."

————

At the hospital, while Emily retrieved information from the Emergency Room receptionist, Jackson turned on Ben. "What happened?"

Ignoring him, Ben stared blankly out the waiting room window.

"Ben!"

His head snapped around, eyes wide with fear and anger. "What?"

"What happened to Genevieve?"

"I'm not sure." Preoccupied with his thoughts, he stepped away to pace between the rows of plastic chairs for a bit before talking through the events that landed them there. "We were having fun at the swim-up bar when out of nowhere, she said she wasn't feeling well and wanted to go upstairs. The next thing I knew, people were yelling for an ambulance. I didn't realize it was for her until I saw her lying on the ground by the gate."

"Did you go to her?"

"Of course, but she was unconscious. Damn it," he growled to release some of the tension.

"Maybe she just had too much to drink," Jackson speculated, relieved to see Emily entering the waiting room. But the devastated look on her face sent his system into a nosedive. He wanted to protect her from this heartache and shelter her from the stresses to come.

Meeting her halfway, he wrapped her in his arms and stroked her long braid, still coarse with sand and saltwater. "What did they say?"

"They're running some tests. Oh, Jackson. I'm so scared."

"Did they say what the tests were for?"

"No. Since I'm not technically her family, they wouldn't tell me anything more."

For several hours, they huddled, paced, and sat in silence until a doctor called for Emily.

"Ms. Olsen tells me you're traveling with her," he said when she joined him near the entrance.

"Yes. Is she okay?"

"She's recovering. Has she passed out before?"

"No. Well, she got dizzy yesterday, but nothing serious. Is that what happened?"

He nodded. "She has a concussion and a gash on her head that needed stitches."

"Do you know why she passed out, Doc?" Ben asked.

"Based on the long sun exposure and high level of alcohol in her system, I'd say it was heat exhaustion combined with low insulin."

"Low in—as in diabetes?" She grabbed Jackson's arm to steady herself as she struggled to comprehend the news. "How did I miss the symptoms?"

"This isn't your fault," he soothed, but she continued to vibrate with guilt.

"You can see her after she's been transported," the doctor added before stepping away.

"Transport?" Emily asked panicked again.

"Out of the E.R. and into a recovery room. She'll be fine," he added. "No need to worry."

"But that's my jam."

Hearing her attempt to joke, settled Jackson's nerves at bit.

The doctor smiled. "One of the nurses will let you know when she's settled. It will be at least a couple of days before she can be released. We need to monitor her a little while longer, and she'll need some diabetes management training."

"Understood." Returning to their seats, she dug into her bag for her phone. She called Genevieve's secretary and then, her own office to let them know neither would be returning as originally scheduled.

"Is there anyone else we can call? Any family members?" Ben asked, needing to make himself useful.

"Unfortunately, G doesn't have any family. She's been on her own most of her life."

"She's lucky to have you," Jackson said, rubbing her back, his touch soothing her.

"Whenever she'd get fed up with her group home or get into a fight with another kid, she'd run away. She'd stay at our house sometimes. Other times, we couldn't find her for days. It broke my heart every time. On her sixteenth birthday, she left that horrible place and never looked back."

"It really says a lot about her character that she overcame that. A lot of kids don't."

"She's unstoppable once she puts her mind to something, but don't try to talk her out of it. She's as stubborn as she is resourceful." She forced a smile. "Now, she has yet another obstacle to overcome. It isn't fair."

"Emily," Ben began. He sat in an adjacent chair, his elbows resting on his bouncing knees, trying unsuccessfully to hold it together. "I'm so sorry. I should have done more. If I had gone with her, she might not have fallen." When he noticed his hands shaking, he scrubbed both down his face.

"Ben." Taking his hand, she gently guided him into the seat beside her. "You couldn't possibly have seen this coming, and I think you've already figured out that G's a proud woman. She would have seen help from you as a weakness and refused."

"I would have done anything she needed had she asked."

"I know, but don't hold your breath."

"I'm glad you're okay," Jackson said as he entered Genevieve's room and joined Emily on the far side of the bed.

A bandage covered the left side of her head, her long dark hair flowing wildly over the pillows beneath her. The skin under her lazy, bloodshot eyes was darkened by exhaustion. She looked small and weak in the large room—a vast contrast to the woman he'd come to know.

"I'm still in one piece but could do without this hideous gown," she said slowly so not to agitate her injuries. Her eyes followed him into the room, then glanced back at the door. "Where's Loose Lips?"

He spun around. "He was right behind me a minute ago."

Poking his head out the door, he scanned the bustling hallway, the familiar combination of machines beeping, carts rolling, and nurses chattering transporting him back to London. The stinging aroma of medicine and bleach gripped his senses, and once again, he fought to stay alive.

Dropping his head, he propped himself up with his hands on his knees, memories, panic, and helplessness hitting him all at once. Repeatedly, he told himself to hold it together. He was not strapped to a hospital bed. He wasn't dying. Breathe in, breathe out, he willed, but reality slowly slid out from under him.

"Jackson?" Emily asked, rushing to his side. "Are you okay?"

He focused on her voice until a blurry shape appeared beside him. A hand on his back had him shooting up and fumbling for her. With her in his arms, he held on tight, his sanity tipping into hazardous territory. He painted a picture of her in his mind as the feel of her body slowly registered. The sweet, familiar scent of her lavender shampoo soon followed. And moments later, the past separated from the present.

"Jackson, you're shaking. What's wrong?"

"I'm not a fan of hospitals," he finally whispered as the agony melted away.

"I'm so sorry. I didn't think." She placed a hand on his sweaty chest, her eyes widening at the feel of his pulse, racing at an unhealthy rate—his heart on the verge of bursting. "Please come sit down, and we'll get you out of here soon."

"Stay with me, and I'll be fine."

Reaching for his hand, she kissed him before leading the way to the small couch below the window.

As Emily and Genevieve talked, he held on tightly to her, relaxing as best he could. He felt like an anxious child who couldn't manage on their own and hated himself for the burden. Emily already had her friend to worry about.

A knock sounded on the door, and after Emily cracked it open to look out, she flashed a smile over her shoulder that animated her entire face.

"Who is it?" Genevieve asked.

Instead of answering, Emily held open the door, allowing Ben to squeeze through with a bouquet of yellow flowers and a massive teddy bear. The bear, complete with an oversized cowboy hat, boots, and a gaudy leather vest made Genevieve giggle.

He set the flowers down on the shelves under the television, pasted on a goofy sideways grin, then positioned the man-size bear in front of him. "When I heard about a mighty fine lady taking quite the spill today, I jumped on Gertrude—that's my trusty horse—and hurried on over here lickety-split to see how she was a feelin'." He strolled slowly toward the bed with every drawn-out syllable.

"I also come bearing a message from an outrageously handsome fella named Benjamin. He said he was right sorry for what happened at that there pool, and if he could do anything to make that mighty fine lady feel better," he paused and moved the bear to show his face, "he'd do it."

Leaning down, he kissed her nose, careful not to cause any discomfort. There's the man Emily had faith in. Jackson could see it now.

"Thank you, cowboy."

While Ben had Genevieve's attention, Emily turned her focus back to Jackson. "Can we go talk for a minute?"

Outside, they located a shaded bench in a courtyard near the hospital entrance and sat facing each other. She looked down at his hand in hers, searching for how to begin. When she raised her head, the navy eyes that usually burrowed into his soul were now distant, uncertain, and full of unshed tears.

She sucked in a long breath. "Being with you has been a dream, and I want to spend every second I can with you."

"That's what I want, too."

"Good." The corners of her mouth turned up, but it didn't have the same radiance as her authentic smile. "It broke my heart to see you struggling in there. Jackson, I can't watch you go through that again."

"What are you saying?"

"This is so hard." Tears pooled on her lids but didn't fall as she took a deep breath. "What do you think about getting a head start to Savannah?"

"When? Today?" Since meeting her, he'd tried not to think about the day he'd have to say goodbye or how difficult it would be. He wasn't prepared to go through it just yet.

"Asking you to leave is not what I want."

"It's not what I want either."

"But I'll be here with G, night and day."

When her eyes closed and she struggled to wrangle her emotions, he rose and drew her into his arms. "Okay. I'll go."

"You know why I'm asking this, don't you?"

"Yeah." But knowing the reason didn't make it any easier.

"I need you to run fast, Jackson Vane. Hurry back to me."

"Like lightning," he promised and kissed her forehead. "I'll take a cab back to the hotel. Have Ben call me when he has a minute, will you?" He handed her the car keys but couldn't bring himself to touch her again. If he did, he'd never be able to do what she asked.

"Be careful, and call me often, so I know you're safe," she yelled after him as he walked backward toward the main road. She blew him a kiss—a farewell kiss he wanted no part in.

The goal of running to Orlando in honor of veterans had been enough to sustain him through the difficult times. But a chance to spend more time with Emily? That had the power to liberate him from everything that smothered his drive between runs. He may not have been ready to say goodbye, but he could endure anything with her as his homebase and guiding light.

———

Emily

When the sobs took over, she collapsed onto the bench, shaking with both regret and relief. A head start meant having him back sooner after she returned home, but she left too much unsaid and worried he hadn't fully understood why she sent him away.

Wiping the heartbreak from her cheeks, she breathed deep. She could do this. Genevieve needed her, and two weeks wasn't a long time. She could do this, she repeated with growing uncertainty and headed back inside to deliver Jackson's message to Ben.

In the room, she found him sitting on the couch reading a magazine while Genevieve slept. "How long has she been out?"

"She fell asleep shortly after you left and doesn't seem to be in any pain." He surveyed Emily's tear-stained cheeks with caution. "Jackson on his way up?"

"No." She handed him the keys and dropped down beside him. "I asked him to go."

"Why?"

More sobs rocketed out of her without warning, causing Ben to snatch the tissues off the table.

"Why, Emily?" he asked again, handing her the box. "Did something happen?"

She shook her head and explained what she witnessed with Jackson's reaction to the hospital room and the intentions behind her request.

"It was awful. The look on his face broke me, and he left without complaint or a kiss goodbye." She searched Ben's face for answers. "Did I mess everything up?"

"No, of course not." He took her trembling hand in his. "He probably didn't want to make leaving more difficult with a long goodbye."

"It definitely would have. I might have changed my mind had he stayed a second longer."

"Don't worry. He'll be fine."

"Thank you, Ben." She wiped her cheeks with a tissue. "What will you do now that he's leaving?"

"I guess I need to pack up everything and get to the next location. I can't imagine him wanting to go far tonight, so we'll be nearby if you need us."

"Don't tempt me," she said with an uneasy grin. "Call or text me if anything happens, and please take good care of him."

"I will."

He stood, and she did the same, reaching her arms around his middle before he could step away. Shock from her turning to him for comfort struck him immobile at first, his arms hovering around her like he didn't know what to do with them. She didn't care. She needed the warm comforts of a hug from someone she trusted. Someone she knew would show up.

As his hands threaded together on her back, he sank into the embrace, giving her exactly what she needed as she knew he would.

"Tell Genevieve I said bye, and that I hope she feels better soon," he said when she released him moments later.

He'd almost made it out the door when Emily called for him. "Yeah?"

He stepped back into the room.

"How about you tell her yourself?"

———

Ben

Forcing himself to look in Genevieve's direction, he found two stunning green eyes focused on him. The sudden urge to flee hit him like a kick to the gut. He may have accepted his relentless attraction to her but deciphering her feelings about him had been near impossible.

The events at the club the night before unfolded like a rollercoaster ride. It started with an explosive adrenaline rush when they kissed, dipped to a lull with the stupid Dwyane incident, then settled into a rhythm he could get used to as she took comfort in his arms afterward. Earlier that day, she flirted with him one minute and dismissed him the next. He had no idea where he stood and knew it didn't matter. He wasn't ready to give up just yet.

"Hi," he greeted, joining her bedside.

"I'm going to go get some water. I'll be back soon," Emily said, winking at Ben as she hurried out the door.

"Why was she crying?" Genevieve asked.

"It's a long story. I'm sure she'll tell you all about it." Scooping a hand under hers, he sat on the bed. "I'm glad you're awake. Jackson and I are leaving tonight."

"Am I that scary in this repulsive gown?" she joked, fighting against her heavy eyelids.

"Absolutely not. You make hospital fashion look sexy as hell."

Satisfied with his compliment, she managed a grin before losing the battle.

"Genevieve, stay with me one more minute, please." He waited for her gaze to meet his again. "We'll be close for the next day or so. If you need anything, text or call, and I'll come right back."

She stayed silent, her eyes glossing. He couldn't tell if she heard him until her free arm lifted and draped around his neck, bringing his cheek to hers.

"Thank you," she whispered, drifting off to sleep.

Memorizing her scent and the irresistible feel of her soft skin, he lingered long enough to make his back ache. But in dragging himself away, irritation added itself to the Long Island Iced Tea sort of emotional concoction she seemed to stir in him. For one miniscule moment, she opened herself to him, and he didn't snatch up the opportunity to ask her what she wanted. Now, he had to leave with no better understanding about his place with her—

Whoa. He backed a safe distance away. Being that close to her and getting to glimpse behind her impenetrable shield influenced him more than it should. Naughty thoughts about dating and, heaven forbid, exclusivity snuck into his dazed head like little snipers. No matter how much he wanted her, that shit had to stop.

But he wouldn't mind if she missed him while he was gone.

———

"I think I'll take you up on that," Emily answered when Ben offered to give her a ride back to the condo to change and pack a few things for their hospital stay.

She left Genevieve a note, then followed him to the car. Once on the highway, Emily fidgeted in her seat and chewed on a fingernail. After the third sigh and another fingernail ruined, he broke the silence.

"What is it, Emily?"

On another audible exhale, her hands dropped into her lap.

"I owe you an apology."

"You do? Why?"

"I was watching you with G earlier. I shouldn't have, but it was nice seeing someone treat her so thoughtfully. Guys usually look at her like she's their last meal, and I hate it so much."

"I'm sure I've looked at her like that, too."

"Yeah, but you were there for her when it mattered, and you treasured her today." She placed a hand on his arm. "I appreciate it, and she will too. Eventually."

She held his gaze until he understood the hidden meaning. Genevieve would be stubborn about letting him in, but he shouldn't give up. She needed him, even if she couldn't see it yet.

Well, shit. There go the damn snipers again, shooting holes in his perfectly crafted bachelorhood.

———

Emily

At the condo, Emily rushed inside, not wanting to be away from Genevieve longer than necessary. She threw open the door, stepping on a piece of paper folded in half on the floor. She picked it up and threw it, along with the key, onto the kitchen counter before hurrying to her room to pack.

Since they would be living at the hospital for the next several days, she decided to check out early. But first, she took a quick shower to rinse off the sunscreen and sand still lingering on her skin.

Thanks to her affinity for organization, she got dressed and tucked her things neatly in her suitcase within minutes. Genevieve's, on the other hand, took more time and attention since her room appeared to have been hit by a tornado. Clean and dirty clothes littered the room without a single drawer or hanger used. Shaking her head, she tossed the empty suitcase on the bed and packed everything in an organized manner.

With the aftermath somewhat contained, she rolled both suitcases into the entryway and gathered the remaining snacks from the kitchen. Reaching for the room key sitting on the counter, she froze. The folded paper she tossed there earlier sat open, revealing a handwritten letter.

Tears stung when she noticed Jackson's name at the bottom, her thoughts jumping to the worst-case scenario— she'd pushed him too far. With her heart at a standstill, she carefully lifted the letter off the counter as if it might burst into flames and forced herself to read his neat cursive.

Dear Emily,

I'm not good with words, so I hope I can find a way to adequately write this letter. Leaving you today was as difficult as I expected it would be. Based on the circumstances, I knew it was coming, but I thought I'd have a couple more days to figure out how to do it. You caught me off guard, and if I hurt you by leaving so abruptly, please know how sorry I am. But if I had to watch you cry or hold you a minute longer, I wouldn't have been able to do what you asked.

As hard as it had been to say goodbye, please know I understand and appreciate why you did it. It's just another reason why I am falling for you. The days and nights between here and Savannah will be long, but I can't wait to continue this journey and hold you in my arms once again.

Yours,

Jackson

He was falling for her. She'd read that line multiple times, wishing she'd summoned the courage to be honest with him the first time he said it. But that didn't matter now. They were together, even when far apart, and she would soon have plenty of chances to say the words she'd held back.

On the way to the hospital, she thought about the saying, "good things come to those who wait," grateful it had been true in her case. She'd spent her entire life believing a fairytale love could exist in real life with the right person. And she'd waited for it. Even though she'd spent some time with a few wrong ones, making her question the dream, she never settled.

She'd always hoped for a blissful happily ever after and secretly prayed for one to find Genevieve. They both deserved an unconditional, life-altering love. Even if one of them didn't believe in fairy tales or true love or princes and white knights, it could still happen. And when Genevieve was blissfully happy with her own dashing prince, Emily wouldn't hesitate to say, *I told you so.*

Chapter Ten

☆ ☆ ☆

Jackson

While waiting for their meals to arrive, Jackson studied Ben from across the table. He'd been sulking since they sat down, and Jackson wondered, with slight annoyance, if he would stay in a permanent pout for the rest of the trip.

"What's up with you?"

"Nothing. Why?" Ben snatched up his glass of water and took a long drink.

"You're unusually quiet, and you haven't gone out once since we left Myrtle Beach. It's been four days. I think we should call a doctor."

"Funny. You're frustratingly chipper tonight. Does that mean you already talked with Emily?"

"It does."

"How is she? Did she mention how Genevieve's doing?"

Ah, the crux of Ben's foul mood. "She did."

"Well, are you going to tell me?"

"Relax, Romeo," Jackson teased. "They're both fine and heading home as we speak. I figured you knew this already."

A hard line formed between Ben's eyes as his brow lowered with a frown. "I've texted, but it's a one-way street. Apparently, I no longer exist."

"So, the ladies' man couldn't wrangle her in, after all. Shocking."

"For your information, I don't mind a little pursuit. Let's see if she can continue to resist when we get to Savannah."

"Can you make sure I'm there? After all her rejections, I'd love to see how you convince her to surrender to your charms."

"Just because you didn't have to work for Emily doesn't mean I can't win Genevieve over with a little persistence."

"You're right. I'm sorry. I have full faith in you."

"Shut up."

"Hey, I'm just happy you're not flirting with every female within range. It's been nice having a little peace for a change."

———

Emily

"Welcome back!" Jillian, the receptionist and her only friend at work, wrapped her in a hug on her first day back. "You look… strung out."

"Thanks."

"Sorry. I just expected to see you more relaxed and rejuvenated. Did you not enjoy your vacation?" She grabbed the tablet she prepared for Emily to use during her appointments and followed her down the hallway.

"No. I did. It's just the ending wasn't as great as the start."

"Is your friend feeling better?"

"I think so." Her last thread of sanity strained with the question and threatened to snap. "Can we talk about it later?"

"Sure. If there's anything I can do to help today, please tell me."

"Thank you, Jill."

She managed to hold it together until Jillian closed the door to her office. Then, the weight of the previous week crashed down around her.

The past seven days had been anything but ordinary. From letting go of everything familiar and landing feet first in the middle of a romance novel to gripping frantically for a safety net when her world rocked out of control. Nothing in her life was as she wanted it to be, and she'd grown tired of pretending long before leaving the hospital.

After Genevieve was released, they hit the road and drove straight through, returning home only ten hours ago. She had just enough energy to unpack before dragging her weakened body into bed. Being home should have brought her comfort and allowed for a reset. But she couldn't eat or sleep while her habitual worry meter short-circuited from overuse.

She worried about Jackson's safety and when she would see him again. Worried about Genevieve, who struggled to reclaim herself after her diabetes diagnosis. Both kept her in a constant state of ache and angst.

With her main support system soaking up the Florida sunshine in their new home, she had no one to turn to for comfort. And for the cherry on top, being at work meant putting on a smile and continuing to pretend nothing happened over the last week to knock her off kilter.

Not to mention she still had Lucas—one of the other doctors at the practice—to deal with. He took a sudden interest in her several weeks ago, and when his advances crossed over into potential harassment territory, she decided to take the vacation she and Genevieve dreamed about. The break should have been enough for him to lose interest and remember why he ignored her for the better part of a year.

It took everything she had left in the tank to keep the flood gates closed and the river of tears at bay. Picturing herself as the brave woman she'd been with Jackson by her side, she pushed aside the pity party and stalked to the fitness room.

"Good morning." Emily set a smile and greeted her first patient, Ms. Cather, waiting for her by the door. "It's great to see you. How did your appointment go with Dr. Allen last week?"

Ms. Cather, who'd yet to regain her speech after a stroke, raised her fist and pushed up a thumb. Then, she grabbed her chalkboard and wrote quickly.

"How was my vacation?" She contemplated an answer. Immediately, Jackson and Genevieve jumped into her thoughts, and longing and regret jammed in her throat. Where had her willpower run off to. Frustrated at the gathering tears she swore she wouldn't shed, she dropped onto the bench next to Ms. Cather and let them trail down her cheeks.

"What's going on here?"

At the sound of Lucas's voice, she shot up and cleared the evidence of her cracking resolve from her face. "Nothing."

Ms. Cather gave him a subtle shake of her head.

"Nothing, huh? My informants tell me otherwise. Go take a break, and I'll make sure Ms. Cather here gets in a good workout."

With the dam cracked and leaking, she had no other choice. She gave Ms. Cather a swift hug and retreated to her office, cursing her weak infrastructure. Why couldn't she be more like G? Just once—and especially that day—she'd love to know what it felt like to not care what people thought or if she let anyone down.

For the next thirty minutes, she leaned back in her chair with her feet propped on the windowsill—the sun streaming over her while she breathed. Her second appointment slot, Joey's usual time, remained unfilled. She hadn't had the heart to fill it to someone else since losing him, giving her more time to tuck away her heartache before facing Rick, her third appointment.

She sighed, knowing he would see right through her poor acting.

Since Jackson was on the road and unavailable to put her world back into perspective, she called her mother.

"How's the unpacking going?" she asked after Eden answered.

"It's... interesting."

"That good, huh?" A loud clatter rang through the phone, then a variety of four-letter words. "Dad sounds like he's having fun."

"You have no idea. I had to get him out of the house for a little sanity yesterday. Told him I had a craving for some chocolate milk. He was gone for over two hours."

"Guess you both needed the break."

"How are things with you, sweetheart? Tell me about your vacation."

In case the tears returned, she pulled a tissue from the box sitting on her desk. "Amazing and terrifying at the same time."

"Oh! That sounds—" Another loud bang. "Did something happen?"

"I met someone."

"Really? I'd love to hear about—Charlie, can you give it a rest? I'm trying to talk to Emily!"

"Oh. Hi, lovie," her father yelled to her from across the room, and Emily's heart expanded. She missed them so much.

"Tell Dad I said hi."

"Emily says hi and to be quiet," Eden yelled, then giggled into the phone. "That ought to do it. You were saying?"

"His name is Jackson, and he's the most amazing man I've ever met—besides Dad, of course."

"Of course," her mother agreed. "Do you have a picture?"

"Hold on a sec." Frustrated that she hadn't taken any photos while they were together, she saved a shot from his social media page and texted it to her mother.

"Oh, my," Eden said after opening the text. "Well, he sure is handsome."

"That's an understatement. And he's so much more than that, but I don't have enough time to list his qualities out for you."

"This sounds serious. Does he live in Myrtle Beach?"

"No. Virginia."

Her mother, who knew her well, heard the disappointment in her voice. "Don't worry. If it's meant to be, it will work out. Don't stress over it. So, what does he do?"

Emily checked the time. "Shoot. Mom, I need to get back to work. I had a short break and wanted to call and check on you."

"Alright. I want to hear more later. And we're fine. Go take care of your patients. They need you."

Her mother was right, she thought as she hung up the phone. Her patients deserved her best, and she refused to let down another patient that day. Deciding some friendly company would do her good, she rushed to the fitness room. As she'd hoped and fully expected, Rick had arrived early.

For the entire appointment, she gave him undivided attention without cracking. He didn't bring up her blotchy face and red eyes. No doubt he noticed. But having four sisters, he knew when he should ignore it or ruin his workout. With an unspoken agreement to keep it light that day, they got the work done without embarrassing either of them.

"How are you feeling?" Lucas asked, leaning on the door to her office with his hands in the pockets of his sleek khaki shorts.

"I'm okay. Thanks."

"Want to tell me what happened earlier?"

"Not particularly."

"Alright, but I think you already know I'm a good listener."

An understanding and empathetic smile sprang to his lips, and she almost considered it. "I appreciate that, but I've got it under control."

"Good. If you change your mind…"

"Understood." She held firm until he backed out of the room, then dropped her head onto the desk. She had control over nothing in her life.

"I thought you were fine," he said, causing her head to shoot up. "What's wrong, Emily?"

He knelt beside her chair, searching her face for information she didn't want to disclose.

"I don't know. Well, that's not true. I do know, but I don't want to talk about it."

"Okay."

"I'm so overwhelmed with everything that's happened recently, and I've experienced every type of emotion imaginable. I'm worried about a few things, and everything I want to control is completely out of reach. We got home late last night, and I haven't been sleeping. I just need some time to readjust my system from all the unexpected changes, I guess." She looked down at her trembling hands and noticed Lucas's rested mere inches from her leg on the chair.

"I thought you didn't want to talk about it."

A giggle spurted out, and along with it, some of the stress weighing on her. Maybe she did need someone to talk to. Shockingly, Lucas made himself available to her as he had when he showed up to escort her to Joey's funeral on his day off. If he didn't act like such a pretentious jerk most of the time, they might have become friends.

"How about I buy you lunch? We can order in."

"That actually sounds nice. Thank you."

"You're welcome. Give me a few, and I'll be back with your favorites from the deli next door." He rose and headed out, stopping to at her. "Turkey wrap with avocado and lemonade, correct?"

"Yes. That would be great."

Fifteen minutes later, they sat on the floor of her office, eating and talking as they had during their get-to-know-you lunch two weeks ago. Like last time, conversation flowed easily, and he was charming, even considerate. But concern that this meeting would end with another indecent proposition kept her from relaxing completely.

"Thank you, Lucas. I feel much better."

"Glad I could help." After cleaning up, he helped her to her feet and opened his arms for a hug.

Suspicious, she searched his face for motives and the lurking surprises she'd come to expect from him. Finding none, she surrendered. It felt good to be embraced by friendly, compassionate arms. Felt even better to forgive.

She no longer had the energy to harbor embarrassment over their kiss or the resentment that festered after he suggested they sleep together. She was partly to blame, after all. She'd given in to impulse while consumed with grief over Joey's death and failed to be stern when he pushed for more.

Grateful they'd gotten through those rough patches, she slid her arms from around his back. "My next patient should be here soon. Thanks again for lunch."

"No problem. See you out there."

Shaking her head, she grabbed her tablet and followed. Her world felt right side up again, giving her the mindset to conquer the afternoon. Although, if someone had told her that Lucas Oliver would be the one to give her that gift, she would have stumbled over herself laughing.

Chapter Eleven

☆ ☆ ☆

Jackson

"This is the worst bar I have ever been to," Ben complained. Other than a few waiters, he and Jackson were the only people in the rugged establishment.

"It's not that bad." Jackson's eyes rolled in response to Ben's usual theatrics. He could enjoy any bar if it had cold beer and good food, but this place had the potential to test that.

It had small town, rustic charm with a side of low-budget scary movie. Creepy taxidermy eyes stared at them from every wall. The neon signs and LED string lights outlining every surface and molding gave the large room a dull, eerie glow. The scent of rust, dried beer, and sweat overpowered any appetizing smells the kitchen might produce. Hopefully, it had seen better days at some point in its existence.

"I seem to recall suggesting we keep looking," Jackson said, coming back from his visual trip around the room, "but *someone* didn't want to waste prime drunk time walking around."

"Whatever. Did you see the cross-eyed deer head behind me?" Ben shuttered, refusing to turn around for fear of meeting the creature's glassy gaze. "This place is disturbing."

"Well, you picked it, so shut up and order."

"Welcome, gentlemen. My name is Levi, and I'll be your server tonight," the waiter greeted with no energy or change in expression, matching the decor. "You ready to order?" He reached for the notepad and pen in his back pocket as a swerving customer jostling a large ice bucket and collection of long-neck bottles knocked him into the table. Catching himself on the wobbly table, he whipped around, anger snapping into place when he recognized the offender. "I should have known."

"Sorry, man. Just trying to find my table."

"It's where it always is," Levi mumbled and collected his notepad from the floor.

"I'll have what that guy is having," Ben announced, pointing at the only other customer, then at Jackson. "My friend, here, promised to hold my hair while I puke, and I want zero memories of this hellhole."

"For one, he doesn't mean that," Jackson corrected and flashed Levi an *I'm sorry* smile. "Second, I never said that and never will. Just to be clear."

"Six." Ben shot up from his chair before noticing Jackson's disapproving stare. "Please," he added and stormed off.

"What's his problem?" Levi asked.

"Don't get me started. I'd like a glass of water, and we'll both have the steak. Thank you." He made a mental note to double the poor guy's tip, then checked his phone. No messages from Emily, but he hadn't expected—

He twisted in his seat at the sound of Ben's cackle echoing through the hollow bar. At another table near the stage, he and the only other customer engaged in an animated discussion. Unconcerned and grateful to have Ben out of his hair, he spun back around.

The day had been long and draining, and he'd give anything for an uneventful, relaxing evening. Focusing on the dull music overhead and the soft bustling noises of the staff nearby, he tried to enjoy the rare reprieve from Ben's relentless questioning and drama.

But the quiet had never been kind to him.

Having zero faith in his ability to relax, he inserted himself into the center of the drama against his better judgement. "What's so funny?" he asked, joining what would soon morph into chaos.

"Have a seat." Ben pushed out a chair with his foot. "This is Nick. He's also a Marine."

The hand not clutching a bottle like a lifeline reached across the table to Jackson. "*Was* a Marine," Nick corrected.

"Once a Marine, always—"

"Yeah, yeah," he said, cutting Jackson off. Snatching another beer out of the bucket, he twisted off the cap and tossed it over his shoulder.

Levi snatched the top out of the air on his way to their table, and Ben's face lit up. "Nice catch."

"I've had lots of practice," he growled, then dropped the top into the second full bucket as he set it down. "Are you going to eat something tonight or drink your dinner again?" he asked Nick.

In answer, he lifted the bottle to his lips and drank.

"Add another steak to my tab," Jackson whispered.

"He hates me," Nick informed them after Levi left. "But I can't blame him. I've made a lot of bad decisions in this bar. Like this one."

"What are you—"

"Woody!" Nick turned and yelled toward the bar. "Three shots! The usual." Spinning back around, he leaned his elbows on the table with a smirk. "I've puked on Levi at least twice. That's all I remember anyway. See that billiard table over there?"

Jackson and Ben followed where he pointed.

"That's the replacement I had to work two jobs to buy after I threw a guy on the first one in a fight." A shoulder tipped up as if it was inconsequential. "Carved my name into the bar counter. Had eleven beers that night. Levi didn't care too much for my art since his grandpa built it out of some stupid tree from his childhood. Got banned for a month while he cooled down."

"Why do you come here?" Ben asked, too intrigued by Nick's stories to drink the beer he ordered. He seemed to enjoy not being the biggest screw-up in the room for once. "It looks like it's been dying a slow death for decades."

"It's early. Wait until the shift ends at the factory out back. Then, it gets interesting. Why aren't you drinking?" he asked Jackson.

"He's a lightweight," Ben answered for him with a crooked grin, raising the bottle to his lips as if to prove he wasn't.

"I try to avoid hangovers." Nausea and headaches don't help accomplish missions—he had first-hand knowledge on the subject—and he'd tolerate zero delays in reaching Savannah.

"Woody!" Nick yelled without turning around. "Where are those shots? And bring two more for my new friends."

"We don't need any shots."

"Speak for yourself," Ben protested. "I would love a shot."

Nick tipped his beer in salute, then turned to Jackson. "I usually drink alone. People tend to avoid me, so if you're going to take the risk and sit at my table, you're doing a shot."

"Fine. And for your information," he said to Ben. "You could never outdrink me."

"Oh, really? I've never seen you have more than a few. Challenge accepted."

"Now, we're talking." Nick slammed his hand on the table, considering the matter settled. "So, Jackson, where were you stationed?"

"Some at Quantico, some in D.C., but mostly Okinawa."

"Don't like to be home, huh?"

"Not in the least." Jackson accepted the open beer Ben handed him.

"I grew up in North Carolina and wanted to stay close. Never did much traveling. There's a base in the state, you know."

"I do."

"But what do I get? I get shipped to Hawaii. The farthest fuckin' base from North Carolina."

"There are worse places to be."

"You don't sound like you wanted to be in the military," Ben said

"Nope. Didn't have a choice."

"Everyone has a choice of what to do with their life."

"Not in my family. You're either a doctor or a Marine. I'm not cut out for either, but four years in the Marines sounded a lot better than ten or more years of school."

"What was your specialty?" Jackson asked.

"Communications." A grin brightened his milky eyes. "I like to talk. What about—it's about time," he complained as Woody set the tray of shots on the table with a growl.

Nick snatched one up and raised it for a toast. "To finally having someone to drink with and talk to that doesn't want to punch me in the face... but it's only a matter of time." Not waiting for the others, he tossed back the shot and reached for another.

Ben did the same, slammed the glass down to the table, and stared at Jackson. "Your turn."

"Are you sure about this? Because the second you look like you're about to vomit, I'm leaving your ass here."

"Never been more sure of anything in my life."

"Alright. You asked for it."

———

"What's the stupidest thing you've ever done?" Ben asked Nick. Over the past hour, while eating and emptying bottles, they quizzed each other on life lessons and adventures.

"How much time do we have?"

"I only asked about the stupidest, not all of them."

"That's easy." Nick cracked his neck, looking suddenly uncomfortable.

"Let me guess, it involves a woman."

"Oh, Benjamin. She's the reason I drink these days."

"Figures." He scowled, surely thinking of his own female-centered problems.

"She showed me a way out of the disaster my life had become. Taught me that I could be truly happy and make something of myself."

"What happened? Where is she?"

"I have no idea. I come here every day hoping she shows up or to learn where she may be."

"Why here, of all places?" Ben asked, looking around the room without hiding his disgust.

"This is where we met, and her family owns it." He pointed at the bar. "Woody, he's her uncle, and that waitress over there is her cousin. Levi is her brother. He runs the place, and like I mentioned, he hates me."

"Dude, there are a ton of women out there. Why put yourself through all this torture? Don't look at me like that," Ben scoffed when Jackson tilted his head and glared at him. "I know I'm one to talk, but this is different. I'm not miserable and could move on if I wanted to."

Nick sighed out his frustration. "I can't. Without her, I have no purpose. No reason to get up in the morning or stay sober."

"How long has it been?" Jackson asked. "Since you've been sober."

"Day of discharge."

"How long ago was that?"

"Two years."

He watched Nick's hand tremble as he lifted the bottle to his lips and thought of Will. He'd consumed an unhealthy amount of alcohol after returning, thinking it would help him cope.

"Levi," Ben yelled when he appeared nearby to wipe down a table. "Why don't you tell Nick where his girl is?"

"This is none of our business," Jackson scolded through clenched teeth, cutting his eyes to Nick hunched over the table, his eyes distant and glistening.

"If she wanted to see him," Levi answered flatly, "she'd be here."

"Wow. If you're not going to help, the least you could do is bring us another round." Ben slapped Nick on the back and waited for Levi to stomp off. "It's time to get this party started and raise a middle finger to them all. What do you say?"

Nick sat motionless for a moment, then slowly raised his head. "I'm all in on that, brother."

Chapter Twelve

☆ ☆ ☆

Emily

Did Lucas really ask her that? With the new day, Emily arrived at work that morning with her spirits high. But once again, it didn't take long before she found herself in yet another strange conversation she couldn't navigate. "Excuse me?"

"Who was that guy you were with last night? On River Street," Lucas repeated.

"Who?" She stared at him as if he'd grown a second head. "George? The gelato vendor?" Foregoing her usual treadmill routine, she ran from her little home to River Street, several miles east, stopping at her favorite gelato stand before jogging back.

"Nice try. I was talking about Dr. Allen's patient."

"Who?" Then, she remembered and squinted at him, trying to decipher the purpose of his questioning. "You mean Cameron?"

Her ex had cornered her by the gelato stand, and they talked for a bit. An uncomfortable invitation to join him at the bar resulted in an equally awkward refusal. It was the second time he'd asked her out since he showed back up in Savannah. The first one, two weeks ago, she ignored. He'd asked by text after she filled in for Dr. Allen and handled his physical therapy appointment. She didn't understand his waltzing back into her life like they didn't have an explosive break up and avoided each other ever since. And she didn't understand Lucas's obsession over the chance meeting either.

She breezed past him to put some distance between them, but he stepped into her path—the newly formed lines between his dark brows indicating he had more to get off his chest.

"We have a strict policy against dating patients."

"Yeah, and I agree with that policy," she said, challenging him. His cheeks flashed red, and something flared in his eyes she hadn't seen in him before. "Jealousy isn't a good look on you, Doctor Oliver."

He closed the breath of space she managed to gain. "Are you seeing him?"

"No. But tell me something, Dr. Oliver. Where's the policy that prohibits employees from harassing their co-workers."

"Do you feel harassed, Emily?"

"Very. Now, unless you have something work-related to tell me, I need to get back to the fitness room."

He lowered his head to whisper in her ear. "I haven't forgotten about us." The heat radiating off him scorched her skin.

"You're delusional. There is no *us*." So much for squashing his growing obsession with her. She'd run out of ideas to make him understand and leave her alone. "Take your hand off me."

"It's only a matter of time, Emily. You might as well give yourself to me."

"Never."

Grinning, his haughty glare traveled down his perfect nose to land on her. "You know, there's a line of therapists begging to join this practice."

"Are you threatening to fire me if I don't sleep with you?" Her eyes dared him to say it. Two can play that game.

"You're very sexy when you're pissed. Go ahead. Get angry all you want. I'm not going anywhere until you're in my bed. Or do you prefer the floor? 'Cause I'm up for—"

Yanking herself away from him, she rushed into the hallway. He'd crossed the line, and she was finished playing games and tiptoeing around him. Something had to be done, officially, if she was going to regain her happy, carefree existence in the job she adored. Once Human Resources got involved, he'd have no choice.

Feeling as though she had a new layer of protection, albeit a paper-thin one, she called Genevieve on the way home to check on her.

"I'm fine," Genevieve sighed into the phone. "Stop worrying."

"Can't. Comes with the best friend title. What were you doing? Did I wake you?"

"No. I'm just relaxing with my feet up on the couch. Been here all day, snuggling with my laptop and phone. It's not as satisfying as a strong, sexy man, but it's all I have." The laugh that followed didn't drip with her usual sass.

"I'm sorry, sweetie. I'll stop by the house and get a few things. Then, I'm coming over to cook dinner. Don't you dare try to stop me."

"Wouldn't dream of it."

After changing, Emily added a container of raw chicken and salad fixings to a cooler bag. The wine bottle on the kitchen counter beckoned to her, especially after the day she had. But with Genevieve and her new restrictions in mind, she ignored it. She was proud of her friend for following doctor's orders to cut back on her drinking, but it hadn't helped sweeten her mood. And it wasn't helping Emily now.

She tossed the bag over her shoulder, catching a glimpse of the back door sitting slightly open, with the motion. Frozen where she stood, her over-stimulated brain immediately thought intruder—*another gift from Lucas*. Had someone been in her house? Were they still there?

Listening for strange noises, she replayed changing in the bedroom. She hadn't noticed anything to put her on alert then and didn't now, allowing her to relax. That morning, she must not have closed the door properly after having her coffee on the porch. Winds from the tropical storm, threatening off the coast, must have pushed it open.

Thinking nothing of it, she shut the door and grabbed the lock, but it wouldn't budge. She was in and out so much with the back porch swing being her favorite spot in the house, she rarely remembered to lock it. She could have missed it jamming along the way.

She added it to her mental list of things to deal with later and hurried out the front door. Genevieve waited for her.

———

"That was the best salad I've ever tasted," Genevieve said, mopping up the remaining salad dressing in the bowl with her last bite of garlic bread.

"Only because you haven't eaten enough today." She gauged Genevieve's bare face, unbrushed hair, and sunken cheeks. "Am I right?"

"Can't put anything past you."

"How are your glucose numbers? Are you checking them like they showed you?"

"Don't worry, Mom. They're fine." She smiled when Emily cocked her head and glared at her with an *I don't trust a word you're saying and you're going to get yourself into trouble* look—her most practiced expression when it came to Genevieve. "You give me that look a lot."

"Because you deserve it a lot."

"Maybe, but do it too often, and your face will stay that way."

Emily refused to dignify that with a response.

"Relax. My numbers will be unpredictable for a while. I've got this."

"I know you do, but I can't help but worry. You've given me plenty of practice."

"At least I'm not boring." She crossed her legs under her and tapped Emily's knee. "Tell me. How was Dr. Horny today?"

"You wouldn't believe me if I told you."

"Oh, please do. My day has been a big pile of shit. And look at me. I need a good story to take my mind off it all."

Emily grinned. "You look beautiful as—"

"Cut the flattery. It will get you nowhere. Out with it."

"Fine." With a sigh, she wished for the wine she passed over at home. If it were there, she'd drink it straight from the bottle. "We didn't talk last night, so buckle up. This one's a doozie."

"Don't keep me in suspense."

"During my first appointment, yesterday, I nearly had a nervous breakdown."

"Why?"

"You know me. When I worry, I don't sleep. It festers until I hit my breaking point."

"I do know you, and I can confidently say that your worrying is unnecessary most of the time."

"Everything is unnecessary to you."

"Not everything." She winked. "Anyway. Your crying is nothing new. What's got your panties all bunched this time?"

"That's quite the list. You, Jackson, my parents moving, Lucas. And I was already exhausted from the trip. All of that compounding together broke the dam."

"I appreciate you worrying about me, but I can't have you making yourself sick over it," she said, taking Emily's hand when her eyes glistened. "If you lose it, then I'll lose it, and we both know you're a prettier crier than me."

"Yeah, right. You never cry about anything."

Genevieve's shoulders popped up with her agreement. "But what about the doctor? I doubt a few tears shed at work is all the juice to squeeze out of this story."

"No. I'm just getting started."

"Good. I want all the juicy details."

"Just before lunch, Lucas came to check on me. He was gentle and sweet but kept his distance, enough to knock my guard down, and I let him buy me lunch. He picked up some sandwiches, and we ate in my office while I talked it out. Surprisingly, he listened like we were old friends, and it helped."

"Jerk."

"Hold that thought. Before he left, he wanted a hug."

Genevieve's face scrunched with suspicion. "What did you do?"

"The usual. I caved. I'm so bad at saying no, and it felt as if we'd gotten past the unease between us. I thought we were finally friends."

"Guys like him don't have women friends."

"Yeah, not when his first reaction to *no* is sexual harassment. He threatened to replace me today if I don't sleep with him."

"No, he didn't. Did you report it?"

"Not yet. He isn't thinking straight. He's jealous."

"Jealous of who? Jackson?"

"No. He doesn't know about Jackson. It's Cameron."

"Cam? Cameron Reid? I thought you reburied him in the terrible boyfriend graveyard where he belongs. How does this guy even know about Cam? You're not seeing him."

Emily's frown deepened. "I'm not seeing Lucas either, so why would he care? He saw me with Cameron and—"

"Stop right there. Why in the world were you with that asshole? And where?"

"Sorry. Like I said, there's so much you've missed." She told Genevieve about running into her ex on River Street, Cameron's invitation to join him and his friends at the bar, and Lucas' reaction the next day. "It's all so bizarre. How is this happening to me? This kind of stuff is usually reserved for you."

"The hell it is. This would never happen to me."

"Whatever. Guys go blind with lust when they look at you and usually multiple at a time."

"I can't help that, and what you're going through is a shining example of why I don't do relationships."

"What do relationships have to do with this?"

"You get attached, then someone in the relationship usually turns into a whack job in the end. In your case, it's always the guy."

"Thanks. But I'm not in a relationship, nor do I want to be, with either of them. I have only one man in my life, and he's perfect."

"Careful." Genevieve pointed an accusatory finger, pinching her lips together. "You used to say that about Mr. Ghost of Boyfriends Passed."

"I never said Cameron was perfect."

"Okay, maybe not, but you attached yourself to him for years, thinking he could do no wrong, and look what happened." She circled a finger outside her ear. "Whack job."

"Well, things are different with Jackson. It feels perfect." Just one mention of his name, and suddenly, he was all she could think about. "What?"

"You blanked out and didn't participate in my Cam bashing party. You're not having second thoughts, are you?"

"Of course not."

"Must be Jackson, then."

"Guilty," she admitted with a grimace, making Genevieve's eyes roll. "Watch it. You do that too much, and you'll…"

"Blah blah blah. For that, I'm throwing you out."

"Why?"

She grabbed Emily's hands and pulled her up. "For allowing a man to interrupt girl time. Get out of here and go call your man. I'm ready to hit the sack and release a little of this built-up tension, if you know what I mean."

"Eww. I do. Thanks for that."

"Any time." After handing Emily the bag she'd used to carry in the groceries, she walked her to the door. "Dinner was great. Thanks for coming over and making me feel human again."

"You're welcome. Now, lay off the vibrator and get some sleep."

"How else am I going to wear myself out?"

"Ugh. You're unbelievable." Spinning around, she escaped down the hallway.

"You should try it. Or maybe a little phone sex with Jackson would suffice."

Emily waved without turning around. "I'm not listening."

"Yes, you are, and you know it would be hot."

―――――

In her kitchen, Emily poured herself that glass of wine she'd wished for earlier and pushed the reset button by dialing Jackson's number.

"Hi, handsome," she greeted when he picked up, jumbling her insides like a dismantled puzzle. "How was your run today?"

"Worth it now that I hear your voice."

"Legs hurting?"

"Yeah. I didn't meet my goal today, but at least it's progress." He let out an audible sigh. "But I'm still on track to reach Savannah by next Friday."

"Really? That's amazing. You really are running like lightning."

"I'm a man of my word."

"Thank goodness," she said, laughing. "By the way, what were you guys up to last night?" She fought the concern creeping into her thoughts, knowing there was no reason for it. "The photos on your sites were interesting."

"Great. I should have known Ben would post something. Interesting is an understatement. It wasn't as bad as I'm sure it looked, and the night had a better ending than expected."

"What do you mean?"

"We met Nick at the strangest bar. He was discharged from the Marines two years ago and reminded me so much of Will." The phone went silent for a moment as Jackson gathered his emotions at the mention of his friend's name. Her heart broke for him. "He's been struggling to adjust, and alcohol is his coping mechanism."

"Oh, no."

"He was already wasted when we met him, and it snowballed from there."

"Ben seemed to enjoy having a drinking buddy."

"Yeah. Another shining example of someone trying to drink away his troubles."

"What troubles could he possibly have?"

"The usual."

"Not enough women there throwing themselves at you three handsome guys?"

"Not exactly, and don't worry. There's only one woman these eyes want to see."

"And I can't wait until you can. So, how did the night end? You must not have passed out in a ditch somewhere since you said it ended better than it looked."

"After I figured out what was going on, I convinced him to go back into rehab."

"Go back?"

"He walked out the week before and went straight to the bar. The sad part is he could only afford a month of treatment, and that wasn't enough to make any real change."

"If he can't afford it, how is he going?"

"I'm his new sponsor. He'll be able to stay longer this time and get the help he needs. Something I couldn't do for Will."

"Jackson, that's so generous of you. Who knows what would have happened to him if you hadn't been there?"

"He has a chance at a new start now. The rest is up to him."

"You're the most amazing man I've ever met. I'm so proud of you."

"Thank you. I just want to help as many veterans as I can, but I think it helps me more than it does them."

"I believe that. There's real power in giving. Warms the soul."

"Enough about me," he said quickly with an audible exhale. "How was your day?"

"I rather talk about you. Your life is way more exciting."

"Fine. Let's settle in the middle. How's Genevieve?"

"Not good. I just came from her apartment."

"Is she still having side effects from the concussion?"

"No, or at least I don't think so. It seems to be something else. She won't talk about it. Maybe she's having trouble adjusting to her new lifestyle. It's a complete one-eighty from what she's used to."

"That's understandable. She's lucky to have you to help her through it." He paused for a yawn. "I guess I should get going. It's late, and I have a critical mission to accomplish. Don't want anything to cause a delay."

"No. That's the last thing we want. Get some sleep and come back to me as fast as you can."

———

Emily had never lost her temper before. Always amenable, first to back down, calm, collected, weak. For the first time in her twenty-six years on earth, she teetered on the verge of erupting.

Every day since returning from vacation, she got through her schedule, frantically glancing over her shoulder, always wondering when Lucas would pop around a corner and embarrass her, corner her, touch her. Constantly on alert, she powered through every minute on sheer tenacity.

Her office was her only refuge—a safe place to lock herself in and Lucas out. The few minutes she'd steal here or there to breathe and recuperate grounded her enough to keep her focus on what mattered—her patients.

After the last appointment on Friday, she retreated to her office and locked the door. She leaned her head against the cool wood, grateful to have finished out the week without any uncomfortable encounters. Lucas kept to himself the last few days, mainly because she made sure she was never alone. He couldn't sneak up on her with witnesses, and she considered the idea and her ability to pull it off a major win.

"Did you wear those tight shorts for my benefit?" Lucas asked.

She spun around. "What are you doing in my office?"

"Making it impossible for you to avoid me."

"Lucas, this has to stop." With her back against the door, she quietly turned the lock and held tight to the handle. "I don't want to be with you."

"The way you kissed me said otherwise."

He glided across the room, stopping close enough to count the evening stubble along his jawline.

"That was a mistake, not a statement."

"It didn't feel like a mistake. I'm tired of waiting, Emily."

"You know what I'm tired of?" Her heart pounded in her ears, but she looked him dead in the eye and fought the impulse to run. "I'm tired of being pursued like a dog in heat. Like my feelings and what I want don't matter."

"Playing hard to get will only make having you that much more satisfying."

"I'm not playing, Lucas. Leave me alone, or I'll file a complaint."

Stumbling back on a hearty laugh, his hand slapped over his stomach. "Oh, Emily. You don't have the balls, but your confidence is adorable."

The afternoon sun streamed through the window and blanketed her desk in a beacon of white light, giving her an idea. She waited while he lowered into her chair and propped up his feet, brazen amusement still on his face. At least this time, his perpetual arrogance played right into her plan.

"Top drawer."

"What about it?" He studied her, his grin slowly fading as he cautiously slid open the drawer. Color rose up his neck, and he eyed her with a new fury before slamming his palm on the desk.

She jumped at the clash, cursing herself for the gut reaction and what it showed him. He retrieved the completed harassment complaint form and scanned it, his frown deepening with every turn of the page. At least he was finally taking her seriously.

"You say here that I touched you against your will." His eyes raised to her as he pointed at the page. "When? Oh," he interrupted before she could answer. "Do you mean when you climbed into my lap on the fitness room floor and wrapped your legs around me? That was so hot, but I believe your lips *and* tongue, mind you, touched me, too." Closing his eyes, he breathed deep. "Good times."

She jumped again when he shot to his feet.

"This is a good one." Tapping on the form, he smiled over his shoulder. "I can assure you that I have better things to do than follow you around, but I must admit, the view is quite nice from back there."

"Lucas, I don't have time for this. Give me the form and get out of my office."

"Let go of the handle and come take it."

"You sound like a spoiled child."

"Wait. I have a better idea." After a few steps, he stood over the small shredder she kept by the desk and pushed the power button.

"Don't you dare."

"Dare? I do love a dare."

He placed the papers into the slot, slicing the salvation she'd labored and fretted over for hours into countless irreconcilable pieces in a matter of seconds. The motor switched off, it's betrayal complete, and Lucas closed his eyes to revel in his victory. Silence hovered in the air like suffocating smoke.

"That was almost as satisfying as having your sexy body in my hands." His eyes flew open to meet hers. "Almost. But let me make one thing clear." He started toward her, and her hand tightened around the door handle. "If you ever go to *my* staff again with even the slightest thought of tainting my reputation…" Pausing mere inches away from her face, he slapped a hand against the door behind her. "I won't be as forgiving or gentle the next time."

Shocked speechless and stuck in an endless loop of one embarrassing and frightening situation after another, her brave attempt to set him straight disintegrated like her ticket to freedom he sent through in the shredder.

"So," he began and assumed a casual stance, his hands in his pockets. "Unless you want to take care of our little problem right here as I suggested, I'd appreciate you opening the door. It's been a long day, and I need a drink."

She could only stare at him. How could he stand before her as though he'd said nothing threatening? Where were all the things she should be screaming to make him back off? He'd offered to leave, and she wanted to get out of there untainted and untouched.

With a turn of the handle, she opened the door.

But just when she thought she was free of him, until Monday at least, he stopped in front of her. His woodsy cologne burned her nose, and a cold chill raised the hairs on her neck as his eyes glided over her again. She stood firm, expressionless, refusing to tremble as he undoubtedly expected.

His gaze traveled back to hers, and a satisfied smile touched his lips. That one sinister motion had her fearing what he might do next. With the building empty, he could hold her hostage and follow through on his threats. And no one would hear her scream.

He opened his mouth to speak, then closed it on a sigh. "You look beautiful today, Emily, as always."

And then he was gone.

Slamming the door closed, she leaned against it and slid to the floor. He knew how to toy with her fears and test her boundaries, mastering the game he'd solidified in stone with this last stunt. And he ensured she had no card to play when he shredded her last hope.

But she couldn't continue like this. Either she needed a plan to stop Lucas or a new job. With that, the barbed wire around her stomach tightened. Both options were inconceivable. He was too powerful, cunning, and always one step ahead of her. And leaving her patients after the progress they'd made together would rip her heart in two.

Helpless and heartbroken, she cried on the floor until the river ran dry.

———

"I can't believe you're going to be here in two days." Lying on the bed, Emily looked at Jackson through a video call. It wasn't the same as being with him, but it soothed the ragged edges of a hard day. "These last two weeks felt like a month."

"Tell me about it. How's Genevieve? Ben's beside himself wondering."

"She's doing a little better, but she's still not herself. Why is Ben… Have they not kept in touch?"

"No. That's the problem."

"Now that you mention it, we haven't talked about him since leaving the hospital." Frustrated, Emily let out a long sigh. "But that's what she does."

"He's hoping to see her while we're there. Think she'll be up for it?"

"I'm sure she will, but if not, they'll just have to figure it out on their own."

"Good. I want all your attention while I'm there."

"Speaking of that. How long do you think you'll stay?" Whatever the answer, she would be grateful.

"I'm not sure. Depends on how long it takes to recover. I've been torturing my body, and I may need to relax for a while." A playful smile sprang across his lips, but it didn't erase the evidence of how difficult the journey had been on him.

"Selfishly, I hope it takes a long time, but I have a few therapies we can try to ease the pain."

"I may take you up on that." A yawn surprised him, and he checked his watch.

"Don't say it," she said quickly. "I hate this part."

"Me, too. I can't wait to see you tomorrow."

"You better run like lightning, soldier. That's an order."

Chapter Thirteen

☆ ☆ ☆

Emily

The brutal wait to have Jackson back in her arms ended when he appeared through the distant haze. When they last talked, she suggested they meet during her lunch break later that day, knowing she'd already taken off work. She wanted to surprise him. And when she got the call from Ben with details on Jackson's timing and route, she rushed out the door to meet him at the Savannah city limits.

But spending every available minute with him hadn't been her only motivation for the extended weekend. She hoped it also added a little insurance to her Lucas situation. He'd kept his distance since ambushing her in her office, and she cautiously considered the matter settled—and just in time, too. Watching Jackson glide over the horizon, she could finally let her excitement latch on.

With the temperature already stiflingly hot and humid, like most summer days in Georgia, he'd tied his long hair up off his neck—a new and incredibly sexy look she hadn't seen on him yet. The effort it took to run these last several miles, accentuated every glistening muscle as if an artist had designed and painstakingly carved each one to perfection. And she couldn't wait another second to trail her fingertips over them all.

Climbing out of the car, she leaned against the side and waited. It took only a few strides for him to recognize her, and his pace quickened. Her heart, now light and full as a balloon, beat faster with every step that brought him closer. His hands reached for her face to kiss her with the sweetest tenderness before she could remember to breathe.

"What are you doing here?" he asked, drawing back and pressing his lips to her forehead and cheek.

Enjoying the feel of the tiny shocks his lips left on her skin, she ran her hands down his chest and abs. He felt as glorious as he looked. "I couldn't wait and wanted to surprise you."

"I'm so glad you did. God, you're beautiful." He took her in his arms, then quickly stepped back. "Oh, sorry," he said, cringing at the new wet splotches on her shirt.

"A little sweat never hurt anything." Taking his hands, she wrapped his arms around her waist, and kissed him until the last two weeks of longing for this moment erased from her mind. "Ready to get out of here?"

"I was ready the second I saw you."

Once in the passenger seat, he leaned back to enjoy the cool air conditioning on his heated skin.

"I thought you might need these." She handed him a towel and bottle of water. "It's a hot one today."

"This was sweet of you. Thanks."

Getting to watch him rub the towel over his face and torso was all the thanks she needed. Her cheeks burned hot when he noticed her gawking. "I got you something else," she added to distract herself from climbing into his lap. She reached into the back seat, handing him a small gift bag with a wide smile.

"What's this?"

"Open it."

He reached inside, and pulled out a dark blue t-shirt, letting it fall open to reveal the design. *My Heart Belongs in Georgia* was printed inside a white outline of the state.

"I couldn't resist."

He took her hand and brought it to his lips. "It's perfect."

To her disappointment, he put on the shirt, covering up the view. But she had to admit, he looked handsome in it, as he would in anything. The man could wear a paper bag, and she'd still melt into a puddle.

"So." She cleared her throat and the lump forming there to keep the melting at bay. "What do you normally do when you reach a stopping point?"

"Now that I have you, all I need is a shower and some food. Did Ben give you the address for the hotel?"

"He did." She put the car in drive and headed in that direction. "Have you been reading the comments on your social media sites?"

"Not for a while."

"The pictures of you are breathtaking, but the comments are just as special. Jackson, you're making a difference with so many people. You should read them."

"Okay. I'll look the next time I'm missing you."

———

After a short drive, they parked at the hotel with plans to pick up the room key and luggage from Ben.

While Jackson showered a few feet away, Emily checked the air conditioner under the window and turned the dial. Was it hot in there? Needing a distraction from thinking about his naked body in the next room, she paced the room, slowing in front of Jackson's suitcase.

It sat open on the rack near the dresser, his running shoes tucked underneath. The perfect rows of tightly rolled T-shirts, shorts, and socks—all systematic, neat, and purposeful—brought a smile to her lips. Only the necessities and nothing out of place. An organized system she could relate to and appreciate. She wondered if he'd always done that or if it came from his military training. Maybe Eleanor taught him. Either way, she had another thing to love about him.

He soon emerged from the bathroom, his hair down and wavy with moisture. The crisp white T-shirt with the Marines logo printed on his left chest framed the wide breadth of his shoulders and down his V-shaped torso, complimenting his tan skin.

Feeling bold, she crossed the room, her impatience to do more than admire him growing with every step. His eyes locked with hers and read her intention. Reaching an arm around her waist, he offered what she craved most—him.

At first contact, she forgot where they were and the cautious and proper woman she'd always been. He tended to do that to her in every situation, but this wasn't just about lust or simply missing him. Love guided every decision, every touch. Like a pricked guitar string, his hands and lips sent a potent sensation strumming through her body. Too overcome by it, she couldn't stop the moan from vibrating inside her throat.

"Welcome to Savannah," she said for a distraction when he separated from her suddenly. He did that whenever his control faltered, and he needed to readjust his grip around it. Leaning her head back, she took in the lazy, remorseful eyes staring back at her and smiled. Maybe that indestructible resolve of his was starting to crack.

"I don't usually get this type of reception when I enter a city," he said with a little more rasp than usual. "I have to say, Savannah is my favorite."

"Second best news I've heard all day. Time for step three."

"Great. I'm starving."

Taking him by the hand, she led the way downstairs and to a restaurant two blocks from the hotel. While waiting for their meals to arrive, they sat at a small corner table and talked about Emily's work, hobbies, and family.

"Sorry. I tend to ramble. All we're doing is talking about me."

"Good thing it's my favorite subject."

She tilted her head with a grin. "It's your turn, Jackson Vane. Tell me something about you."

"I run a lot." He smiled, quick and charming, making her heart stutter.

"Funny, but not really what I meant."

"Okay. What do you want to know?"

"Did you talk to anyone or do anything that you haven't already told me about?"

He considered her question for a bit. "I visited a P.O.W. memorial not too far from here, and it made me think of someone I served with."

"Is he still captured?"

"No. Released and discharged about a year ago. We served together during my second tour, but since I haven't talked to him since, I tracked him down and called him."

"That's wonderful. What's his name?"

"Logan Carter."

"How's he doing?"

"He's roaming, trying to heal."

"Roaming?"

He let his frustration out with a rush of air. "It happens to some veterans after they come home, especially after trauma. You feel lost and have no idea what to do next. Life becomes about survival and getting through one day at a time."

She reached for his hand. "Did that happen to you?"

"Yeah. I couldn't figure out how to move forward until I could walk on my own, and even then, it still felt like I was trapped in a maze. Sometimes it gets too hard to see through all the pain and loss. But Logan is taking it to another level."

"What do you mean?"

"He's roaming figuratively and literally. He wanders from town to town, working when he can. Mentally, he's suffering from the abuse he endured while captured. I'm not sure he'll ever be free of that."

"I'm sorry, Jackson. That must have been hard to hear. But at least he's home, and the healing process has begun." His compassion for his friend touched her, and she loved him more for it. "Speaking of healing. How are you doing?"

A server stopped by with their meals, and he waited until they were alone to answer. "Other than the migraines and the pesky joints, I feel great, especially now that I'm with you."

Her lips tipped into smile, as he wanted. "Good. What about your path forward? Have you had any ideas?"

"No." Irritation over having to admit it scrunched his face while he cut into the steak he'd ordered.

"Well, I have full faith that you will, and it will be amazing."

"I hope you're right, but so far, there's only one thing I know for sure about my future."

"What's that?" she asked, ready to be his biggest supporter.

"I want you in it."

She forgot to hold her flirty smile when her heart came to a halt. Focusing on the softness in his eyes as he stared into hers, she realized he meant it. She'd been too afraid to think about the possibility of having a lifetime with him.

But her feelings came unexpectedly like true love should and were too powerful to ignore.

"Jackson—"

The server interrupted again to refill their glasses, saving Emily from embarrassing herself and giving her a chance to realign the conversation to a topic that didn't make her heart want to explode.

When their plates were empty and the bill paid, they strolled downtown. At a souvenir shop, he purchased a stack of postcards, featuring photos of Savannah.

"Who are those for?" she asked.

He held up five cards one at a time. "Eleanor and her family. Ms. Beasley, who's taking care of the house while I'm gone. Billy's parents, Will's family, and Callie, of course."

"Of course."

She noticed he left out his own parents. In all the hours they'd spent talking, he never mentioned them. But before she could ask, something behind him caught her attention, and she took off.

"What do you see?" He followed her to the back corner of the tiny shop.

"Our condo in Myrtle Beach had a clock just like this one." Picking it off the shelf, she ran a finger over the bright colors of the ocean waves and seashells painted on every side. "I wanted to buy one to remind me of our trip but never got the chance. I'd forgotten about it until now."

"Let's get it. No one has to know it came from here."

She grinned up at him. "No one but us."

After checking out, she waited while he addressed each postcard, then escorted him to a satellite post office.

"Where to next, my beautiful tour guide?"

She showed him around downtown, walking through Forsyth Park, past historic estate homes, and under massive Oak trees with cascading Spanish moss. She often went there when she wanted to relax on long weekends and get lost in the beauty that had flourished despite the grueling test of time.

"I love these old houses. So much character and history. What about you? Do you like modern or historic houses?"

"I'm not sure I've ever thought about it."

"Think now. Do you like…" She spun around to look for an example and settled on a yellow Victorian with tall gables and a forest-green door. "Do you like that one?" She pointed, then looked at him, enjoying the way his lips pressed together while he pondered.

"It looks like a Barbie house."

"Hmm. Maybe that's why it's my favorite." Laughing, she searched for another. "There. The navy one is more masculine, and the wide porch would be great for people watching during the day and listening to ghost stories at night."

"Ghost stories? I didn't take you for the type."

"Doesn't everyone like ghost stories? Especially stories told in a haunted house?"

"How do you know it's haunted?"

"Says so on the sign out front. These houses are famous for their uninvited guests, and there are tours for you to see for yourself. I thought everyone knew about Savannah's spirits."

"I've lived under a rock for the past two years and overseas for the eight before that. Guess I have some catching up to do."

"Guess so."

To escape the heat for a bit, they stopped by an ice cream shop, finishing their last bites on a shaded park bench.

"That one," Jackson said without warning and pointed his spoon across the park. "I've been thinking about it, and I can't believe I like that one."

She followed his spoon, her eyes landing on a gray stone Colonial with a wrap-around porch. "Good choice. Classic with no ghost warnings out front."

He laughed. "I thought you liked ghost stories."

"Stories. Not real ones." She glanced over the river at the forming rain clouds in the distance. "Can I ask you something?"

"Sure."

"You seemed to be surprised by your favorite. Why?"

"There's a lot I still don't know about myself. I've lived in camo gear, military bunks, and foreign places my entire adult life. Everything I had or have now first belonged to someone else." He let out a slow exhale. "I have no clue what kind of car or house I'd buy if I had a choice."

"Okay. Why don't you start with some easy questions and build from there?"

Eager for the game, he twisted toward her. "Like what?"

"What's your favorite food?"

"Roasted chicken and asparagus."

"I thought you'd know that one. Favorite type of music."

"That's a hard one." He paused to flip through the options. "Most of the guys in my unit liked seventies rock. It played all the time, so I guess I'd go with that. What about you?"

"Nineties pop." She laughed when he grimaced. "It's fine. I didn't expect my sexy rocker to agree with me. Do you prefer beaches or mountains?"

"Mountains."

"Chocolate or hard candy?"

"Neither."

"Figures." She rolled her eyes with playful disapproval. "Wine, liquor, or beer?"

"Beer."

"Skydiving or bungee jumping?"

"Skydiving."

She straightened in wonderment. "Have you done it?"

"A few times."

"Where?"

"Switzerland, Chili, Australia."

She shook her head, envious of his courage and full passport.

"What's your favorite color?" When he hesitated, she had to ask the obvious question. "It isn't Army green, is it?"

"Heck no. If it was green, it definitely wouldn't be Army green. I'm a Marine, remember?"

"How could I forget? But Marines wear camo, right?"

"Yeah."

"Isn't that the same thing?"

Thunder clashed closer this time, making her flinch.

"We should get out of here before that storm hits," he suggested, adding her empty cup to his and tossing both in a nearby trash can.

Sliding her hand into his, she savored the tingles creeping up her arm from his touch. "How about we go to my house?"

"Sounds like heaven."

"What's Ben doing tonight?" she asked on the way back to her car.

"Who knows. Probably trying to locate the elusive Genevieve."

A snort-laugh burst out of her. "That's a good nickname for her."

"Can you believe he didn't go out or flirt with anyone between Myrtle and here? Not once."

Genuine shock stopped her feet, tugging Jackson into spinning to face her. "You're joking."

"I swear."

"I knew he was head over heels for her."

"That's an understatement, and why he's not handling her silence very well."

"Has he tried contacting her?"

"Many times."

Since Genevieve hadn't mentioned it, that meant… She smiled. "She likes him."

"Not talking to him means she likes him?"

"G doesn't date," she explained, resuming their stroll. "She'll meet someone while out, enjoy his company for a night." She shook her head, showcasing her disapproval of Genevieve's one-night stand habit. "Then never talks to him again. But her experience with Ben has been different, and she's trying to prevent doing something she thinks she doesn't want."

"Sounds complicated and a lot like Ben. But once he met her, all that stopped for him."

"That's sweet. Maybe we should help him out and invite them to dinner," she said, already regretting the idea. She wanted more Jackson, not more distractions.

"Why do you have to be so nice?" Brushing his lips over her fingers, he opened the driver's side door of her car.

While she waited for him to join her, she started the engine and air conditioner. Savannah humidity in mid-May never held back any sweltering punches. "Believe me, I don't want to entertain them either," she continued once he'd buckled into the passenger seat. "But if we can get them together now, maybe they'll leave us alone the rest of the time you're here."

"Not only are you nice, you're smart, too. Deal."

Before taking off, they each called their friends and made plans to meet at a restaurant on River Street that evening. Genevieve balked at first, attempting an excuse to prevent her from attending, but she caved after a little persuasion. Ben, of course, needed no convincing.

———

Jackson

Soon after arriving at Emily's, they nestled on the couch, grateful for the solitude.

"I like your house," he said, taking in her bright living room.

"Thank you. I like it, too."

When he chuckled, she lifted her head off his chest to meet his gaze. He'd be content to stay cuddled together all night if the option arose.

"Where are you going to put your new clock that's not from Savannah?"

"Oh, right." She tilted her head toward the white floor to ceiling bookshelves around the fireplace without taking her eyes off him. "On a shelf somewhere, but out front where I can see it and think of you."

"Good plan."

"Speaking of clocks, I should go change for dinner. It's almost time to leave." Scooting onto her hands and knees, she straddled him, her hair tumbling around his face. "Have you figured out your favorite color yet?" Her sultry voice ignited little fires of awareness all over his body. "I can see if I have something to match."

His hands itched to touch her, stop her from going, but he shoved them under his legs instead. "Not yet. Surprise me."

Amusement bloomed on her face with the challenge before trotting off to her room.

And just in time. A second longer in that position and she would have gotten more than she bargained for.

He felt the magnetic pull toward her before she emerged from the hallway and stood to take in the full view. The short emerald dress she wore exposed her shoulders and gathered at the waist. The flowing skirt and small ruffle at the bottom, softly skimmed her mid-thigh.

"How about that," he mused as she spun to reveal a slit in the loose fabric down her back. "Green *is* my favorite color."

"Just not Army green." Looking confident and beautiful, she went to him and draped her arms around his neck.

His hands found their way to her bare back, making her shudder and melt into him. God, he loved those primal reflex responses of hers.

"I'm glad you like the dress."

"I like it a lot, but I like you in it more." And probably out of it, he thought against his will and wondered how she'd look naked in the late afternoon light streaming through the open blinds.

"Ready?"

The word *no* popped into his head. He wanted to stay there with her in the uninterrupted quiet, holding her through the night. But since she wanted to go and looked at him with love in her eyes, he nodded. He'd do anything she asked and go anywhere, so long as they were together.

———

Not surprisingly, Emily and Jackson were the first the arrive.

"Ben likes to make an entrance," Jackson complained as he slid into the booth before Emily.

"G, too. They're more alike than she wants to admit."

"Don't say that. I can barely tolerate one Ben."

Although the restaurant was packed and buzzing with Friday night excitement, their booth, tucked in the dark, rear corner, provided a seductive amount of privacy. When the server left with their drink order, Jackson wasted no time, framing her jawline and bringing her lips to his. Her pulse revved under his fingertips, and as he'd come to expect and appreciate, she absorbed every emotion he poured into her and doubled it in her response.

"How about we ditch the happy couple at the first opportunity?" he suggested, adoring the way her thick lashes glided open at the sound of his voice.

"My thoughts exactly." Her eyes dropped to his mouth and parted, inviting him back.

Wanting nothing more than another taste of her, he leaned—

"Can you two give it a rest?" Genevieve interrupted before he could satisfy that craving.

He rested his forehead against Emily's, he said with slight irritation, "Hi, Genevieve."

"Great to see you, too. Now, release my friend so she can return to this planet. Hey! Welcome back," she said as Emily sat back in her seat with a sigh. "Regret inviting me yet?"

"Never. Glad you could join us."

"I had nothing better to do tonight and gotta eat on schedule." Her eyes glanced at the ceiling before returning. "Did you order—" Snatching up the menu, she opened it without another word.

"Order what?" Emily got out before Ben scooted into the booth beside Genevieve, who no one could see around the menu she held up.

Jackson swallowed a chuckle at the awkwardness Ben infused into the gathering. Emily had been right about Genevieve's reaction to Ben. The warrior she'd been when she arrived scurried away the moment he arrived.

"Sorry, I'm late," he said, setting a small gift bag on the table. "Hi, Genevieve."

Lowering the menu slightly, she flashed a tight-lipped grin before getting back to reading the entrée list as if it held the answers to life's biggest mysteries.

"It's great to see you again, Ben," Emily greeting with a pat on his arm. "What's in the bag?"

"Something for you and Genevieve."

"Really? How sweet of you."

Accepting the gift, she removed the tissue paper and two thin picture frames. Each held an identical photo of them sitting on the beach, their eyes alive with laughter. The dark ocean and several colorful umbrellas faded in the distance and framed the shot.

"Oh, Ben. I love it. I didn't know you took this photo." She handed the second frame to Genevieve.

"He's sneaky like that," Jackson joked. He'd been a daily victim of Ben's stealthy photo maneuvers since they left Richmond.

"Isn't it a great photo, G?"

"It is. Thank you."

Ben's enthusiasm deflated to match Genevieve's, and Emily cast her a disapproving look. He'd hoped for a more favorable reaction and a ticket back into her good graces for the weekend.

"Thank you, Ben," Emily said, placing the frames back in the bag. "This was so thoughtful of you."

As the night went on, the conversation remained light and fun, allowing space for Genevieve to relax. She actually seemed to enjoy herself. That is, until he and Emily announced their exit, leaving her alone with Ben. He could almost feel the eye daggers she threw at their backs as they escaped.

————

Ben

"Do you ignore every guy you kiss?" The question had been scratching the back of his throat all evening, and the last two reasons to keep it to himself just left the building.

"I haven't ignored you."

"Not responding to a single call or text is the definition of ignoring someone. You could have at least told me to piss off." He tried not to whine, but the pulsing burn in his chest told him he wasn't pulling it off.

"Look, I'm dealing with a lot right now, and I didn't want to give you the wrong idea."

The frustration that had burrowed inside him and festered like an infected wound since Myrtle Beach cracked open the irritating scab and oozed out. "What idea do you think answering any of them would have given me?"

"The wrong one. Now, let me out. I want to go home."

She waited impatiently for him to obey. He wasn't in the mood. "Not until I get an explanation."

"I don't owe you anything. *You* kissed me and almost got us killed, mind you. *You* followed me to the hospital. *You* texted me after you left." Her anger rose to match his and smoldered in her eyes.

That fire, the one she so effortlessly ignited inside him, sent up smoke signals for an urgent retreat. All of which he quickly disregarded.

"I never asked for any of that," she said with finality, like the *I appreciate you* look and the *I like you more than I'll admit* hug she gave him before he left the hospital didn't say otherwise.

"Maybe not in words, but your body and your eyes did. You liked all of it, except for the almost dying part. Don't try to deny it."

"Fine. I don't deny that you're a good kisser, but that doesn't mean I want a relationship. Especially with you, of all people. In fact, it's the last thing I want."

The declaration hit below the belt and throbbed. To return the blow, he cupped her neck with both hands and crushed his lips to hers before she could protest. Near ravenous for her, he felt the jolt—that undeniable connection between them—and the surprise that came with it. She fought him at first, but when his tongue tangled with hers, she molded against him, gripping his hair into a fist. Her back straightened to get better access to him, dissolving every remaining ounce of his frustration with the motion.

Wind and thunder roared outside. Or was that what she did to him? Something stirred inside him every time he touched her, and the storm grew louder and more intense the longer she stayed in his arms.

"Let's get out of here," he whispered before catching her bottom lip in his teeth.

Angling her head to reposition her mouth over his, she pressed against him, begging for his hands to explore, possess, and excite. Something he was happy to do.

Blinding spectacles of warm tingles and booming shockwaves shot through him as she maneuvered onto his lap, the table forcing them closer. She straddled his hips and kissed him hard, indulging in the sensations he ignited. A guttural moan rumbled in her throat as his hands explored her thighs and waist for a bit longer. She rose to her knees, giving him more access. God, he loved the way she moved… but not when that writhing took her away.

With her feet firmly planted outside the booth, she disconnected from him. His eyes flew open, to find her out of reach and glaring down her nose at him.

"I'm leaving, and don't even think about following me."

With a pivot, she sauntered away, leaving him dazed and reaching for her.

Chapter Fourteen

★ ★ ★

Jackson

What do you think Ben and G are talking about?" Emily asked him as she drove down East Broad Street.

"He's probably grilling her about not answering his texts."

"Yeah. She's not going to handle that well. I feel sorry for him."

"Don't. He needs to be reminded that he's not God's gift to women."

"He's not?" She gasped with exaggerated surprise, making him laugh. "How disappointing."

Further down the road, she pulled over and parked. He shifted in his seat as flashes of lightning illuminated her face. The look she gave him wasn't one he'd seen on her yet.

"We're at a crossroads here," she began. "I can go straight and take you to your hotel or turn left to head back to my place."

He knew what that second option implied. He hadn't been with a woman for over a year. It hadn't even crossed his mind. But he also never wanted—no, needed—someone as much as he did Emily. With her permission, he wouldn't hold back and allow that night to change everything between them.

He nodded, and she didn't hesitate. Putting the car in drive, she turned at the intersection—hope, passion, and love swelling like the approaching storm.

Parking in her driveway minutes later, the dark threatening clouds spilled buckets of heavy rain. Laughing, they rushed to the door and stumbled inside, soaked to the skin and dripping.

The dim porch light shining through the windows and the frequent sparks of lightning provided the only light in the room. Stopping in the small area between the foyer and living room, she stood before him and slipped off her sandals, her eyes never leaving his face—the electricity between them overpowering any lingering amusement.

Her hand moved to the thin straps of her dress, pushing the left off her shoulder and then the right. His eyes followed the soft fabric as it collapsed around her waist and as her thumbs dug in behind it above her hips. He knew what came next, and he couldn't breathe. She wiggled and pushed until the dress fell to the floor, exposing the thin lace fabric of her matching undergarments clinging to her damp skin.

Fingers he could barely feel twitched to the drumming heartbeat in his ears, eager to explore every inch of her. He'd go to her and satisfy that hunger if her beauty and surrender hadn't rendered him wholly powerless. Hell, he didn't know how he stood before her now. On second thought, he did. It was her. She recharged and steadied him simply by her presence alone.

Taking on the task herself, she closed the space between them, and his body sprang to attention. She clutched the hem of his shirt, lifting it over his head, then ran her hands lightly down his chest and abs. Everywhere she touched screamed at him to return the favor.

She watched him, her chest heaving with rapid breaths, while he trailed a finger down the side of her neck and gently pushed a bra strap off her shoulder. A low unrestrained moan oozed from her throat when he kissed her there—the same sound he'd been using as a signal to stop before he crossed a line he shouldn't, now fueling his next move.

"You amaze me," he whispered on his way to her parted lips, and she met him the rest of the way. Circling her arms around his neck, she dragged him closer, the weight of his body knocking her backward. The backs of her thighs collided with the couch, and she wrapped a leg around him for balance.

The motion had him yanking back to breathe. Her simple caresses were enough to tip him over the edge. But this was his undoing. Reading him as she always did, she placed a hand on his cheek to calm him, then led the way down the hall.

He sat on her bed while she lit candles around the room, pouring an impossible voltage into their already charged connection. After starting the last flame, she turned and floated into his arms.

Not wanting to rush a moment he'd remember for the rest of his life, he held her tight, his cheek resting against her stomach. In carving every detail into memory, understanding came with it.

His failures with Avery, the strange sensation urging him to leave Richmond, the hardships of his journey to that point, all of it happened for a reason. To strengthen and prepare his heart to not only fall in love but accept love in return. To finally start healing a part of himself he thought would stay forever broken.

———

The feel of Emily's soft fingertip tracing the outline of his jaw gently lulled him back into a reality no dream could ever match.

"Where did you come from, Jackson Vane?"

"Virginia," he answered on a chuckle, immeasurable happiness consuming him.

Smiling, she ran a finger down his chest and along the contour of each defined ab. Her touch sent his contentment spiraling, turning his breathing ragged and unstable. The storm may have given way to the calm outside, but desire churned inside him.

Closing his eyes, he clawed for the control he once held within his grasp before she shattered it. "I have a hard time restraining myself when you do that."

"Maybe I don't want you to."

———

Emily

"I feel like I'm floating through a rainbow and cotton candy clouds," she whispered against his neck, her leg and arm draped across his body.

"I'm right there with you." A satisfied hum vibrated in his throat. "And you know what else?"

"What?"

Linking his fingers with hers, he kissed her forehead. "I don't need the trip to Orlando to find myself anymore. With you, I know who I am and who I want to be."

Overwhelmed by her feelings for him, three words tickled the back of her throat. She wanted so desperately to set them free, but her history flashed through her mind and silenced her. A magnet for beautifully broken men, she had a talent of supporting and guiding them through their struggles. Her mother always said she had a light within her, and maybe that was why all three of her past, and seemingly strong relationships failed. Even after they emerged from the darkness, that incessant light kept pointing them toward something better. And that always meant someone else. She loved, she fixed, and they left—a pattern she hoped would be broken with Jackson.

"What are you thinking about?" he asked and pushed onto an elbow to face her squarely.

She shook her head, trying to forget about what might happen someday and soak in every sweet moment she had with him. Nothing else mattered.

"Whatever it is, you can tell me."

It was true. She could tell him anything, and he wouldn't judge or shut her out. So, why had fears crept into her mind?

"I was just thinking about you," she said, retreating a little when his eyes darkened with sadness.

"I hope not."

"What?"

"You look so troubled."

She touched his cheek to settle his concerns. "It's not what you think. Sometimes, it feels like all this is a dream, and I'm going to wake up one day to find that you no longer want me." Feeling foolish, she dropped her gaze, but he gently lifted her face with a finger under her chin.

"Nothing in this world," he began, leaning in to kiss her cheek, "could ever make me not want you. Since that first night, you've been my everything."

"Oh, Jackson." Drawing him close, she cherished him and the dreams he made come true. However long she had with him—days, months, years, a lifetime—she would treasure every second. Tilting her head back, she surveyed the man who gave her strength to tackle her fears and leaned into it. "My sweet Marine, I'm so in love with you."

———

Jackson

The next time Jackson opened his eyes, the room glowed in the golden light of the rising sun. He watched Emily sleep for a bit, replaying the previous night in his mind. From giving in to their desires to holding each other in contented slumber, all had been unlike anything he'd ever experienced. But it was her confession of love, accompanied by a conviction he'd yet to comprehend, that moved him the most. His only regret was that he'd been too overcome with emotion to tell her that he felt the same. A regret he planned to remedy before he left.

As she curled into him and her muscles went lax again, his thoughts transitioned to the future—the life they could have together after his journey. Lazy Saturdays in bed, dinners on the back deck after work, maybe some kids running around underfoot one day. But would she move to Richmond? All his loved ones would be there soon, making the place he'd avoided for most of his adult life finally start to feel like home. What if she wanted to stay in Savannah and made him choose—her or Richmond?

Such a ridiculous reason for his blood pressure to spike, especially since they'd barely—

"Everything okay?" she asked sleepily, placing her hand on his cheek. She turned his face and pressed her lips sweetly to his until his heart rate resumed a normal pace. "How can you be so tense? My muscles feel like warm milk this morning."

"Side effects of years without you. Old habits die hard."

"Well," she began, drawing herself on top of him. "Is there anything I can do to take your mind off that old nasty habit?"

"Hmm, this is a good start." His hands slid up her back. "Suddenly, I'm feeling a lot better."

Lowering, her lips hovered over his. "What am I going to do with you?"

"Whatever you want."

Laughing, she dropped her head onto his shoulder. "Good to know. Now, tell me what's making you so anxious."

"I can't remember." He shifted to his side and placed her on the bed, brushing stray whisps of hair from her face. "You seem to do that to me."

"Fine. Be all tough if you want, but the next time you feel an old habit pounding in that gorgeous head of yours, please tell me. I want to help."

"You are. Being with you helps more than you know."

"Good. It's where I want you to stay." She snuggled inside his arms, giggling when her stomach growled loud and fierce. "Guess I worked up an appetite. Interested in breakfast?"

"Maybe. My brain gets all fuzzy when you're naked."

"Funny." With a kiss to the tip of his nose, she threw back the sheets and jumped out of bed. "Feel free to relax. I'll make us breakfast."

Propping himself up against the headboard, he watched her blow out the candles still holding on and slide on a short pink robe before leaving the room. Amazing how much his life had changed after spending one night with her, sending him into a whirlwind of feeling content, hopeful, and absolutely terrified at the same time.

In a matter of a few weeks, he'd gone from being buried alive under mound of regret and pain to overwhelmingly happy in love. He worried it couldn't be as real as it felt.

Needing advice and something to soothe his fickle nerves, he called the one other calming force in his life.

"I'm sorry I haven't called in a while," he said after Eleanor answered and grimaced. "It's been a little busy lately."

"That's okay. I'm excited to hear from you. Where are you now?"

"Savannah, Georgia."

"How wonderful. Savannah's such a beautiful place. Last we talked, you were on your way to Myrtle Beach and having a tough time. I've been worried about you. How are you doing, sweetheart?"

"Eleanor, you wouldn't believe me if I told you."

"Try me. I love the unexpected."

He listened down the hall for Emily. A few clanking pots and sizzling noises told him she was still in the kitchen. "I met someone there."

"Wow. That what a wonderful surprise. Does she live in Myrtle Beach?"

"No. She lives here in Savannah."

"Oh, I see."

She paused, undoubtedly fighting with her curiosity before settling on a safe response. Knowing he'd made her squirm with the news brought a smile to his face.

"What's her name?"

"Emily."

"Tell me about her. What does she do?"

"She's a physical therapist." He braced for her reaction.

"Well, that's ironic, isn't it?"

"I'm not going to answer that."

"Smart boy. What's she like?"

"I'm not sure where to begin or what it is about her. Eleanor, when I'm with her, the anxiety, the noises in my head, the pain, all of it disappears, and I can breathe again."

"I know what that is, my boy. It's true love."

Air caught in his lungs and held. Hearing Eleanor validate his feelings, meant more than he expected. "I—"

"Breakfast is served," Emily sang, bouncing into the room with a tray of food before noticing him on the phone.

"Having breakfast together, are you?" Eleanor teased, amusement animating her voice. "All I have to say is, it's about time. Call me again when you're not so *busy*. Love you, sweetheart," she added, disconnecting before he could respond.

He stared at the phone, shaking his head at the first woman to steal his heart, then set it aside.

"You look guilty. Was that another woman? Should I be jealous?" With a wink, she set the tray on the bed and climbed up.

"It's just Eleanor. I hadn't spoken with her in a while, so I called to check in."

"I'm sure she appreciated that."

"And she approves," he said, accepting the plate, overflowing with a large omelet and fresh fruit, she handed him.

"Approves of what?"

"Of us."

She'd opened her mouth for a bite of cantaloupe but froze with the confession. Setting down the fork, she took his hand.

"That makes me happy. I know how much she means to you." She poured two cups of orange juice and set them on the tray. "Do you have any plans today? Anything you wanted to get done?"

"No. My only plan was to be with you. Every second, remember?"

"That's right. Good plan. Well, I suggest a lazy Saturday at the house—What?" she asked when he held back a smile, pretending to be distracted with breakfast.

"This tastes amazing. What's in it?"

"I don't think so, buddy. What was that smile about?"

"Nothing, really. While you were sleeping, I wondered what a lazy Saturday would be like with you. But I wasn't thinking of today."

Setting the tray aside, she took his plate and climbed onto his lap. "Did you imagine me feeding you breakfast in bed?" She stuck a chunk of watermelon with a fork and held it out for him to remove it with his teeth.

"I didn't, but now I wish I had." Running his hands down her thighs, he kept his eyes on her. The short robe, tied loosely around her waist, exposed the insides of her breasts.

"Did you imagine long bubble baths and full-body massages?" She set the fork onto the plate and gathered his hand in hers. Beginning with his fingers, she rubbed the muscles in his hand, arm, and shoulder before moving down his chest and hips.

His head dropped back against the headboard, air seeping out of his lungs when she began massaging his sore legs. Her magical hands slowly erased the nagging stiffness. "When did you say that bubble bath would be happening?"

"Whenever you're ready."

"Ready." He scooped her off the bed and threw her over his shoulder, ignoring her squeal. He no longer wanted to see her in that robe, teasing him with slivers of her smooth skin. He wanted all of her.

Setting her down on the bathroom rug, he turned on the hot water in the white clawfoot tub and set the stopper. She reached for something on the counter, stopping at the sound of his voice.

"Eyes on me."

Her lashes fluttered with the command, her breath coming out jagged as his hands found their way inside her robe. Moving up her sides, he covered her shoulders and pushed the silky fabric lightly down her back.

"You forgot… the bubbles," she stammered, her voice barely above a whisper. Watching her come undone under his touch would never grow old.

"Where?"

She raised a weakened arm to point to the nearby cabinet.

Grabbing the bottle, he reached around her to squeeze the solution into the bath. Thick, white foam immediately coated the water, the fresh scent of lavender blooming through the room.

He helped himself to the taste of her skin while the tub filled, then helped her inside.

"Will you tell me what Eleanor said when you told her about us?" she asked, color tinting her cheeks as he lowered in behind her.

He collected the soft sponge and ran it softly up her arm. "She said she was happy for me, and…it was about time."

A giggle popped out of her. "What does that mean?"

"Since I got back, she's been urging me to date."

"Did you?"

He dipped the sponge under the water and swiped it slowly over her stomach. "I tried once."

"Why didn't it work out?"

He looked down at her. "Are you sure you want to talk about this?"

"No." A sheepish grin emerged on her face. "It's not fun to imagine you with someone else, but I want to know everything about you. Your highs and lows, the people in between."

"Okay," he began, unsure if he should be talking about his one and only relationship nearly two years ago. "At the time, I was lonely, and we'd just lost Will. Avery is his cousin and my physical therapist at the time."

"Hmm." She bit her bottom lip.

"What's that smirk for?"

"You have a very specific type."

"Apparently."

"What happened between you?"

"I couldn't give her what she needed and knew I never could." He considered the differences in him between then and now. The doubt that crept in with Avery never took flight with Emily, soothing the guilt he still felt over hurting her. Because no matter what he had done, their relationship had been doomed from the start. She wasn't Emily. "But I am eternally grateful for her. She helped me find a path forward."

"How?"

"Most importantly, she got me walking again with her creative therapy. But the day she got angry and——"

She leaned back to see him. "What did you do?"

"That's not important." He had zero interest in rehashing the bathtub incident while he ironically sat in a bathtub with the woman he loved. "When she got angry and stormed out, it snapped me out of the rut I'd settled into. That's when I ditched the wheelchair permanently."

"Stormed out, huh?" Pinching her lips, she hid her amusement.

"Wasn't my finest moment. What about you?"

"You want to know about my ex-boyfriends?"

"Definitely, not. Maybe something less torturous. Tell me something I don't know about you."

"I have a weakness for banana splits," she confessed, settling back against his chest in the spot she fit so perfectly.

"Really? You don't look like you've ever eaten junk food."

"I could say the same about you," she teased. "Since I know it's my guilty pleasure, I just stay away from it."

"I hope you don't stay away from everything you like." He kissed her temple to reiterate his point and ran his hands down her sides.

"There are some things I love more than banana splits, and I can't resist those."

"Oh, yeah? Like what?"

"Like cheeseburgers."

His fingers curling into her ribs garnered another squeal. Instinctively, she squirmed and fought against it, causing water to spill over the tub's edge.

"I mean you. I love you more than ice cream," she yelled through the tickles and splashes.

He released his grip. "That's more like it."

Reaching up to wrap her arm around his neck, she leaned back and pulled him down to her. He kissed her with a new tenderness, pouring out his heart through the connection. His patient hands moved in a trance over her skin and made him weak with want all over again. She gave without restrictions, trembling under his touch again like it was another first.

"You're shivering."

"You do that to me," she confessed, opening her eyes.

"I'm so sorry," he said, the cold water finally registering. "Let's get out and get you warm."

He shifted to climb out of the tub, but she grabbed his arm to stop him, smiling in response to his concern. "You're sweet to worry, but I'm okay. Better than okay thanks to you. Although, all this talk about ice cream and cheeseburgers has me hungry again."

"We did get a little distracted during breakfast."

"You can distract me like that any time you want. Lazy Saturdays are my new favorite day of the week."

"How about we order in and keep the lazy going?"

She twisted onto her knees to face him. "Sounds heavenly."

"Agreed." Draping his arms around the edge of the tub, he took in the beautiful view. "But I'm now thinking of devouring you instead."

When she inched closer, his hands dropped into the water to shift her legs into straddling him. "That sounds even better."

Shooting out of the water, he carried her to the bedroom. "We'll eat later."

Chapter Fifteen

✫ ✫ ✫

Emily

When the doorbell rang, she sprang out from under the sheets. "I'll get it."

"Oh, no, you don't. You stay right there." Jackson slipped on his shorts. "It's my turn to serve you in bed, and that thin piece of fabric you call a robe is not fit for visitors."

"Fine. I'll save it only for you."

She watched him leave the room, then fell back against the pillows, more in love than she'd been yesterday. They spent Lazy Saturday doing little more than making love and talking. Now it was mid-afternoon on Sunday, and they'd yet to leave the bed.

"That smells delicious," she said when he reappeared with the food. And seeing him casually walk around her house shirtless was even better.

"I don't think I've ever been this hungry. What did you order?"

"A little of everything." Sitting up, she crossed her legs and let the sheet fall into her lap.

"Good. I could eat everything."

"How about a glass of wine to go with it?"

"Coming right up." He dropped the bag onto the bed and jogged out of the room, soon returning with a bottle of white wine and two glasses from the kitchen.

"I could get used to this kind of treatment." She watched him open the bottle, and after handing her the full glass, he disappeared into the bathroom. "Where are you going?"

"Thought you might want this." He held up her robe before settling onto the bed.

Touched by his thoughtfulness, she slipped her arms inside and tied the strap around her waist. "I assumed Lazy Saturdays that turn into Lazy Sundays meant clothes were optional."

"I like the sound of that. Maybe we can get back to it after we eat." Reaching into the bag, he flashed her a smile.

"Don't you think we should get out of bed today?"

"We got out of bed yesterday."

She thought of their bubble bath and the heat it sparked between them. "I mean to do something that requires us to put our clothes on."

"Why would we want to do that?"

"Good question. Forget I brought it up."

"Too late." He handed her a container of salad and a fork. "If you'd like to do something that requires clothes…" He smirked. "Let's do it. Have anything in mind?" He tossed a bite of chicken into his mouth and closed his eyes, letting the flavor seep into his tongue.

"You normally train while you're stopped in a location for a while, don't you?"

"Yeah. But I'm not sure my legs still work after Lazy Saturday."

Another of his earth-shattering smiles flashed in her direction, awakening every nerve ending in her body. He had a way of turning her into a fumbling mess with those casual blue-eyed glances.

She shuffled quickly through her brain, now successfully reduced to pieces, to form her next thought. "How about we go on a run together? I can show you my route, and you can get in some training."

"Your route? I thought you preferred the treadmill?"

"I did. You see, I met a man recently, and he inspired me to hit the road instead. I can run about seven miles."

"Impressive. He must be an awesome guy."

With a nod, she shifted to her hands and knees. "He's the most amazing," she began and inched closer, "caring, bright, gorgeous man who takes my breath away and makes me feel treasured and beautiful."

"That's because you are, and he is the luckiest man on this planet." He kissed her softly. "When do we leave, Sergeant?"

"Whenever you're ready, soldier," she said, laughing.

"I still don't love that nickname."

"You'll live. Now, eat. I need you to keep your strength up. I'm not done with you yet."

———

"We're never going to get out of here if we don't focus," she complained.

As they cleared the containers only moments before, their eyes met, sending them right back to where they started. Passion and pleasure, love and emotions taking over.

"I'm okay with that." He grabbed the bottom of his shirt to take it off again.

Pointing at him, she shook her head. "Don't you dare. We have a mission to accomplish, remember?"

"Hmm."

It took strength and willpower, but they dressed and soon made their way to the living room. When she opened the front door, he pushed it closed from behind, surprising her. She spun around in time for him to devour her how he wanted, his hands squeezing her waist as if she kept him upright.

"That will hold me over for a while." The sexy voice that could lull her into submission at will now hinted of strained desires.

She could relate and would have felt sorry for him if she wasn't so damn proud of herself drawing that passion out of him.

"You have to stop doing that," she complained, her eyes gliding open to meet his. How could she run with knees he reduced to jelly with those dangerous lips? "I take it back. Never stop doing that." Twisting his shirt in her fist, she yanked his mouth to hers. *Devour away*, she managed to think before her mind went numb.

"You were right. We should… take a break," he managed between ragged breaths.

"I don't want to." She captured his lips again, and it took every ounce of determination she had not to drag him back to the bedroom.

"This was your idea. Remember?"

"Fine." Her head dropped back against the door with a thump. "But you'll have to wipe that very hot but smug grin off your face before I move a muscle." She waited and watched while he adjusted his gorgeous lips.

"Sorry. Can't control it when I look at you."

"Fair enough." Satisfied, she tossed open the door.

Her blood already pumped hot and fast from his kiss, but she followed along as he led her through his warmup routine to keep from doing it again. Plus, he looked too good in his element to interrupt.

"How long is this route of yours?" he asked, lowering into a lunge, and distracting her with bulging thigh muscles.

Her eyes trailed up to his mouth, now smirking at her. She cleared her dry throat to refocus. "It's about three and a half miles and ends at River Street. I usually run there and back for an even seven. We can continue down the river to extend the distance if you'd like."

And they did. At River Street, they took a different, longer route back to her house. Hunched over inside the door, gulping for oxygen that didn't seem to exist, she shot daggers at Jackson with her eyes as he stepped past her as if they'd gone for a casual stroll around the block.

"You did well, Sergeant. I'm proud of you." He kissed the top of her head and handed her a bottle of water. "Mind if I take a shower?"

Unable to form any words through her labored inhales, she waved toward her bedroom and held the cold bottle to her burning throat. The run challenged her more than she thought it would. She'd wanted to impress him, but she found herself cramping and gasping long before they reached the house.

Several minutes passed before she could hear more than her heartbeat thumping in her ears. The refrigerator motor kicked on, a car passed by outside, and the water ran in her shower. Awakened by the thought of Jackson nude in the other room, she propelled from the door with newfound energy.

———

"Work up an appetite again?" she asked when she found him rummaging through her refrigerator after their shower. He'd already set out the blender, almond milk, and berries on the island counter.

"I hope you don't mind. I was looking for ingredients to make a protein shake."

"Top shelf in the back." She pointed to a cabinet beside the refrigerator and took a seat at the island.

Reaching over several boxes of pasta, he located the powdered protein. "Perfect," he whispered and closed the door.

She watched him cut and transfer ingredients to the blender, struck by how natural it felt having him there. But as with most things, his visit came with an expiration date.

"Jackson, can I ask you something?"

"Sure."

"Have you decided when you'll leave?"

He held up a finger, then pushed the button on the blender to start the loud motor, giving him time to contemplate his answer. When the mixture merged into a milky mauve color, he turned off the machine. "I was thinking Tuesday. Since you have work and I need to keep making progress, it seemed like the logical choice."

Although she tried not to allow it, her posture deflated. "I understand. Just doesn't make it any easier to accept."

"Believe me, leaving you a second time will be nearly impossible."

She forced a smile before slipping off the seat to grab him a cup. As she reached into the cabinet, he took hold of her hand and gently tugged her into his arms.

Sobs set her body into motion. "I told myself to be strong and not make this any harder than it already is. I want to be your rock and support you no matter how far apart we are. I just don't know how to do it." After having him to herself that weekend, his upcoming departure was going to rip her at the seams.

Tensing with his own emotions, he stroked her hair, still dripping water down her back. "We'll find a way together," he said to ease her worry, but the words sounded empty. They both needed answers, a plan, and a guarantee that what they built wouldn't fall apart in his absence.

"Why don't we invite Genevieve and Ben over tonight for a distraction?" he suggested. "We should enjoy these last days together and not think about goodbyes. We already know they suck."

A laugh burst through the tears, and she nodded in agreement. "So true." Sliding her arms from around his waist, she wiped her face.

Once in her room, she dialed Genevieve's number.

"Hi, stranger. Good to know you're still breathing," she teased, but Emily couldn't join in the banter as Genevieve expected. "What's wrong? Why are you calling?"

"Nothing's wrong. We're inviting you over tonight," she got out between sniffles and yanked a tissue from the box in the bathroom. "Jackson's calling Ben."

"Wow. I didn't know spending time with us was so upsetting."

"Sorry, let me back up. Jackson and I were talking about when he would leave, and I got upset. He suggested some time with you and Ben would cheer us up."

"I see. Bring in the entertainment, huh?"

"G, I didn't mean it like—"

"It's okay. I can accept that I'm fun to be around."

"How about six o'clock? I'll cook dinner."

"Sounds good. See you then," she said but called for Emily before she disconnected.

"Yeah?"

"What did he say?"

"Who? Jackson?"

"Yeah. When is he leaving?" she asked cautiously.

"Tuesday."

"I'll be there at five."

———

Jackson

In the kitchen, while Jackson drank his shake, he called Ben instead of texting.

He answered on the first ring. "What's up, man? I was just thinking about coming to check on you."

"No need. Can you cancel my hotel room? I won't be needing it."

"Hell, yeah. It's about time you got laid," Ben said, laughing.

With a sigh, he held the phone away from his ear until Ben stopped whistling and carrying on. "We're having dinner here tonight if you want to join us. No hard feelings if you have   "

"Is Genevieve coming?"

"I think so. Emily's talking with her now."

"Then, I'm game for another round of rejection. She can't resist me forever."

"Whatever. Just be here at six and bring your good behavior with you. I don't want anything to upset Emily tonight."

"What do you mean? Don't I always behave?"

Frowning, Jackson suddenly wished he'd texted. "I'll send you the address. Oh, and bring my suitcase too, please."

"Sure, no problem. Hey, buddy?"

"Yeah?"

"Tonight's the night I'm going to win her over."

"Good for you, but if it goes south, Emily can't find out. Understood?"

"Yeah, yeah. Oh ye of little faith."

Second-guessing his suggestion to entertain their crazy friends, he slammed down the phone. He and Emily should be enjoying their time together without distractions before he…

No longer hungry, he poured the remaining shake down the drain, then headed to the bedroom to find Emily.

––––––

Emily

"Ready for this?" she asked him when a car pulled into the driveway, draping her arms over his shoulders.

"I'm never ready to share you."

"Don't worry, it will be over soon, and then, we can get back to Lazy Saturday, part two."

"Deal." Leaning down, he kissed her one last time—his promise of more to come when they were alone again. "And you can get the door while I start the grill." He lunged at the plate of seasoned steaks, sitting on the counter, and hurried out the door.

"Coward." With a satisfied sigh, she turned to greet Genevieve as she let herself in.

"You look happier than you sounded earlier."

"I had a little nervous breakdown, but I'm better. Thanks for coming."

"No biggie. I'm just here for the food."

"Ha. What's this?" She accepted the bottle of wine Genevieve held out for her. "I thought you were supposed to be laying off the alcohol."

"Relax. I haven't had a drink since we met for dinner the other night. Doc said I could have one occasionally. Today is an occasion."

"Fine, but I'll be watching you."

"No doubt. Where's lover boy?"

"Which one?" Emily flashed a smile over her shoulder before grabbing two glasses from the cabinet.

"Not funny."

"Jackson's out back, and Ben hasn't arrived yet."

"Good."

"I'm dying to know." She leaned on the island counter after Genevieve claimed a seat at the small island. "What happened with Ben after we left the other night?"

"Ugh. I don't want to talk about it." She reached for the glass Emily filled.

"Why not? Did he grill you about not texting him?"

"How did you—" She rolled her eyes, answering her own question. "Yes, he tried to get a rise out of me, but it didn't work."

"What thrilling story did you come up with as an excuse?"

"Emily, I do not have to answer to him. If I wanted to talk, I would have let him know. I didn't. End of story."

"Right. I just thought maybe there was more to it since you didn't tell me he was texting you."

"It's not a big deal. Men message me all the time. I rarely answer any of them, and I don't tell you about them, do I?"

"No. My mistake." Emily held up her hands, backtracking. "Well, he should be here any—" The doorbell ringing had her stopping and staring at Genevieve with eyes wide. "He's early. Too excited to see you, I bet."

With a wink, she jogged to the front door.

———

Genevieve

Taking a long sip of wine, she welcomed the soft caress on her scratchy throat. If their encounter at the restaurant was any indication of how sloppy that evening might be, a little buzz should help her endure it without losing her shit over it.

She straightened to adjust her low-cut top. Showing extra cleavage never hurt anyone. For her entertainment, she'd flaunt her God-given assets and drive Ben mad. Of course, she'd dismiss his attempts to get closer to her, but a few harmless games could bring back the spice she'd been missing from her life.

His flirting should be off the charts and desperate now that Jackson had announced their departure date. A satisfied grin touched her cheeks before readjusting the expression to one of practiced indifference.

Bring him on.

"Hi, Ben. Thanks for coming. Don't you look handsome?" Emily said from the foyer, and Genevieve cursed her body for trembling with anticipation.

"Aww, shucks. Thanks, Miss Emily."

"Enjoying the southern accents, I see. Come in. Genevieve's in the kitchen, and Jackson's on the back porch. If you're thirsty, there's a six-pack and some sweet tea in the fridge."

"I believe I could go for a beer," he said, entering the kitchen. "Thanks, Em." He opened the refrigerator door and grabbed two bottles. "Genevieve," he said flatly before exiting through the back door.

What the—

"That was weird," Emily said.

"What?"

"He barely acknowledged you."

Yeah. What the hell? "I'm fine with that," she lied.

"Man, whatever you said to him the other night must have gotten through."

"Good. Maybe I can enjoy the evening without him drooling on me."

"Come on," Emily smiled over her wine glass before taking a sip. "He's cute, and he smells good. He can't be all that bad."

"What's for dinner?"

"Alright." Emily's narrowed eyes scowled at her. "I'll play along. Steak, steamed asparagus, and baked potatoes."

She watched Emily set the vegetables, cutting board, and knife on the counter, noticing something was different about her. And there could be only one cause.

Emily stopped chopping. "What?"

"You're glowing, and it's freaking me out. What have you been doing since you ditched us at dinner the other night?" Although, it wasn't hard to figure out, she was dying to hear how her tender-hearted friend described it.

"We didn't ditch you."

"Yes, you did. You left me alone with him." She tossed her thumb over her shoulder toward the back porch. "And without warning."

"Okay. We kind of did that, but you two needed to talk. He was pining for you, and you were being stubborn… not surprisingly."

"Now, you've crossed the line."

"What line? I like Ben, and I know you do, too." Emily pointed at her friend. "You just won't admit it."

"I don't understand a word you're sayin'. Besides, weren't we talking about you? What have you been doing all weekend?"

When Emily's smile morphed into meek pride, Genevieve's braced herself against the counter in mock astonishment. "No way."

"What? Is it so hard to believe that I've had a *lot* of mind-blowing sex with an incredibly beautiful and sensitive man for forty-eight straight hours?"

"I hate you."

"No, you don't. You're happy for me." She flashed her wide grin before tossing the chopped asparagus into a bowl.

"You're right. I am. Does he know?"

"Know what?"

"That you're in love with him."

Somehow, the question caught Emily by surprise. She should have expected her best friend, who knows her better than anyone, to recognize this life-altering moment. "Yes, he does."

"And does he feel the same?"

"In Myrtle Beach, he said he was falling, and everything he's done and said since makes me believe it. But he hasn't said those three words yet."

"And you're not wondering what's holding him back? I know you and how your romance novel brain works."

"I don't want to lose him." Her vision blurred without warning, and just as fast, Genevieve circled the island to wrap her in a hug.

"Oh, honey, that's not going to happen. Why would you say that?"

"I know he feels strongly for me. I'd be a fool to think otherwise, but he's going away for who knows how long. What if he meets someone else?"

"Do you really think that will happen?"

"Distance can mess with relationships. Maybe he'll stop missing me. Maybe he's better now and doesn't need me anymore. I don't know."

She smoothed Emily's hair. "There's something you're not saying. What's actually bothering you?"

"My track record is always in the back of my mind, taunting me and making me second guess everything. I hate it, but I think it's more that he's told me practically nothing about his life in Richmond or what's waiting for him there."

"Have you asked him? You have a right to know."

"Do I? We've known each other less than a month, and I haven't exactly told him everything either. He doesn't know about Lucas." She cringed at the thought of what Jackson might do if he found out.

"There's nothing to tell. You've taken care of that situation."

"I hope so." Needing something to do, Emily scooped up the remaining vegetables and tossed them into the bowl. "Lucas played it off, but he was furious the last time I saw him. And since then, he's kept his distance like he's on the prowl, a patient one, waiting for the right time to pounce."

"Then quit," Genevieve suggested and took a sip of wine.

"I can't quit." Securing the lid on the bowl, she tossed it in the microwave and pressed a button to start it. "I love my job and my patients. I can't leave them after all the progress we've made."

"You can if you're terrified to be there. You should think about yourself and the hell with everyone else."

"Easy for you to say." She paused when the oven timer sounded. "That's your mantra."

"It's worked so far. You care too much about other people. Focus on what you want for a change."

"Believe me, I've done only that all weekend and have indulged plenty. You'd be proud of me."

"Oh, really? Then, do tell. I could use another juicy story to wet the whistle. I've hit a dry spell in the men department."

"You're joking. I don't believe you."

Genevieve glared at her. "Where would I meet someone? I've barely left my apartment since we got back."

"And why is that? It's not like you."

She waved her hand to dismiss it, not interested in speaking the truth. "Doesn't matter. I'm sportin' a desert down there, so spill."

Before story time could begin, the back door flew open, adding Jackson and Ben to the room.

Genevieve dropped her head to the counter. "The drought continues."

With a laugh, Emily accepted the plate of cooked steaks as the microwave chimed. "Dinner's ready. Let's eat on the porch."

———

By the time the sun dropped beyond the horizon, casting warm undertones across the sky, all plates and glasses had been emptied. Emily stood to collect the dishes, and Ben bounded up to do the same.

"I'll help," he offered. "Gotta take a piss."

Genevieve shook her head in disgust, but at least his full bladder gave her alone time with Jackson. "So, you're leaving on Tuesday?"

"That's the plan. Are you going to miss us?"

"Not in the least, but Emily will."

Raising the beer to his lips, he drank slowly, unimpressed by her comment.

"Here's my problem," she continued. "We know very little about you. What will you do after Tuesday or after you go home?"

He took a deep breath before answering. "I know you care about her, Genevieve, but that's none of your business."

"Do you love her?"

Silence.

"Do you love her?" she pressed. She wanted to see him angry. In her experience, the truth always came out in bursts of anger, and she often learned a lot in those moments. "Or is she just another notch you can brag about to your buddies back in Richmond?"

He shot to his feet, the chair rocking on the deck floor from the sudden movement. "You're right," he agreed, glaring down at her, his broad chest heaving. "You don't know me."

Snatching his beer off the table, he stalked past Ben on his way through the door.

"What's wrong with him?" Ben asked and reclaimed his seat at the table.

"He wasn't a fan of having to answer for his actions."

"Tell me you didn't."

"Didn't what?"

His pinched lips and glower showcased his annoyance, and she less than cared for it.

Tossing her hands in the air, she bit back. "What?"

"What did you do?"

Sighing, she draped an arm over the chair, hoping she looked detached from her confession. "I asked him if he was serious about Emily or if she was just a notch. That's all." Saying it aloud sent a pang of regret through her stomach but not much. Because she hadn't yet been convinced Jackson was being real with any of them.

"Wow."

"Look, Emily is my best friend, and I don't want her to get hurt." She swirled the wine in her glass, convinced she'd done nothing wrong.

"You've got a lot of nerve."

"Excuse me. Who do you—"

"Jackson is the most honest person I've ever met, and I already told you he hasn't been with a single woman since we left. He's given you no reason to question his intentions." He paused, carefully selecting his next words. "It's obvious that he cares for Emily, and you could see that if you'd open your stubborn eyes to what's right in front of you."

He watched her, waiting for her response as the double meaning hung in the air. "You don't have anything to say?"

Having reached his limit, he puffed out his frustration with a push of the chair and stormed inside, leaving her alone with her conscience.

———

Jackson

For Emily, the group put aside their arguments and enjoyed playing games the rest of the evening. They laughed until they cried at how terrible Ben was at charades. After that, the girls won in a landslide at Pictionary, and the guys took the pot at poker.

Given her arrogance when they started, Jackson seriously thought Genevieve would challenge his vast experience at cards, but she was either easier to read that he expected, or their argument knocked her off her game.

"Can you believe Jackson didn't play board games or watch movies growing up?" Emily asked the others.

"Shit, man. I knew you were different from the rest of us, but that's just wrong." Ben shook his head. "What did you do for fun?"

"I liked adventure and being outside. Movies and board games were too stationary."

"What did you mean when you said Jackson is different?" she asked, curiosity alive in her eyes.

Ben cut his eyes to Jackson for permission. He didn't object but gave Ben a warning look to proceed with caution.

"Jackson's childhood wasn't like us normal folk," Ben began, reveling a little too much in the attention. "He was the most popular kid in school and the star running back on a football team that went to the state championship every year. As if that wasn't enough, he also had these looks." He grabbed Jackson around the bicep before he could avoid it. "Everywhere he and his friends went, the girls followed. And to top it off, he lived in a big stone castle with a moat at the edge of the city. So, like I said, not normal."

She turned to Jackson and laughed. "A castle, huh? I knew you were my Prince Charming. Now, I have proof."

"For the record," he said to the group. "It's not a castle, and there is no moat."

———

By ten o'clock, Jackson had had enough of entertaining their guests. While getting drinks in the kitchen, he urged Ben to make his exit and give him some alone time with Emily.

"You pay for the ride, and I'll get Genevieve out of here, too," he promised with a dramatic wink and held up his beer. "I've had way too many of these."

"Great." He would have done anything Ben requested to get them out of there.

"Oh, and Genevieve told me what she said to you. She was out of line, and I told her so." He swayed a little in his shoes as a burp caught him off balance. His fist flew to his mouth, and he went pale like he might vomit.

With a grimace, Jackson reached for the trash can, but Ben held up a finger to stop him.

"Like I was saying," Ben said, resuming his normal drunken posture. "Not only was she wrong to say it, but she's wrong about you. You're a good guy, Jackson. You didn't deserve that."

"Thanks, buddy. I appreciate it. Now, get the hell out."

Chapter Sixteen

✫ ✫ ✫

Jackson

When Jackson awoke the next morning, the house and other side of the bed were empty. Frustrated, he sat up and fumbled for his phone to check the time, finding a note from Emily instead.

Hi Sleepyhead,

Meet me for lunch at 12? I will be counting the minutes until I see you again.

Love,

Emily

Using the address she included at the bottom, he mapped the route and calculated that he had two hours to waste. After a workout in the backyard, he took a shower, then called Harrison to check in.

"How can I leave tomorrow?" he asked when the conversation turned to his trepidation over the next step in his journey.

"You'll find a way. You always do. Just remember why you're doing this. If she truly loves you, she'll be there when you get back."

"That's not what I'm worried about."

Disgusted with himself, Jackson switched the call to speaker and wiped his damp hands on a kitchen towel. He had to figure out how to go on without her and not fall apart. He was stronger than this. He went to war, came back from the dead, and learned to run again on two busted legs. A few weeks without Emily should be easier than that, right? She wasn't leaving him. He could still talk to her by phone, and maybe she'd meet him on some weekends. But even then, being away from her for weeks on end would be the most difficult thing he'd ever have to do.

"I believe she will wait for me," he continued, "but I'm concerned I may not be able to accomplish my goal without her. I can't ask her to leave her life for this."

"No. You can't. This is your journey, and you need to finish it. When you do, you'll have found what you need to start the rest of your life—with her, if that's what you want. Stay focused, my boy. It will work out how it's supposed to."

Putting the phone away, his frustration with the situation and his disappointment over his inability to manage his emotions, made him want to quit for the first time since losing Will. Forget Orlando and his search for meaning. Did it really matter anymore?

He ran his hands over his face and let them drop to the counter. *Damn, it did*. It meant everything. To him, his family, and now Emily. What would she think of him if he gave up halfway through his goal? How could he honor those he loved and his country by being selfish?

Unable to sit around in the quiet, vacant house a minute longer, he retrieved the spare keys to the car from his suitcase and headed to town early. While he waited, he browsed through the nearby shops and stopped outside a jewelry store when a necklace in the window caught his attention. He could picture it sparkling around Emily's slender neck and quickly made the purchase. With the gift bag in hand, he walked the few blocks to her office.

"I got you something," he announced when they were seated in a booth at the deli next door and held up the tiny pink bag.

She exploded with excitement, his chest expanding with her. Accepting the bag, she dug a hand inside, flashing him an affectionate look as she pulled out the small black box. She opened the lid, her finger tracing the gold necklace and diamond heart pendant on the soft felt.

"Jackson, it's beautiful." Amazement still on her face, she raised her gaze to his. "I love it."

And I love you, he thought as she carefully removed the chain.

"Will you help me put it on?"

With the latch secured, he ran a hand over the delicate chain along her neck, loving how it draped over her skin, before reclaiming his seat.

"Thank you. I'll wear it every day and think of you." Reaching for his hand, she smiled sweetly. "What have you been doing all morning?"

"Staying busy. I worked out, called Harrison, and wandered around town until it was time for lunch."

"Who's Harrison, if you don't mind me asking?"

"Oh, sorry. Billy's dad. Harrison's been a father figure to me for most of my life. I'd love for you to meet him one day."

"I'd love to. Does he—" A perky waitress, who seemed to only notice him at the table, interrupted to take their orders. "Wait a minute. I know you." She pointed her pen at him.

"You do?"

"We haven't met… in person anyway. I've been following your memorial run on social media and commented a time or two. I can't believe you're in Savannah. Can I get a picture with you?"

"Sure," he agreed reluctantly and waited while she searched for her phone in her apron.

"Do you mind?" She thrust the phone at Emily.

Holding back a laugh at his cringy response, Emily agreed, making his nerves crackle a bit.

After a few poses, the young waitress zeroed in on him again. "It's such an awesome thing you're doing. My grandfather and father both served in the Navy." She whipped her head toward the front door when the bell chimed. "I need to take care of that. I'll be back to get your order in a minute, sweetie."

"You're going to have to get used to that, sweetie," Emily joked, laughing when he slumped back in his chair.

"Never."

"Ah, come on. You have a lot of followers, not surprisingly, and there's the whole magnet thing. It's going to happen more and more the closer you—"

Her face went stone white over something she saw across the room. He followed her stunned gaze to their waitress, escorting a tall man in a light-yellow shirt and khaki shorts to a table several rows over. "What is it?"

"It's nothing."

She wanted to ignore whatever bothered her, but color hadn't returned to her cheeks, and the lack of sparkle in her eyes made him uneasy. "It doesn't seem like nothing, Emily. Who is that man?"

"He's one of the doctors at the office, but I really don't want to spend the limited time we have together talking about him."

Her answer did not settle his concern, but before he could ask more questions, the waitress reappeared to take their orders.

"What were we talking about?" Emily asked to change the subject after the waitress scurried off. "Oh, right," she answered herself. "Harrison. Does he live in Richmond, too?"

"Yes."

"Why did you say he was a father figure to you? Was your father not around when you were growing up?"

He shifted in his seat, searching for the words. "Can we add my father to the list of things not to talk about today?"

"That's fair."

"In all sense of the word, Harrison is my father. After returning to the States, I regret not reaching out to him sooner. Like Eleanor, he would have helped with my emotional healing." He forced a grin. "It's something I'm still working on."

"Other than the hospital incident, you seem to be doing great. Is there more you're struggling with?"

"Yes. But when I'm with you, every horrible piece of it goes away."

Touched, she reached for his hand. "I'm glad I can give you that."

"You give me more than peace, you know."

Her free hand rose to the necklace and held the diamond heart between her fingers—a symbol of his love for her. "I know."

———

Emily

When the time came for her to return to work, they rose to leave, but someone calling her name over the bustling lunch crowd had her silently cursing to herself. How had she forgotten about Lucas?

She put on her best smile and waited for him to approach. No way would she close the distance and give him any reason to believe she encouraged his behavior.

"Lucas, hello." Standing close to Jackson, she felt his muscles alert and hoped he couldn't sense how uncomfortable this encounter was for her.

"Aren't you going to introduce me to your friend?"

What she wouldn't give to slap that unwarranted arrogance off his face.

"This is my boyfriend, Jackson. Jackson, this is Dr. Lucas Oliver. He is one of the founding members of the practice," she added in her most flat and professional tone.

"Nice to meet you, Dr. Oliver." He reached out his hand, and Lucas took it.

"I was unaware you had a boyfriend," he said before addressing Jackson. "Call me Lucas. Are you from the area?"

"No. Virginia."

"Interesting. That's quite a distance away. How did you two meet?"

"It was nice seeing you," she interrupted, "but I need to get back to work. Enjoy your day off." She pushed Jackson toward the door.

"Speaking of that," Lucas began. "I need to talk to you… about work, of course."

"I'll pay the bill and wait for you outside." Jackson ran a hand across her back as he left, telling her he'd be close by if she needed him. And thank goodness. She had the sinking feeling that Lucas planned to make a scene.

She watched him walk away, then whipped her head back to Lucas. "This little meeting has nothing to do with work. What do you want?"

"You didn't tell me you were dating someone."

"Because it's none of your business. God, you're unbelievable."

She turned to leave, but he grabbed her arm. Her eyes snapped to him and burned with the same fire she felt in the pit of her stomach. He hadn't expected her to react that way, the shock in his eyes telling her as much, and it gave her the confidence she needed. "Take your hand off me."

Dropping his hand slowly, he glanced over at Jackson, who had yet to leave the restaurant, and amusement danced across his face.

"Emily, your boyfriend is watching. You better be careful, or he might start asking questions about us."

"There is no us. Never was. This is all a game you're playing to stroke your overactive ego."

"I have to say, I'm enjoying this new aggressive side of you, Emily. It's very sexy."

"I am so sick of this. I'm warning you, Lucas. Just one more word, and I'll—"

"You'll what? File charges? Sue me? You don't have it in you, but it's cute when you say it."

"I guess we'll just see, won't we?"

Pivoting, she stalked away, the room spinning faster with every step. She'd never spoken to anyone that way, but she'd also never been so livid. As nausea replaced the smolder in her stomach, she refused to let Lucas win again. Willing a smile to keep her lunch where it belonged, she linked her arm with Jackson's and headed outside for some much-needed fresh air.

"You don't care for him, do you?" he asked, breaking the silence.

Instinctively, her hand went to her warm cheek, surely giving her away. "Is it that obvious?"

"I learned a lot about reading people in the Marines. Yes. Your feelings were obvious, and he's a pompous jerk."

A laugh bubbled out of her throat, releasing the Lucas-infused tension in her muscles. "You have no idea."

———

After escaping work and the Lucas reminders there, Emily leapt into Jackson's arms. When she saw him waiting for her on the front porch, she barely put the car in park before jumping out. "I missed you so much."

"Have a good day?" he asked, setting her back on her feet.

"It was okay, but being home with you is much better."

"I like the sound of that."

"Wow. You've been busy," she said, admiring the cut grass and fresh straw under the newly trimmed bushes and trees. He'd also planted several colorful pansies around her front steps. "I can't believe you did all this."

"I was bored."

"I might just keep you around, soldier." Cupping the back of his neck, she drew his lips to hers. "No wonder I love you so."

"I also fixed the drip in the kitchen sink and the back doorknob that wouldn't lock," he continued, following her inside and closing the door behind him. "You know that's not safe, right?"

"I had it on the to-do list. I thought you were going to hang out with Ben today."

"I tried, but he was busy."

"Busy? What does he have to do?"

"Not what...who."

"How did he meet someone already? Wait." She peeked through the oven window. "Are you cooking dinner?"

"Yep. Eleanor's specialty. She taught me how to cook it when I was a kid."

"It smells amazing. What is it?"

"Beef Wellington."

She stared at him, her mouth falling open in disbelief. "You're kidding."

"Nope. Why?"

"It's like one of the hardest things to cook, but I'm not surprised you can do it."

"Don't be impressed yet. You haven't tasted it."

Wrapping her arms around his waist, she took in the feel of him. She would miss these moments the most. The casual life moments he made unforgettable. "Did you make dessert too, my Prince Charming?"

"No." His lips tipped into a sly smile. "I thought we could have each other for dessert."

Those gorgeous lips of his traced the curve of her neck to the sensitive space under her ear, making her lose all interest in food. "It drives me crazy when you do that."

"Really? What about when I do this?" While he continued to explore her jawline, his hands slid under her shirt and circled her waist.

"Insane. Don't stop."

"And this?" He covered her parted mouth with his own, drinking in everything she offered as if he needed it to survive.

In that moment, she felt the same. Before Jackson, she'd been living half a life. The other half started when his blue eyes found hers and glowed with wonder across a crowded room.

Grabbing hold of his shirt, she yanked it off, ready to show him how much he meant to her. Without him, she never would have known how it felt to be truly fulfilled and loved whole-heartedly.

———

Jackson

With her face tucked into the curve of his shoulder, he brushed away the hair that had fallen over her shoulder. Kissing her soft skin there, he realized he'd never seen her look more beautiful. But as his brain began to function again, the oven timer sounding off provided a shameful reminder of what he'd done.

"I'm sorry," he whispered against her throat.

"Mmm. For what? Making me go clinically insane?"

"I wanted our last night to be romantic, and the kitchen isn't that."

She sat up to face him, letting her arms linger on his shoulders. "Please don't apologize for what just happened. It was sexy, spontaneous, and very satisfying. I wouldn't have changed a thing."

Lifting her off the counter, he set her feet on the floor in front of him.

"There are no words to adequately explain how much I love you. You are my reason for breathing, my everything."

"Oh, Jackson, I love you, too. I am irrevocably yours."

———

Emily

They awoke at the first light of dawn, their need to take advantage of every remaining moment too overpowering to sleep. But knowing his inevitable departure grew closer with every tick of the clock prevented either from genuinely savoring it.

She turned and buried her face in his neck. How was she going to say goodbye later? "I'm not ready."

"Me neither."

"Will you call me every day? No matter what?"

"Of course."

The promise soothed her frayed nerves, but not enough to settle them completely. "I'm not ready," she repeated, but she never would be, and the longer she put it off, the more it would wreck her. "I guess I should get dressed for work."

"Okay. I'll make breakfast."

"Wow. Dinner and breakfast. How lucky can one girl get?" Her voice quivered, overshadowing her attempted flattery.

"I think I'm the lucky one." Taking her face in his hands, he kissed her forehead. "Now, get going so you're not late."

With no energy left to put up a fight, she cried in the shower and skipped most of her usual routine. What was the point? Misery over what laid ahead had taken hold, and after drying off, she felt drained and beaten, courtesy of her fragile and unpredictable emotions.

Frustrated, she tossed on her robe and headed to the bedroom to dress. But standing in front of her dresser, adrenaline ran rampant through her system. She hadn't opened a single drawer since getting ready for work the day before, yet some sat slightly ajar.

With an unsteady hand, she pulled one open to find the contents no longer organized and folded neatly like she kept them. She opened another and then another, and her hands sprang to her mouth. Her T-shirts and shorts, socks, and random garments were strewn about like someone had rummaged through them in a hurry.

"Breakfast is ready," he announced, stopping in the doorway. "What's wrong?"

"Were you in these drawers yesterday?"

"No."

"I didn't think so," she admitted, mainly to herself, then forced a smile. "I'll be right there."

After selecting the items she needed, she shut her overactive imagination inside. That morning, she didn't have time to worry about something she couldn't explain. She'd think about it later when she wouldn't be wasting her last precious minutes with Jackson.

———

"This is really good," she told him after taking a bite of the omelet he'd made.

"Why do you sound so surprised?"

"I'm not in the least. You seem to be great at everything," she added with a sheepish grin. "Speaking of that, I'll never be able to look at my kitchen island the same way ever again. Thank you."

"My pleasure."

She leaned forward, her hand on his thigh, and waited for a kiss. "I'm going to miss this."

"Me, too, but remember, it's temporary."

"Thank goodness. I do hope you find what you're looking for. You deserve it."

"Thanks, but if I don't, at least this trip was a success in other ways."

"Oh, yeah?" She set down her fork and shifted in her seat to face him. "How?"

"I found you—my favorite success story." He kissed her fingers before continuing, sending a convoy of tingles down her spine. "I also got to see Eleanor and convince her to move back to Richmond."

"Really? You didn't tell me that. I'm so happy for you," she said, and meant it. But knowing Eleanor would be back in Richmond when he returned answered the question she'd been too afraid to ask.

"Thanks. She was living with her daughter and three grandkids in southern Virginia. Although she'd never admit it, they were struggling. I'm buying them a house, and Harrison offered her daughter a better job."

"That's wonderful. And you also got to meet William."

He lifted her hand to his lips, touched that she remembered. "That's right. I talked to Sydney yesterday.

She started packing for their own move back to Richmond."

"Wow. Looks like you're going to have a large welcome home party." Any remaining doubts about where he'd want to live after his trip vanished. If they were to be together, she would have to join him in Virginia. She had a lot to think about while he was away.

Noticing her inner dialogue, he tugged her into his lap "It's not going to be easy, but we'll get through this."

"We will," she agreed to convince herself and wished for the positivity to stick while they were separated. "Maybe I can visit you some weekends when you stop to rest." She looked down at her watch, and a lone tear slid down her cheek.

"You have to go, don't you?" With his finger, he gently lifted her chin to discover her eyes full of tears and blurring her view of him. "I love you."

"I love you. More than you know."

He followed her to the door and held her tight while sobs shook her body. "Please don't cry."

With a deep breath, she wiped her heartbreak from her cheeks. "Be careful and call me every day. Promise me."

"I promise. Every day."

————

Jackson

Letting her go took all the strength he had. Watching her leave drained life from him. And as her car disappeared around the corner, he collapsed to the floor, unable to pretend a second longer that her absence didn't rip him in two.

Attempting to wrangle his wavering commitment to keep going, he replayed every moment he'd spent with her that weekend. If he could tuck the memories away, maybe they'd help him get through the days leading to Orlando.

He wanted to remember her many animated expressions, her smile, the sounds she made when he touched her, her radiant skin when they made love, and the way she fit in his arms. But he treasured telling her he loved her and the look in her eyes when she said it back the most.

How could he run that day or any day without her? He already felt weak, overwhelmed, and defeated after only half an hour.

"What in the world happened to you?" Ben asked when he found Jackson hunched over on the porch, the front door still open. "You're letting the gnats in. Get up, you big fool."

Jackson wiped his nose with the back of a hand and stood when Ben hooked his arm and pulled.

"You look like shit."

Yanking free, he ignored the comment that didn't help one fucking bit. "Stay here."

After throwing the rest of his things in the suitcase, he dropped it at Ben's feet and stalked to the back porch.

"The goodbye not go well?" Ben asked when he returned with a pile of dirty dishes and silently placed them one by one in the dishwasher. "As you know, I have nowhere to be, so I'm not leaving until we talk about this."

Trying desperately not to snap, Jackson breathed slowly while loading the last of the dishes.

"Fine. I'll just sit here and wait you out." As he reached for a stool under the island, Jackson whipped around.

"Damn it, Ben. Yes, it was miserable, and I have no idea how to do this." With his hands on the counter, his chin dropped to his chest. He despised feeling weak and letting his anxiety mount beyond a level he could control. It would soon debilitate him if he didn't find some semblance of normalcy.

"So, Jackson Vane is human after all." He placed a hand on Jackson's back. "Can I give you some magical Ben Stevens advice?"

Crossing his arms over his burning stomach, Jackson stepped away to lean against the counter. "Why not."

"I have the answer. Are you ready?"

He answered with a silent glare.

"That's what I thought. Here it is. If it gets difficult to continue without her, keep going *for* her." He opened his arms, prepared to receive the praise that advice deserved.

The words *keep going for her* echoed in Jackson's thoughts. "You're right."

"I know. She not only loves you but what you're doing. So, make her proud," he added before strutting out of the room.

While Ben loaded the car, Jackson stood in the foyer and looked around Emily's house one last time. He'd lived with her for several days there, getting a glimpse at the life they would soon have together—unconditional love, adventure, and undeniable passion. All things he didn't have when he started this journey and couldn't have without her.

Feeling as if he could conquer anything he set his mind to, he stepped outside and closed the door. Wherever his path took him from there, he was ready to complete the mission for Emily, for Will, for himself.

Chapter Seventeen

★ ★ ★

Emily

After a long workday, Emily walked with Jillian to the parking lot since nothing good ever happened when she was alone.

"Thank you for being there for me today, Jill. You're a great friend."

"No problem. If Jackson was my boyfriend, I'd be a mess too. He's so stunning."

"I know. My knees turn to jelly when I look at him."

"So, what will you do while—" she paused when Emily's phone chimed.

Retrieving it from her bag, she checked the text message, and her hand sprang to her lips.

"Who's it from? Jackson?" Jillian asked, excited for a little romance.

"No. His friend Ben. He sent me their location for tonight."

"Well?" she pressed. "Where are they?"

"They're only twenty minutes away." She looked up from the phone, her eyes wide with hope. "I'm going to do it."

"Yeah, you are. Go surprise that gorgeous hunk of man, and don't think about tomorrow."

Squealing with excitement, she wrapped Jillian in a hug, then jogged to her car. Before taking off, she texted Ben to ensure Jackson would be in his room when she arrived. Since they'd made plans to meet for dinner in an hour, she had time to pack for the night.

At home, she tossed a small bag on the bed, goosebumps raising the hair on her arms as she turned toward her dresser. A stranger had been in her house and in those very drawers recently. Despite attempting to conjure up other possible explanations, only a break-in made any sense. She made a mental note to call the police, but *after* she got her fill of Jackson.

Less than thirty minutes later, she parked at the hotel and headed upstairs to his room, her heart racing at the rare spontaneity. It was unlike her to follow her heart without thinking through all details. But everything changed when he came into her life, and she loved the courage he gave her.

If she'd jumped off the cliff when they met, she soared with no parachute at that moment. With a knock, she braced for impact. But the door flew open, and she landed softly in his arms, her legs wrapping around him, before she could utter a single word. Their lips forged together as he hauled her inside, passion and longing rejuvenating her weary spirit.

"I think it's obvious that I'm happy to see you, but what are you doing here?"

Freshly showered and shaven, the scent she'd come to associate with home enveloped her like a warm blanket. It had only been ten hours since she last saw him, but with the way her system strained for him, it might as well have been a month.

"Ben texted me your location, and I missed you."

"I knew he'd prove useful one day." Taking her hand, he kissed her fingers. "I want you."

"You have me. All of me."

———

"Hi, handsome," she said when Jackson emerged from the bathroom in nothing but running shorts the next morning, the bright morning sun highlighting him like the masterpiece he was.

"Aren't you looking satisfied this morning?"

"Very."

He sat on the bed, brushed the hair from her shoulder and kissed the tender skin there. "Thank you for coming to see me."

"I couldn't sit at home knowing you were so close. How far will you go today?"

"Not sure. But I feel so amazing I might set a record today."

"Ha. In that case, come back to bed. I'd like to lay a little while longer in your arms."

For the next hour, contentment settled over them while they talked.

"I realized the other day that I don't know much about your life in Richmond," she confessed and ran the back of her hand softly down his chest. His smooth skin and the familiar scent of his woodsy soap and shaving cream warmed her soul.

"There's not much to tell. It's just me living day by day in my dad's house."

"You mean castle."

He smiled. "Nope, since it's still not a castle."

"That's not what I heard."

"Your source grossly exaggerated the description."

"I don't know." She giggled, happier than she'd ever been. "He's very trustworthy."

"I think you should do a background check before you believe that."

"Funny. What about your parents? Do they still live there, or did you lock them in the dungeon?"

"Both my parents have passed."

"Oh, Jackson. That was insensitive of me. I'm so sorry."

"There's no reason to apologize."

"Can I ask how?"

"My mother died when I was twelve and my father last year—both from cancer. We weren't close, and they were absent most my life. Eleanor and Harrison raised me and are my parents without the official titles."

She tried unsuccessfully to imagine growing up without her parents. They were her foundation and had given her the most colorful childhood. "I know you don't like talking about your father. Did you not get along?"

"That would be an understatement. Everything else in his life was more important, and it got worse after my mother passed. Every time we were together, we argued. As I got older, we just stayed out of each other's way. Needless to say, he was less than thrilled to have me in his house after my discharge."

"You were injured and struggling."

"Doesn't matter."

"That must have been very difficult on you."

"Not really. I had Harrison when I needed him, and Eleanor is a formidable influence, forever on my side."

"I can't wait to meet them, especially the famous Eleanor. I'd like to thank her."

"For what?"

"For being there for you so you can be here with me now."

He tightened his arms around her. "How much time do we have?"

"Enough."

———

"I should have reported it sooner," Emily told the officer. "But I was distracted." She glanced at the kitchen island he huddled over, taking notes on a report, and blushed.

"I don't think this was a random break-in. Whoever did this was looking for something personal to you or wanting to scare you. Do you have any ex-boyfriends, co-workers, or acquaintances that might want to get back at you for something?"

"No. I get along with almost everyone." She grabbed a water bottle from the refrigerator and passed it to the officer before taking one for herself.

"Thank you. You said *almost* everyone. Is someone coming to mind?"

She sighed. "I threatened to file a sexual harassment complaint on a co-worker recently, but I couldn't imagine he'd do this." Lucas wouldn't stoop to rummaging through her clothes. No matter how infuriating he'd been, he wasn't a common criminal. "What would he gain from it?"

"Blackmail, personal items to satisfy a fetish, you name it. I've heard many reasons over the years. None have surprised me, but the first act usually evolves into something more later."

"You don't think this is a one-time thing?"

"No. Break-ins like this rarely are." He walked to the back door and tested the lock. She confessed that it didn't work before but had been fixed since. *Thank you, Jackson.*

"So, what happens next?" she asked, snapping her head toward the front door when it swung open.

"Emily! I'm so sorry it took so long to get here." Genevieve rushed to her side and hugged her close. "Everything okay?"

"Yeah. I'll fill you in later."

"That's my cue," the officer announced with a shy smile. Noticing his confidence had flown out the door with Genevieve's entrance, Emily pinched her lips to hide her amusement.

"Um," he attempted, cleared his throat, then cut his eyes to the report in his hands.

Probably waiting for the blood to return to his brain, she mused.

"Uh, we, uh, have a few more tasks to complete before we get out of your way. Stay soon…I mean, stay safe, and I'll call you soon to check in." He let out an audible sigh and a load of embarrassment, tipping his hat as he left.

"Thank you, Officer," she called after him and beamed a smile when he couldn't bring himself to address Genevieve.

"I don't see what's so funny about this."

"Oh, really? Since when?"

"What are you talking about?" Irked, Genevieve slumped down on a stool.

"That officer could put two sentences together before you got here. Now, he's a blubbering mess." She cleared the tricky little laugh that tickled her throat and slapped a hand over her mouth when it threatened to leak out again.

"Whatever." Genevieve slid off the stool and headed for the wine cabinet. "I can't believe you're not taking this seriously."

"I am taking it seriously. Are you feeling all right?" she asked when Genevieve emerged with a bottle in hand.

"I'm fine."

"Are you sure? You don't seem like yourself." She watched Genevieve select two glasses and insert the corkscrew into the bottle. "Normally, you'd have something to say about an attractive man in uniform stumbling over himself because you simply stood before him."

"I didn't notice, nor do I care."

"Hmm."

Setting aside the cork she expertly removed, Genevieve filled the glasses before noticing Emily watching her. "What is it now?"

"I'll repeat. Are you feeling okay?"

"Jesus, Em. Can I please have a glass of wine without the third degree? I'm here because some asshole has broken into my friend's house. I'm on edge, damn it."

Emily's hands flew up in surrender. "Got it. Thank you for coming," she said with more force than necessary and let out the tension molding her muscles with a long exhale. "Now, give me that glass."

Later that evening, Genevieve sat on the couch while Emily paced and recounted the events that led to the investigation. She mentioned the door that wouldn't lock, the messy dresser drawers, her strange encounter with Lucas at the deli, and her unfortunate decision to delay calling the police.

"Did you give the officer Lucas's information?" Genevieve set her glass on the coffee table to address the issues she heard.

"No. I really don't think he would do this. He's incredibly forward and an arrogant jerk, but I don't think he's the type to break into my home and rummage through my drawers."

"He threatened you, Emily. I wouldn't put it past him. What did the officer say?"

"He thinks I was targeted by someone who wants something from me or to get back at me."

"And after everything that's happened, you don't think Lucas wants to get back at you?"

"No. Maybe. I don't know."

"He sounds volatile to me. But if it's not him, who else could it possibly be? You're unnecessarily nice to everyone, even when they don't deserve it."

"Thanks."

"Have you told Jackson?"

"Oh my gosh, no. He'd worry, and I don't want to cause him any more stress. He needs to focus on his journey. It means so much to him."

"It does, but I'd bet you and your safety mean more."

With a shrug, Emily sat on the couch and let her vision blur. "I miss him so much. It's only been a week, and it's hard already."

"I know." She took Emily's hand to comfort her, but her own eyes filled instead.

"Why are you getting emotional?"

"Probably my out-of-whack hormones." Genevieve swiped at the corner of her eye with a finger.

"If that were true, you'd be fuming, not crying, and telling me to suck it up, he's just a man." She laughed until Genevieve's lip quivered. "Oh no, honey. What's the matter?"

Looking disgusted with herself, Genevieve snatched up her glass and drained the contents. "He *is* just a man, and I hate them all."

"No, you don't. You adore them and a little too much sometimes."

"Well, I hate missing them."

"Missing? Who are you missing enough to shed a tear over? You never—" In shock, she watched Genevieve rise and stalk to the wine bottle on the dining room table for a refill. "You've got to be kidding me. Ben?"

She growled in response and took up pacing where Emily left off.

"G!"

"Yes. Shit. Yes. He got under my skin and a lot of other parts, too."

Emily considered the hidden meaning and Genevieve's bizarre spurt of emotion. "Holy Hell! You do like him. I knew it." She rose to give her friend a squeeze.

"What are you doing?" Genevieve pressed her arms tight to her sides, refusing to participate in the hug.

"Celebrating, of course. You finally came to your senses. He's such a sweetie, and—"

"Hold on right there." Wiggling free, she slumped back onto the couch. "Don't you start writing a romance novel. This does not have the happy ending you're conjuring up in that unrealistic world of positivity you live in."

"What? Why?" Joining her, Emily waited with concern.

"You know why."

"No. I can think of the excuses you've told yourself, but I want to hear you attempt to explain it."

"I don't want to talk about him."

"Why? So you don't have to admit that you're screwing up an opportunity to be loved by a good man?"

"Emily, no man is ever going to control my life."

"Who says Ben is trying to control you?"

"No one, and that's exactly why this is so aggravating. He's completely taken over my life."

"How? You've barely talked to him."

"I think about him when he's gone. I wonder about a future with him when we're together. Every man I see reminds me of him."

Emily held up a hand, trying to understand the news, then combed her fingers through her hair. "I'm so confused. You were adamant that you weren't interested in him, and you two acted like strangers at dinner both times. Did something happen after you left?"

"He tricked me into going on a date with him." She cringed. "A real date where he picked me up, and we went out."

"I have a feeling he didn't have to twist your arm."

Genevieve answered with a guilty shrug. "He did a little. I was stubborn."

"What else is new? How'd it go?"

"Another twist in the Genevieve and Ben saga." She stood and took a long sip of wine. "It was amazing. We talked and laughed. He's more fascinating and intelligent than he lets on."

"Not surprising."

"He put no pressure on me, freeing me to be myself. No guy has ever seen that."

"You let Ben see."

"Yeah, and now look at me."

"I am, and I see you, too. You let him in because you knew you had no reason to protect yourself. I'm so proud of you."

"I wish I was." She fidgeted to hide her frustration, then her eyes warmed. "He looked so cute in his white button-down shirt and khakis. And he brought flowers, Em."

"How sweet." More details aligned in Genevieve's eyes as she stared back, words unnecessary. "Don't tell me they were—"

"Carnations, yes."

"How could he know?"

"I have no idea, but it couldn't have been a coincidence. No one buys carnations on purpose."

"You do."

Genevieve smiled and held up her glass in salute. "Ever since Charlie gave me a bunch for high school graduation. It was the first time anyone had ever given me flowers, and I felt so special."

"That's Dad for you."

"But Ben? I can't wrap my head around it. Had I known he was bringing flowers, I would've expected the typical obnoxious red rose or something safe like daisies. I was lost when I saw the soft yellow and white blossoms."

Emily marveled at the irony of her friend's weakness for the simple flower. The two didn't match. "Did the usual happen after dinner?"

"What usual are you implying, Emily?" She grinned and took a sip to hide it.

"Don't play innocent with me. I not only see you, I know you."

Genevieve puffed out her frustration. "No. It didn't."

"You're joking."

"I wish. I invited him in *as usual* when he took me home, but he turned me down."

"The nerve of him." She laughed when Genevieve shot her a disapproving glare. "I bet that's never happened before."

"No, and I was crazy mad. He didn't even hesitate. What game was he playing? It wasn't like we hadn't been sleeping together already."

"What? You slept together before the date? How did I not know that?"

"Come on." She tipped her head on a frown. "Your head was so far up Jackson's ass you didn't see daylight for days."

"True, but that was over a week ago. You've been keeping this hot little secret from me. I can't believe Ben ended the drought. I need details. When? How?"

"The first time was when we left your house in the cab."

Emily's heart kicked into gear. "You had sex in the cab?"

"Lord, no. I don't care for an audience, but I wanted to." She winked and flashed a spirited smile. "Jackson knew. He didn't tell you?"

"No." *What the hell?* Why was everyone keeping secrets from her? "How did he find out? Did Ben tell him?"

"When he stopped by to see Ben the other day, I was there. I had hoped to keep our being together a secret. Glad to know he doesn't blab everything to you."

Emily sulked, then perked up, remembering. "Wait a minute. He did tell me, sort of."

"What does that mean?"

"He said they couldn't hang out that afternoon because Ben was busy." She pinched her lips, trying not to let loose the snickers building in her throat. "When I asked what Ben was doing…" With her self-control faltering, a wild burst of laughter soon took over.

"What's so funny?"

She continued to cackle, her stomach aching from the effort until, with considerable effort, she tamped it down enough to speak. Resting her hand on her sore belly, she continued. "Jackson said…" Another laugh threatened to interrupt again. "He said it wasn't *what* he was doing, but *who*." She slapped her thigh and threw back her head in laughter. "It was you!"

Genevieve pretended to be annoyed as Emily amused herself, but a crooked grin gave her away. "I'm glad you are finding this so entertaining."

"Oh, yes. It's better than a good movie. I can see your face." She demonstrated how she envisioned Genevieve reacting to Jackson exposing her secret—a wide-eyed, Heisman Trophy pose with jazz hands instead of a football—and the friends laughed until they cried.

"I've missed this," Genevieve said when she could breathe again.

"Me, too." Weeks had gone by since the friends spent any significant time together, all the distractions since their trip to Myrtle Beach putting an unfortunate distance between them.

Emily dabbed at her wet eyes, then grabbed Genevieve's hand. "Can I give you some advice?"

"Sure. I know I can't stop you."

"Call him. Tell him you're thinking about him and see what happens. I bet he will be thrilled to hear from you."

"I'm not so sure about that, but it doesn't matter. I can't call him."

"Why not?"

"He's already wrecking my life, and he's not even here. I need to get him out of my head, not add more of him to it. I barely recognize myself now as it is."

"That just means you care for him. Why is that so terrible?"

"Because I'm scared, damn it!" She slammed her empty glass down on the table. "And it's a horrible, disgusting feeling."

Emily patted the cushion next to her until Genevieve stopped revolting and joined her. "Being scared to lose someone you care about doesn't make you weak. It makes you human."

With a sigh, Genevieve reached for a tissue and wiped her nose.

"What are you going to do?" Emily asked.

"I have no idea. I don't even know how he feels."

"Yes, you do. It's obvious he likes you."

"He likes how I feel, how I look. What about the rest? Does he like *me*? I'm a lot to handle in large chunks." She attempted a smile, but it wavered. "Does he see a future for us? Does he even want more than a summer fling?" She swallowed hard, her eyes darting to her lap. "I can't believe that entered my mind."

"He's different, G. He cares for *you*, not just your beautiful outer layer. He showed that every time something happened. You two need to talk."

Genevieve slowly shook her head, her frown tinged with defiance.

"Don't let him get away, G, or you'll regret it."

"On that note." She squeezed Emily's hand and stood to gather her bag. "I'm going home."

"Why? Was it something I said?" Laughing, Emily wrapped her in a hug.

"Are you going to be okay here alone?"

"Yeah. I don't think the coward who did this is man enough to break into my house while I'm here."

"Maybe, unless what he wants is you, and he's just waiting for you to be alone. I can stay, or you can come to my place."

"Thanks, but I'll be fine."

"Alright. But be extra cautious and lock your damn doors."

Chapter Eighteen

✯ ✯ ✯

Jackson

It had been a grueling ten days since Jackson last held or touched Emily. Sleepless nights, lonely days, joint pain, migraines, raging wars. The concoction worsened every passing day without her.

Just as he feared.

He struggled to run the usual fifteen to twenty miles, and most days, he could only manage one outing. He'd made progress, but the more he ran, the farther away his goal seemed to be.

The first weekend after he left Savannah, he thought about jumping into the car and driving back to stay with Emily for a few more days. He spent hours rationalizing the idea, even going as far as grabbing the spare keys out of his suitcase. It wouldn't be cheating or quitting. He'd just be enjoying a weekend getaway for a bit of therapy called

Emily Robertson. Then, he'd get back to the mission where he left off, repaired and ready to endure the next round.

But in the end, he couldn't get himself to do it. Leaving might jeopardize the integrity of the journey, and he'd come too far to risk it. The hardship would make him stronger in the end. It had to.

While he laid awake that stormy night, he took Emily's advice and read the social media comments. He hadn't looked at the photos since she showed him a few at dinner after their first date, and there were dozens of pictures he hadn't realized were taken.

Most were of him running through various towns and terrains at different times of day—Ben and his covert monitoring. But the photo of him kneeling in the rain in front of a war memorial in South Carolina had hundreds of comments.

The last photo showed Jackson sitting with a homeless veteran he met two days ago in southeast Georgia. The man couldn't speak but appeared to have appreciated the hot meal Jackson provided. His baggy shirt, smudged with days-old dirt, looked as if it could fall apart in the next gust of wind. Before he left, Jackson gave him the extra T-shirt he carried in his bag and enough cash to buy several more meals.

Although the photo was new, many comments had already been added. He read each one, the last comment moving him to tears. It explained that the man's family had been looking for him for two years. He'd suffered brain damage from an explosion while serving during the Vietnam War and wandered off from his long-term care facility. The photo helped his family locate him and take him home.

Other comments came from those who'd lost their spouses and found comfort in following his journey or sons and daughters of veterans encouraging or thanking him. Emily had been right. The kind words and personal stories left under each photo gave him more reasons and motivation to keep pushing forward.

For hours, he read the comments until he dozed off with the phone in hand. True slumber had eluded him since leaving Savannah, and he hadn't realized he'd slept through the morning until an impatient knock rumbled on the door. Jumping out of bed, he rubbed his tired eyes and opened the door without checking to see who stood on the other side.

"What are you still doing here?" Ben asked and stalked past him.

"Come in, please. No. I don't mind." Frustrated with the intrusion, he sighed and followed Ben into the room.

"Seriously. What's going on? You were supposed to be on the road hours ago." Ben dropped into the chair beside the bed, his elbows resting on his thighs.

"Change of plans."

"No shit. What happened?"

"I fell asleep." After yanking the first shirt he saw from his suitcase, he pulled it on.

"That's what the night is for and doesn't explain why you're still here."

"You're in a great mood this morning."

"I could say the same about you." Ben stared him down.

"I figured you'd be happy about a later start."

"I'm messed up, man. That woman. The Goddess of all women has destroyed me. I can't sleep. I can't eat. I think about her all day and night." Spinning around, he stomped back to the chair and fell into it. "I'm going insane not having her." He ran his hands over his disheveled hair and down his face again, letting them fall into his lap. "Why hasn't she called me?"

"Have you tried calling her?"

"No. I can't."

"Why not?" Jackson sat on the bed nearby, expecting the conversation to be long and confusing.

"I told her I wouldn't."

"So?"

"The next move is hers. Either she wants me, or she doesn't. I can't keep riding this rollercoaster."

"Sounds like she doesn't. Maybe it's time to step away."

"Easy for you to say. How would you feel if Emily stopped talking to you?"

"Our situation is vastly different. It's not a fair comparison. Genevieve's been through a lot lately. She probably just needs more time."

"It's been, what? Ten days? How much fuckin' time does she need?" He shot up, paced to the dresser and back to flop into the chair again. "She just doesn't want me. I feel like the world's biggest idiot."

"She's trying to figure some things out, and you're not an idiot. Maybe a little feral and annoying, but not an idiot." When Ben snapped his head around and narrowed his eyes in response, Jackson flashed a grin.

"Why did I ever think I could get a woman like her? I'm just a wild, unemployed artist with nothing to offer her."

"You forgot annoying," Jackson deadpanned.

"What?"

"Unemployed, wild, and annoying. You forgot annoying."

With a growl, Ben threw a pillow at Jackson, and he snagged it out of the air.

"Running back, remember? I can catch and run."

"I hate you."

Laughing, Jackson stood. "Come on. We need to keep our eyes on the goal. Don't worry about Genevieve. Everything will work out as it should." He held out a hand, and as he pulled Ben to his feet, he slapped the pillow hard against his stomach. "Now, get out."

"You know," he said, coughing from the unexpected blow to the ribs, "you say that a lot."

"You deserve it a lot."

―――――

Emily

On the verge of erupting, Emily sat across from Gregory Kline, Human Resources Director. She twitched at the chaotic dysfunction on his ornate wooden desk—papers, knick-knacks, pencils, and photo frames strewn about without purpose. But she'd lost her temper long before his disorganization sent her system rebelling.

"Miss Robertson, calm down, and let's talk about this."

"Don't patronize me. I've been talking. Have you been listening?"

"Yes. I heard that you and Dr. Oliver had relations, and you've since misunderstood his comments and actions toward you."

Speechless, her body shook with a longing to clear the clutter from his ridiculous desk with one swoop of her arm and wipe the condescending smirk off his face.

"Mr. Kline, I have been groped, pinned against walls, cornered, and harassed countless times. The most recent being yesterday when he put his hands on me in front of patients."

That instance snapped the last fraying thread of patience she had, and she submitted a newly completed sexual harassment form to human resources that same afternoon. This meeting, her second with H.R. staff, proved her complaint would be going nowhere.

"I have not had any *relations*, as you called it, with Dr. Oliver. I was crystal clear when I told him to stop following me and touching me against my wishes. I want nothing to do with him personally."

"That's not what I heard."

"Excuse me?"

"The story circulating around the office is an intimate moment happened between you in the fitness room one night not too long ago. You've been seen flirting in the hallways and your office on breaks or after hours. You've gone on lunch dates and taken time off together. That doesn't sound like a woman saying no and being harassed by an attractive and wealthy doctor, capable of advancing her career." He tapped a pen against his palm, waiting for her response.

Unbelievable. Lucas beat her to the punch and undermined her entire case with skewed details. "There has been no flirting on my end. He's chased me like a wild animal on a hunt, and the one time we were together outside of work was for a patient's funeral. I hardly call that spending time together."

"What about the fitness room incident and the lunch dates? What are your explanations for those?"

"I'd just found out my patient died. I was vulnerable, and he kissed me. It never happened again." Her heart pumped so fast she felt dizzy. "As for the lunches, a fellow co-worker asked me to join him. They were not dates."

"I have witnesses who say they saw more than two co-workers getting to know each other. Emily, I don't see any harassment here. I see a woman trying to fit in and advance her career, and when that didn't happen, she cried harassment. It happens all the time."

She stood to protest too fast, emptying her veins of life-preserving blood, and she had to use the chair for balance. The room spun, and her lunch threatened to make an appearance all over his arrogant face. To keep her composure, she paused to settle her stomach, but part of her wished to see his gaudy, impeccable suit covered in vomit.

"Well, Greg, since Dr. Oliver has you in his back pocket, *you* can tell him that I quit, and both of you can go to Hell."

Snatching her bag off the floor, she stalked out and hurried down the hall. Panic sank into place and crowded her lungs. She couldn't breathe. Couldn't think about anything but getting out of there. She snatched an empty box from the storage room along the way to her office, thankfully without detection. After locking the door—a new habit, thanks to Lucas—she slid to the floor and let sobs bombard her body.

With her legs folded up, she dropped her head to her knees and mourned the loss of a job she adored. How had this happened? She didn't want to quit, but they'd left her no choice. Greg had all but called her a liar and would have spun every truth she told. Without a care for her feelings, they'd disrespected and disregarded her. They'd won, and she was a fool.

Once the building emptied, she packed up her picture frames, books, and certificates and took one last look around through a wall of tears. She remembered the first day she walked through the door. The smallest office in the building came with a dented, second-hand desk, but she loved it and what it symbolized.

She'd been so naïve then. Her entire life she struggled to see the negative in situations and people. Always made excuses for when someone wronged her and let their actions influence her mood, her thoughts, her decisions. Well, no more.

By the time she loaded the box into the car, day had given way to night. She'd spent the last few hours digging herself out from beneath a mound of sorrow and suffocating regret. Breathing deep, she filled her lungs with the cool evening air, realizing she'd emerged unscathed with freedom as her parting gift.

Too rattled to be alone, she stopped by Genevieve's apartment to give her the news.

"What an asshole," she decided when Emily finished reporting on her day.

"I have never been so angry and insulted. He practically told me that I had encouraged Lucas and made up the story for attention. I wanted to scream."

"You should have, but it wouldn't have made a difference. Sounds like he'd already made up his mind. What are you going to do next?"

"Good question. Celebrate getting rid of Lucas with some retail therapy. Have a panic attack. Mourn the loss of my patients with a few bottles of wine and a box of tissues. After I emerge from that, I guess I'll start searching for another job."

"No. As your best friend and the person who understands you best, I forbid it."

"You forbid me? From doing what?"

"Working."

"How can I do that? My bills aren't going to pay themselves."

Genevieve eyes took a trip to the ceiling and back. "You have money saved. Don't waste this amazing opportunity you have. Take some time for yourself and enjoy life for a while. You work too hard, and the career will be waiting for you when you get back."

"And where would you have me go, my most humble, all-knowing friend?" She laughed, starting to warm to the idea. She had saved for the past two years and could use some time off between jobs to bury some baggage.

"I have the perfect answer. You should find Jackson and finish the journey with him."

Emily's heart skipped. "I can't believe that never crossed my mind." Could the idea be fate be bringing them together again? It would answer how she managed something so completely out of character. She ached for him more with every passing day. "But I don't want to get in his way."

"Oh, shut up. He would be thrilled to have you. Just think of all the amazing things you two could do along the way."

"You make an irresistible point."

"When do you leave?"

Emily began running through the list of things she'd need to do, calculating the time it would take, until something hard smacked across her arm. "What was that for?" she asked, rubbing her sore tricep.

"Stop planning and just go for it." Shooting up from the couch, she motioned for Emily to join her. "What do you have to lose?"

"Right. I'll leave tomorrow." Determined to take the leap and do what always scared her, she grabbed her purse from the nearby chair, then stopped—her mind raced with too many glorious ideas to keep track. She'd started with the most exciting one. "Come with me," she told Genevieve, clutching her shoulders.

"What?"

"Pack a bag, and let's go together."

Genevieve shook her head, her eyes wide and frenzied. "Why should I go? This is your adventure. I plan to live vicariously through you for a change."

"Screw that. Let's go surprise both Jackson and Ben."

"Whoa. Slow down." She tossed up her hands and stumbled backward, needing space to breathe. "Damn it."

"G, what's wrong?"

Absently, she cursed to herself and paced the small empty space until Emily led her back to the couch.

"Talk to me."

"I can't go." She wrung her hands until her knuckles went white.

"You're going to hurt yourself." Separating Genevieve's hands, she held them gently. "He cares about you. He's waiting, probably very impatiently, for you to make the next move."

"Shit, Emily. I don't…" Pulling her hands free, she shoved her fingers through her hair. "I need to… What if he's already moved on?"

"There's no way he gave up that easily."

"What if I let it go on for too long, and he can't forgive me? What will I do if he turns me away?"

Emily studied her friend and reveled at the reversal of their typical roles. "What if he doesn't? What if he accepts you with open arms, and you're blissfully happy? Isn't it worth the risk?"

"I don't know."

"Come on. Isn't taking crazy risks your thing?"

"This isn't the same as starting a business or talking to strangers in a bar."

"Yes, it is. Answer this question: Why do you like him?"

"Isn't that obvious?"

"You need to say it out loud."

Genevieve glanced down at her trembling hands, stalling the inevitable. Emily wouldn't give up on this without a fight. "He brought me flowers."

"Very sweet. What else?"

"He makes me laugh and knows what I like without me having to say it." Her eyebrows wiggled, garnering a sigh from Emily.

"And…most importantly?"

After a deep breath, Genevieve's shoulders drooped in surrender. "He makes me happy."

"That's right. And you aren't as happy pining for him."

"I don't pine."

"Sure, you don't." She winked. "What are you going to do?"

After some mulling, Genevieve snatched her phone off the coffee table and pressed a button.

"Does this mean what I think it means?"

She held up a hand, letting her conversation with the person on the other end do all the talking. "Hey, Steph. Sorry to be calling after hours, but I need you to cancel all my upcoming appointments. I'm leaving town tomorrow." She winced, her body curling into itself like she expected the ceiling to fall with the decision. "Yes, that's right. Just forward my calls to my cell, and I'll keep up with emails… No. I'm not sure how long I will be gone… Call me if you need anything."

Emily managed to hold in a scream until she hung up. Another exciting adventure with Jackson as the destination was exactly what she needed to set her world right once again.

"You're sure about this?" Genevieve asked. "I'm not going to regret this later, am I?"

"I've never been more confident of anything in my life, but what you do when we get there is up to you."

"I think I'm going to be sick."

"In the words of the all-knowing G—shut up. I've never seen you back down from a challenge or worry about what might be. Follow your heart, and what happens after that will be amazing." She wrapped her arms around Genevieve. "Do what feels right. Isn't that what you told me in Myrtle Beach?"

"I wish I had your positivity."

"After all that's happened, the only thing I'm positive about is how much Jackson and Ben care for us. Let's go get our men."

Chapter Nineteen

☆ ☆ ☆

Ben

Wᴴat's wrong with you?" Jackson asked as if he didn't have a care in the world, adding salt to Ben's wounds. Despite his best efforts to cheer Ben up, it hadn't worked. "Her Highness still hasn't called yet?"

Jackson had begun referring to Genevieve as 'Queen' because of her lofty attitude and because the allure of her ruled Ben's life now—a situational change neither of them cared for.

"You better stop calling her that. When you let it slip one day around Emily, she's going to punch you in the face." Thinking about it made him smile despite his foul mood. "If I don't do it first."

"Ha! I'd like to see you try," Jackson teased, knowing he wouldn't dare start a fight. They'd grown close since leaving Savannah, often commiserating over their loneliness.

That day, Ben could focus on nothing except his silent phone. He spent too much of his free time convincing himself that he'd be better off without the woman of his dreams and his life back to normal. But how could things ever be normal again? Especially after he'd had a taste of her—a flavor not so easily forgotten. He'd paint the sky her favorite color if it would make her come back to him.

Shit. His heart raced with a new realization. What if she wasn't playing hard to get and was relieved to have him out of the way? What if the first time they made love was also the last? What if she'd been with someone else since he left?

Air escaped his lungs as panic consumed him. He slammed his hand on the table and shot out of the booth, desperate for oxygen, sanity, a way back to Savannah.

The small restaurant, filled with hungry and suddenly irritated locals, had gone silent, and all eyes fumed at him for the interruption. He quickly decided to panic in private next time. With an awkward wave, he slumped back into his seat.

"What was that?" Jackson stared at him as if he'd spontaneously burst before him. Despite feeling like he had, he only experienced a brutal, unforgiving slap back to reality.

It may only be eleven in the morning, but he desperately needed a drink. With a wave to their server, he ordered a beer, then set his brooding eyes on the parking lot outside to contemplate his depressing situation.

His entire adult life, he'd avoided relationships. Too many of his friends had fallen under the spell of a woman and lost themselves in the process. After watching it happen over and over, he vowed to avoid that particular sickness. He wanted to party, take pictures, and do as he pleased with no ball and chain. No pledges or long-term anything. That was the perfect life. So, how in the world, after one glorious night with Genevieve, had he become everything he despised?

Lovesick.

Snatching the beer that had magically appeared in front of him, he chugged until Jackson's phone rang, surprising him. Beer dribbled down his chin, and he quickly wiped it away, trying to look like he had his shit together when a server arrived with their meals.

"It's Emily," Jackson said absently and rose to take her call outside.

Lucky bastard.

Hunching over the plate with his elbows on the table—his strict upbringing forgotten—he took a bite of the burger he ordered, and all he tasted was jealousy.

Jackson had everything. He didn't have to work for Emily's affection or wonder how she felt. He knew her heart because she told him and showed him every day. Frustration replacing hunger, he dropped the sandwich and watched Jackson pace outside while he talked with woman he loved.

Why couldn't he have the same opportunity with Genevieve? One text or call was all he needed. He didn't ask her to marry him for fuck's sake. But the more time that passed without a word from her, the more unsure he became of so many things—his flailing sanity being the most concerning.

He not only dreamed and thought about her incessantly, he also saw her—on a trail, in the store, or on the hotel balcony. In these appearances, she reached for him, smiled in his direction, or simply stared at him, gripping his senses enough to think she was actually there.

Sick of being tortured, he spent his free time brainstorming how to get over her instead of enjoying their trip. He no longer recognized the pitiful excuse for a man he saw in the mirror, and it had to stop.

Running his hands through his hair, he tried to shake her out of his mind and summon the energy to eat as Jackson slid back into the booth.

"Emily says hello." He picked up his fork and stabbed a piece of broccoli.

"You didn't talk very long."

"She only had a few minutes between patients." With a frown, Jackson dropped his fork with a clank on the plate.

"Now, who's sulking?"

———

Genevieve

"I've got their location," Emily said after hanging up with Jackson.

"Oh, God. Okay. It's getting real."

"Relax. He's going to be happy to see you."

With a sigh, Genevieve kept her eyes on the road, ignoring the various red-flag thoughts trying to steal her attention. "Where are they?"

"At a restaurant not too far from here. If we hurry, we might be able to catch them before they leave."

Following the map on her phone, Emily directed every turn. But slow mid-day traffic added a complication she hadn't calculated into the commute.

"I could walk there faster than this," Genevieve complained. The line of cars ahead stretched beyond the horizon and crawled along the highway at injured turtle speed.

"Yes." Emily waved the phone in the air. "Found another way there. Take the next exit."

Finally arriving at the restaurant, they rode through the parking lot in search of a sign Jackson, Ben, or the car. On the last turn around the building, disappointment set in.

"Looks like we missed them. We should park and regroup." She pushed on the gas then just as quickly slammed on the brake, causing Emily to brace herself against the dash.

"What is it?" Emily followed Genevieve's blank stare out the windshield to Ben strolling toward them, his attention on the phone in his hand. "You can do this, G. Go get him."

But fear of the unknown kept her glued to her seat. Would he accept her, scream at her, walk away without a word? How would she respond to each of those possible reactions? Her mind sprang from one terrifying reaction to the next. Why hadn't she thought through this ridiculous plan before jumping into the car?

But through the dread, she hadn't missed how handsome he looked with the sunlight shining on his hair, making the caramel-shade appear more golden. The dusting of stubble along his jawline or the deep curve of the broad shoulders she gripped when he—

"G," Emily urged.

"Right. I'm going." She let out a long exhale and opened the door.

As she climbed out, the movement caught his attention, and he stopped beside the front bumper—his eyes opening wide enough to see the olive specs in his soft brown irises. Of all the possible reactions she could have listed, never would she have guessed he'd go pale, gaping at her as if he'd seen a ghost.

———

Ben

His sick brain just didn't know when to quit. Another random vision of Genevieve appeared before him in high definition. This time, she wore less makeup than usual but never looked more beautiful. A light breeze tossed her hair over her shoulder, and he smelled her favorite lotion— honey and vanilla.

Crushing his eyes closed, he begged for her memory to release him. Hadn't he told himself to move on and somehow conjure up a level of sanity to find himself again? When he opened his eyes, the torture would be over, and he could go back to reconfiguring his life.

Damn it! Taking in his surroundings more mindfully this time, he heard the car's motor running and felt heat from the engine. He stared into the green eyes he too often dreamed about and noticed something new in them—insecurities mirroring his own and something else.

Could it be? Surrender?

"Ben," she murmured, and his eyes blurred as terror and disbelief suffocated him again.

He'd finally taken a swan dive off the cliff of reality. After all the pointless promises to take back control, he'd advanced from not only seeing her but hearing her, too.

"Genevieve?"

"Are you all right?"

No. He was losing his damn mind. His body refused the oxygen he gulped, and he teetered on the verge of puking. Bracing himself on the nearby car, the hood burned like fire against his sweaty palms. He yanked it away, sincere concern for his well-being stealing his focus, until the car door shut.

"Fuckin' tell me." Panic rose faster this time, and he raised a hand to stop her—or it—from moving closer. "Are you really here?"

"What?"

"Are you here, or am I seeing things?"

"I'm here, Ben. What's going on?"

As he rubbed the warm skin on his palm, he thanked the universe that his twisted mind wasn't messing with him again. Now that his head had been cleared of ghosts, he was more confused than ever.

"Why?"

She swallowed hard. "Why?"

"Why are you here?"

"To bring you something you left in Savannah. I thought you might be missing it."

"Oh." He kicked the gravel on the asphalt and shoved his hands in his pockets, feeling unsteady in her presence. "What is it?"

"Me," she said softly, watching him.

Needing a moment, he held her gaze, trying to find the hidden meaning. There had to be one, right? She couldn't possibly be there saying she wanted him after the way she'd treated him. Running through a list of potential motives had fury boiling in his gut.

"Let me get this straight," he began, tasting the bitter steam now rising into his throat. "You drove all this way after ignoring me for two weeks…"

His sharp reaction caught off guard, and her eyes widened in disbelief. "I—"

"Let me finish." He took a step forward, and she flinched. Seeing the dismay in her eyes stung a bit, but he had too much to get off his chest to stop now. "Why, Genevieve? I didn't ask for much. Just a text or a phone call that said I wasn't dead to you."

"I'm sorry. I was scared."

"Scared of what? I've done nothing but give you space, affection, understanding, patience. Whatever you needed."

"I know. I was afraid of losing myself and what I've always believed in."

"I felt the same way once, but that didn't stop me."

"Stop you from what?"

"From giving a shit."

"Twenty-seven years alone is a hard habit to break."

"So?" Damn, she was beyond stubborn. "If it's worth it, you break it. You were worth it to me."

"Were." At the past tense comment, evidence that he'd given up, she looked away, blinking too fast for his comfort. "I had to protect my heart," she said in a near whisper.

"I'd never hurt you, Genevieve."

"I know." Her two trembling hands ran over her hair, sending a gush of annoyance through him. All this tension and regret could have easily been avoided had she not been so hell bent on pushing him away.

"Do you?" he asked, needing the truth.

"Well, I didn't fully until Savannah. The time we spent together there changed everything."

"How? From where I stand, nothing's different. I'm still chasing, and you're still running away."

She shook her head. "I'm here now... not running."

"And why is that? I need to hear you say it."

"It's quite the story."

With the way her eyes watched him, she expected a sarcastic comment from him. He didn't the energy, and he hadn't forgiven her yet—couldn't even entertain the notion without answers.

"On the way to my apartment after our date, I began to dread the next day. I could feel myself missing you, and you hadn't even left yet. It made me more determined to save myself from the heartache sure to follow."

Tiny drops of hope began to sprinkle on the anger and regret smoldering inside him. "You missed me?"

She lowered her eyes before answering. "Yes."

"I don't know what to say."

"You could start with you missed me, too." She said it in a way that made him think her walls had crumbled on the way to him.

He ran a hand over his face, stopped at his mouth while he considered her suggestion, then let it drop. "You haunt me every fucking day. I can't focus, eat, sleep. If I even try to look at another woman, all I see is your face. Your infuriating, frustratingly stubborn…" He paused when her shoulders drooped. "Beautiful face."

Closing the distance between them, his hands cupped her waist. He lingered softly over her lips and let days of strain and longing slip away. Too many times to count, he'd begged God, the stars, fate, anything that would listen for this exact moment, and he planned to savor it. But she threw her arms around his neck, deepening the kiss and melting his meticulous control with her tongue.

"Where do you think you're going?" he demanded when she separated from him. When he leaned in to reclaim her mouth, she mirrored him.

"I need to know." Her eyes reluctantly met his, looking unsure of herself for the first time. "Does this mean you forgive me?"

Crushing his lips to hers again, he felt her muscles go lax as she gave herself to him. No more wondering, worrying, chasing. Finally. "I'll think about it," he teased before continuing where he left off to give her tongue something to do other than utter the complaint undoubtedly forming.

"Excuse me," Emily called, emerging from the passenger side of the car.

"Oh. Hi, Em. I didn't realize you were here, too."

"I noticed." She flashed him a *thank you for not giving up* smile. "I'm glad you two are back together, but do—"

"We're not back together," he said flatly.

"We're not?" Genevieve pushed on his chest in protest, but he didn't budge. "Did you make that decision all by yourself? I didn't drop everything to—"

He pressed a finger to her lips, silencing her. "As I was going to explain," he got out before she swatted his hand away, "we were never together in the first place, thanks to Miss Stubborn here." He tilted his head at Genevieve and rolled his eyes with a playful smile. "So, we can't be *back* together."

Turning to the only woman to ever take his breath away, he knelt on one knee and reached for her left hand.

Emily gasped, her hands slapping over her mouth.

"Genevieve Elizabeth Olsen…"

"That's not my name," she deadpanned.

"I know." He didn't, but he also didn't see anyone keeping track. "Just shut up and let me talk. Genevieve Olsen." He paused for dramatic effect and flashed his best smile. "Will you be my girlfriend?"

She let out in a breath of relief. "Of course, you big buffoon. Why do you think I drove all the way down here?" She laughed when he picked her up and spun around.

"Hey, you two big buffoons, I'm still here." Emily waved at the happy couple. "Where can I find Jackson?"

"Sorry, Em. He left a while ago. You can surprise him at the hotel," he said, returning to Genevieve. "God, you're stunning." With his forehead on hers, his hands moved over her waist and hips. "I can't believe you're here."

"How far away is the hotel?"

"We're leaving," he announced and dragged her along to his car.

————

Emily

"Don't worry about me," Emily called after them with a touch of sarcasm. She felt forgotten and insignificant, but she couldn't bring herself to be upset about it. She was happy for them, and the joy of their reunion put a little magic in the air. Soon, she and Jackson would make some of their own. "I'll follow you."

Sitting in the driver's seat of Genevieve's little yellow sportscar, she waited for Ben to back out and lead the way. But instead, the car remained parked for over ten minutes.

"You've got to be kidding me." As she positioned a fist over the horn, the car's taillights lit up. "Thank you."

At the hotel while they waited for Ben to check in, Emily leaned closer to whisper to Genevieve, "You just couldn't wait until you got to the hotel, could you?"

She hummed in response without taking her eyes off Ben. "The man is insatiable, and no, we couldn't."

With Jackson's room key in hand, she left the happy couple lip-locked in the lobby and let herself in. She planned a surprise for her own man and had just enough time to change and tuck her suitcase away before a key inserted into the lock. The long wait to see him finally over.

The door slowly creaked open. With her heart hammering in her ears, she emerged from the shadows to Genevieve and Ben undressing frantically between kisses, their suitcases forgotten between the door and the frame.

"Hello," Emily said to announce her presence and prevent burning her eyes with what they'd planned to do next.

"What are you doing here?" Genevieve asked, caught between feeling annoyed for the interruption and proud of her friend. A smirk emerged as she took in Emily's barely-there white lace teddy.

"I could ask you the same thing."

"This is my room." Annoyance tainted Ben's tone. "How did you… Oh."

"You gave her our spare key, didn't you?" Genevieve smacked him on the arm. "Idiot."

His eyes sparkled with the witty comeback forming on his tongue, but Jackson entering the room surprised them all.

———

Jackson

He saw Emily first, and his legs stopped working. The filtered sunlight through the sheer curtains seemed to shine only on her and her tantalizing bare skin.

Hoping his lonely heart hadn't manifested his fantasies, he went to her and took her face in his hands. "I dreamed of this moment so many times. How is this possible?"

"I needed to see you."

Ben cleared his throat in a not-so-subtle request for privacy. With a low, airy growl, Jackson removed the extra T-shirt from his backpack, slipped it over Emily's head, and took her hand.

"I won't be leaving tomorrow morning as planned," he said, pausing beside Ben on the way to the door. He accepted his room key, then turned to Genevieve, who clutched the front of her shirt, struggling to hold it together. "Genevieve."

"Jackson."

On the way out, Emily grabbed her suitcase, and soon, they found their own privacy a few doors down the hall in the other room.

"I can't believe you're here." He kissed her before sitting on the bed and pulling her into his lap. "I didn't think I'd see you again until this was over. Don't you have appointments?"

"I quit yesterday." She studied her hands linked with his for a beat, showcasing the turmoil the decision caused. "This is a big moment for you, and I want to be a part of it."

He couldn't believe what he heard. "You want to come with me to Orlando?"

"More than I've ever wanted anything in my life."

"That makes me so happy." He brought her fingers to his lips, noticing the oversized shirt she wore and remembering what waited for him under it. A shot of adrenaline raced through his veins, awakening his tired muscles. "I want a do-over."

"A what?"

Rising off the mattress, he set her on her feet and took hold of the shirt he put on her only moments ago. He drew it up over her head, tousling her hair and making her giggle when he flung the shirt across the room. "Stay here."

She waited while he jogged to the door and stepped into the hall. Seconds later, he reentered, stopping just inside to rake his eyes over her.

"What are you doing?"

"Seeing you for the first time, the way I was supposed to."

"Well, soldier. What do you think?"

He strolled closer, his gaze never leaving hers. "I think you're the most beautiful woman I've ever seen." He trailed his knuckles lightly across her cheek, then down her arm. "And that white is my new favorite color."

"Since white's a combination of all colors, that means all the colors are your favorite. Even Army green."

His fingertips traced the decorative edging of the fabric between her breasts, silencing her adorable nervous rambling. "I love the lace pattern here."

His name escaped her lips in an airy plea.

"Not yet."

Lifting her arm, he spun her around. Transparent lace continued down her sides and across her lower back, leaving the rest of her bare. He gathered her silky hair in his hand to see more of her, then threaded three fingers through the strands.

"How do you know how to braid hair?" she murmured when he began folding the sections into place.

"Callie."

"Ahh. And why did you take so long to do this? It's incredibly sexy."

"Really? Wish I had known that sooner."

Reaching the end, he moved to the tiny ribbon at the top of the lingerie, his lips finding her neck as he untied it. "Me too."

Chapter Twenty

☆ ☆ ☆

Jackson

Emily rolled over in his arms, her eyes fluttering open to find him awake. The dark room lit only by the amber glow of the rising sun shining through the window behind her covered her face in shadows.

"Hi," he said with a long exhale, feeling like himself again in her arms.

She brushed a lock of hair off his forehead, her eyes following then meeting his again. "Did you want to do anything today?"

"Does it happen to be Saturday?" He tightened his arms around her, burying his face in her neck.

"Wanting to be lazy today, are you?"

"You make it impossible to want to do anything else."

"We could continue where we left off in Myrtle."

"Going to a hospital doesn't sound like much fun." He chuckled.

"No, it doesn't. I was talking about the beach."

"Oh." He smiled against her slender shoulder before planting a kiss there. "Whatever you want."

———

After spending the day connected to Emily in the sand and water, it took everything he had to leave for an evening run. But her promise to be waiting for him naked in bed when he returned had him skipping his usual warm-up.

Through the entire course, he'd envisioned the moment their bodies would reconnect and ran faster than his legs wanted to carry him. Ignoring the ache, he arrived at the next hotel ahead of schedule to find her exactly as she promised. He joined her, foregoing greetings and formalities, and reignited the flame left simmering while he'd been gone.

Now, in the dim light, he focused on every curve of her face, the pure sapphire shade of her eyes, and the intoxicating sensation of his world realigning.

"You know what I realized today?" she asked, fidgeting with the sheet.

"That you can't wait to do that again?"

"Well, yes," she giggled, "but that's not what I was going to say."

"What did you realize, my love?"

Her eyes softened at the sentiment, warming him from the inside. "We're a few days from St. Augustine. How do you feel about stopping to visit my parents?"

"When was the last time you saw them?"

"The week before we left for Myrtle. They moved to Florida while we were there. I miss them so much and would like for them to meet you."

"Have you told them about us?"

"Yes, but we haven't talked since you came to Savannah. So much has changed." Her eyes glistened with fresh tears before she hid them away.

"Why do you worry?" He placed a finger under her chin and lifted her face, grateful to find her eyes dry again. "From what you've told me, I bet they will support you no matter what's happened."

"I'm just scared they won't understand my recent decisions. I don't want to disappoint them."

"Not possible."

"Hope so. But there is one thing I'm certain about." She smiled and ran her hand up his chest, stopping over his heart. "They're going to adore you."

"I'm excited to meet them." And nervous. Meeting his girlfriend's parents would be another first. He had no past experiences or reference points and no idea what to expect.

Sitting up and rolling him onto his back, she climbed on top of him. "You make me so happy, Jackson Vane. What would I ever do without you?"

"Let's make sure you never have to find out." Framing her face, he brought her lips to his and lost himself in her love.

———

Emily

The sun in all its glory blanked the room in white light, blinding Emily when she sat up to retrieve her ringing cell phone. Annoyed, she crunched her eyes closed and reached for the phone, knocking it off the bedside table. Before she could retrieve it, Jackson tugged her back to the pillow.

"Ignore it," he instructed, half asleep with his arm draped heavily across her belly.

"Good idea." She snuggled against him, groaning when the phone rang again minutes later. "They're persistent."

"Fine." With a sigh, he released her. "See what's so important, and I'll go take a shower." Crawling over her, he picked up the now silent phone on his way to the bathroom and tossed it onto the bed.

She checked the missed calls, and her heart sank to find both calls were from her neighbor. She pressed the *Call Back* button, and he answered after the first ring.

"Harry, I'm sorry, I—"

"I have some bad news," he interrupted. "I've taken care of what I can, but I thought you should know."

There goes her good mood. "What happened?"

"Your house was broken into again, and they smashed a window to get in this time. I called the police and checked the house. Nothing else was damaged."

"Did the police say anything?"

"No. Just wrote a report about the window. I'm sorry, Emily."

"It's okay. I'll arrange for someone to replace it, but in the meantime, would you mind boarding it up for me?"

"Already done, sweetheart."

"Thank you, Harry. You're the best."

"Just doing my neighborly duty. But sweetheart, what's happening here is not safe. As much as I love having you next door, you should consider moving when you get back."

She thought about her little house—the first significant purchase she'd made on her own, and her home the second she saw it.

"You're a great friend, Harry. I'll think about it." But as she hung up, she'd already made up her mind.

———

After Jackson left, Emily tried to distract her thoughts from meandering down a negative path. She took a long shower, flipped through the TV channels, and cracked open a new book. But after reading the same paragraph for the third time, she headed out to find Genevieve.

"Can you walk with me?" Emily asked when she came to the door.

"Sure. Is everything okay?"

"It's fine. I just need to talk through something."

Once she slipped on some shoes and they said goodbye to Ben, the pair found a private booth in the corner of the hotel bar and ordered a glass of wine. It may be early, but Emily's fried nerves needed dousing.

"What's going on?" Genevieve asked. "Did you and Jackson have a fight?"

"Of course not. He's an angel. It's home."

"Don't tell me the asshole returned."

"Harry found a broken window this morning."

"He called the cops, right?"

She nodded. "They found nothing again. It's so frustrating." The bartender delivered two full glasses, and she took a long drink. "I've decided to sell the house."

"Oh, no. You love that house."

"I do, but I'll never feel safe there. Apparently, whoever is doing this is good at it, and what if he's setting something up? What if he eventually comes after me?"

"It's true. Until they catch him, you won't be safe there. I'm sorry, Em."

"Thank you. I'm going to miss it, but then again, I'll be free to decide my future."

"What do you mean?"

"What if Jackson asks me to move in with him? From what he's told me, he has no intention of leaving Virginia." She lowered her eyes and braced herself for Genevieve's reaction. Her entire life, Emily had been her only constant. They'd never gone a day without each other to lean on.

"I see. You're planning to move?"

"You are the only thing making that possibility difficult to consider."

"As much as I want to beg you to stay, I would never make you choose. You belong with Jackson. Wherever that is."

"Thank you." She placed a hand on Genevieve's. "That means a lot, but what will I do without you?"

"It's not that far. Only a car ride or flight away."

"Not the same." She squeezed Genevieve's hand, then folded a leg to face her in the booth. "Let's talk about you now. How's it going with Ben?"

Her smile said it all. "Better than I could have imagined. Who knew having a boyfriend could be so good?"

"I did. You were just too stubborn to—"

"Yeah, yeah. Well, you got through."

"No. He did. He's special."

"That he is." She bit her bottom lip. "Being with him is out of this world."

"That's because there's more than just sex between you. When I'm with Jackson, it's nothing like I've ever experienced, and when I think it can't get any better, it always does."

Emily studied her friend, who had checked out of the conversation. "G, what is it?"

"He treats me like I matter. How am I supposed to handle that?"

"You don't. You enjoy it and be grateful for him. I can't believe I'm about to say this, but you're overthinking it."

Genevieve tilted her head at the advice she'd given Emily a hundred times and glared playfully. "You're right, as usual." Straightening with her standard resolve, she took a sip of wine. "How about we forget the bad and celebrate all the good in our lives tonight? I could use some loud music and spontaneity. I bet Jacksonville has plenty of places to go. Shouldn't we be there by this evening?"

"If Jackson can get in two runs today. His knee has been bothering him."

"That's where you come in, Doc. Get him feeling better, whatever it takes." She winked. "And let's have some fun."

"I'll see what I can do." Emily watched her for a moment. Because Genevieve rarely worried, she picked up on her cues immediately. "What are you thinking about?"

She waved it away and reached for her glass. "It's stupid."

"What is? Tell me."

After a sip, she slumped back against the booth. "The uncomfortable fact that I'm worried over nothing. I don't waste time with useless emotions like that. That's your job."

"Not funny. But if *you're* worried it must be important."

"It's hard to explain. I guess I'm worried history will repeat itself and mess up what I worked so hard for."

"You're not making any sense. Are you talking about Ben?"

She nodded, dropping her eyes to the glass in her lap. "Can we survive as a couple in an atmosphere where we're used to being single?"

"Didn't you just tell me your relationship is special and you're happy? You can't possibly think he'd be interested in other women at this point." Emily leaned an elbow on the table to see Genevieve's face. "Seriously. You don't have to be concerned about that."

"Should he be concerned?"

"About you? You'd never cheat."

"How do you know? I've never dated. How do either of us know I won't resort back to old habits when presented with an option?"

"Where is this coming from?"

"I've done a lot of things out of character lately. It seems to be a new, disgusting habit." She smiled, but it didn't stick. "Every day, every situation is new territory, and it feels like my good fortune will run out at any moment."

"That's just your insecurities talking, and frankly, I'm shocked you have any of those."

"Ha. Ha."

"What do you want to do? Do you still want to go out tonight?"

She thought about it, then met Emily's gaze with determination. "Yes. I'm dying to shake my ass. Can we pretend we didn't have this conversation? Everything I said was stupid."

"Not stupid. Human."

"How have you survived all these years like that? It's awful."

"You get used to it." Emily patted Genevieve's knee. "Come on. It's almost time for us to check out and meet Jackson for lunch."

———

Genevieve

"This looks like the right place," Genevieve said when they parked outside an old, rusted tin building with a massive neon sign over the double entrance doors. It looked as though it had been through a lot over the years but determined never to give up.

"Well, it's popular, at least." Emily looked out the windshield at the full parking lot. "How did you hear about this one?"

"We talked with a few locals while we waited for you and Jackson to come up for air after lunch."

"Sorry." She snickered then spun in her seat to face her. "Actually, I'm not sorry. We needed that private time, and you owed me."

"Fair enough. Let's go." Genevieve threw open her car door and the others followed.

"Wait. We need a photo," Ben announced and positioned everyone outside the entrance. Then, he turned his phone around, and snapped a picture of all four of them with the sign in the background. "This is definitely going up on the site right now."

Once inside, he said, "You guys get the table, and I'll get the drinks."

"Good idea. I'll help." Emily hooked her arm around Ben's and winked over her shoulder, leaving Genevieve and Jackson alone.

"I've been meaning to apologize for what I said to you at Emily's," Genevieve broke the awkward silence after they were seated by the dance floor.

"Don't worry about it. I've already forgotten."

"I appreciate that, but it was uncalled for. You've done nothing but make Emily happy. I had no right to question your intentions."

"You were protecting your friend. I don't blame you. But I hope you know by now how much I love her, and I would rather die than hurt her."

"I do." She fought the urge to ask him about Richmond and if she expected Emily to follow him after his trip's finale.

"Speaking of her happiness, can I ask you something?" he said, leaning forward, his elbows dropping to the table. "When I'm running, I have a lot of time to think, and something's been eating at me."

"Shoot."

"What do you know about a Dr. Oliver Emily used to work with?"

Shit. "Why do you ask?" she stalled, wishing for a diversion.

"We saw him at lunch on my last day in Savannah, and their interaction was strange."

"She has a strict policy about not dating co-workers if that's what you're asking."

"Good go know. Has he done anything to upset her."

"I'll repeat, why do you ask? She doesn't work there anymore, and she's here with you." She looked around the room, trying to will Emily and Ben to rejoin them and end this uncomfortable conversation.

"I think someone has been breaking into her house. I wonder if it's him."

"Did Emily tell you?"

"Tell me what?"

Damn it. "I don't know. Did she say something to make you think that?"

"She asked me if I had been in her dresser drawers and seemed concerned when I wasn't. And now there's a broken window. I'm worried about her safety. You heard the lock on her back door was broken, right?"

"Yeah." For someone who worried constantly and paid unnecessary attention to unnecessary details, missing a broken lock on a door she used daily had been a concern of Genevieve's, too. "It is strange how—"

"Shots, anyone?" Ben asked, placing a tray of four shots and two overflowing beer mugs on the table.

Emily followed with two glasses of wine.

Genevieve smiled up at them, grateful for the interruption. "You've been up to no good at the bar, I see."

"What were you talking about so seriously?" Emily eyed them both with mock suspicion.

Jackson thought fast. "Genevieve, here, was boasting that she could drain a beer faster than any man. To which I informed her that she could never out-drink a Marine. She didn't appreciate that, not surprisingly." He winked at her.

"Oh, really?" Emily placed a hand on his shoulder. "Sweetheart, I love you, but I'll put my money on G any day."

He pretended to be offended, and Genevieve's grin turned smug as Ben handed her his beer. She raised it, ready for the challenge, and waited for Jackson tag in.

"Alright. Let's see what you've got."

He held up his glass, and on Emily's mark, they chugged until Genevieve's mug slammed down on the table seconds before Jackson's.

"That's my girl!" Ben cheered and planting a kiss on her wet lips.

Jackson turned his attention to Emily as she lowered onto his lap. "I can't believe you bet against me."

"Yeah. Sorry, but I've seen her do that a hundred times. She never loses."

"Everyone's good at something, I guess."

———

Ben

"How's it going with Genevieve?" Jackson asked him after the girls left for the dance floor.

He raised his eyebrows before answering, "Better than a wet dream."

"I don't know how to interpret that."

Ben relaxed in his chair and set his eyes on Genevieve through the mob of bodies moving to the beat. She danced like she moved in bed—confident, fluid, bold, unforgettable. "Things couldn't be better. That's all I'm sayin'."

"Why couldn't you just say that the first time?"

"I'm an artist. I like to be creative."

Soon, Emily returned to Jackson's lap and blotted the sweat beading on her forehead with a cocktail napkin.

"Where's Genevieve?" he asked when he lost sight of her.

"She's out there somewhere."

Standing for a broader view, Ben spotted her in time to see a tall man approach her from behind. His pecs twitched under his tiny T-shirt, too tight for his bulky frame, as he bounced behind her. He could get passed the filthy way the man's eyes undressed her, but his paws sliding into place on her hips, had him shooting off the chair. Why didn't she dismiss him, slap him, kick him in the balls? Why were those sexy hips, swaying to the music against his?

Dwayne and the ridiculous gun incident in Myrtle Beach flashed through his mind as a warning, but he swatted it away. The need to punch something took precedence—the asshole's face would do.

"Take your hands off my girl," he demanded when he reached the duo.

"If she's your girl, why is she dancing with me?"

Valid question. And he would appreciate an answer. He could have looked past this incident, their relationship being new and all, but when she stepped back and glared at him as if he'd been unfair, temper trumped tolerance.

"I don't appreciate being treated like a disobedient child," she yelled over the noise of the club.

"I don't appreciate you letting him touch you."

"We were just dancing. What's the big deal?"

"Seriously? The deal is I'm here with you. Only you. I don't want to dance or talk to anyone else. Why are you here, Genevieve?" When a response wasn't on the tip of her tongue, he sighed and stormed away before she saw how much it hurt.

———

Genevieve

Stunned, she stood frozen on the dance floor, watching the strobe light bounce off Ben's back. What had she done? She'd upset him and pushed him away *again*. So typical of her, she loathed, and it happened just as she feared.

Oh, God.

Her stomach tightened at the thought of how he must have felt when he saw her with someone else. How would she have reacted if he'd done the same? Of course, she knew the answer to that. She would have been furious and told him so, probably with more choice words than he used with her.

She rushed back to the table, expecting to see him waiting for her, but his seat was alarmingly empty.

Oh, God.

"Where's Ben?" she asked the others, squinting to see into the darkness beyond. Occasionally, the lights would flash through the bar and illuminate the scattered tables and crowd, but not Ben.

"I thought he was with you," Emily answered, her smile fading when she noticed Genevieve's frantic expression. "What's wrong?"

"Nothing. I'm going to get a drink."

She grabbed her purse and headed to the bar, praying he'd gone there to cool off. When she didn't see him, she fought with her disappointment and climbed onto an empty stool.

"Can I buy you a drink? You look like you could use one," the man claiming the empty seat next to her said.

"Thanks. I've got it."

"Suit yourself. What's your name, gorgeous?"

Rolling her eyes, she waved for the bartender when he glanced in her direction. He tilted his head in acknowledgement but continued washing dirty glasses at the sink. What the hell? Oh, yeah. She sighed. Ben's curse.

While she waited, she scanned the room for him. She really messed up this time. She put her business on hold, laid her heart at his feet, and somehow still sabotaged everything. Even after all he'd done to show her how much he cared.

When the bartender finally arrived, she ordered a ginger ale and dug into her purse for her debit card. "Shit."

"Something the matter?" the man beside her asked.

"I must have left my wallet at the hotel." She dug through the contents of her purse again, begging her wallet or a random credit card to magically appear.

Her neighbor motioned for the bartender to add her drink to his tab before she could object.

"Thank you," she said sheepishly, wishing for the first time to pay for her own drink.

"Are you in town for business or pleasure?"

"Not business."

This guy was not the usual type to approach her. Preppy with mischievous hazel eyes, a boring solid-color collared shirt, and obsessively pressed khakis. He may be easy on the eyes, but she would give anything to be sitting there with Ben instead.

"Thanks again." She raised the drink the bartender dropped off, then hopped off the stool.

"Wait. Can't you keep me company for a few minutes? I'm also visiting Jacksonville and here alone."

He poked out his bottom lip and stared down at her over his all-too-perfect nose. Unimpressed, she slid back onto the stool anyway, deciding that returning to the table without Ben would generate too many questions. She resolved to small talk with Country Club for a few minutes while she figured out what to do next.

"Who were you looking for earlier?" he asked.

"My boyfriend."

Boyfriend, she mused and took a sip, letting the cold liquid soothe her dry throat. Saying that word out loud sounded like a foreign language. Not only because he was her first, but because she found herself in uncharted relationship territory she couldn't navigate.

"Where did he go?" Country Club asked, snagging her attention. "If you were my girlfriend, I would never let you out of my sight."

"Thanks, but neither of us is good at this relationship thing. One of us——" She pointed at herself. "——Was bound to screw it up."

She forced a grin and studied her companion as he held her gaze in the arrogant way that always turned her off. But there was something else—something unnerving about him. With all the men she'd flirted with and taken to bed, none had ever made her uneasy. Country Club, she decided, hid a dangerous side.

"I'm not a fan of dating," he finally said and leaned closer. "There are too many beautiful women out there to settle for one. But I have to say, I've seen none more beautiful than you and your friend."

Genevieve's brow pinched in suspicion at the mention of Emily.

"Sorry," he began and straightened, reclaiming his drink from the glossy counter. "When you look like you do, it's hard not to notice. I saw you with her at the table and on the dance floor earlier."

"Do you always do this?" She kept her eyes on him as he sipped.

"Do what?"

"Stalk the women you find attractive?"

"It's not stalking. I like sex, and you caught my eye as someone who could teach me a thing or two." He smiled when she didn't react to the bold comment. "I'm happy to hear that your boyfriend left. How about we forget about him and get out of here?"

Unbelievable. Had Ben's curse changed her, or was Country Club beyond annoying?

"You know what?" She slipped off the stool and leaned on it, exposing enough cleavage to get his juices flowing. His smile widened, giving her his full focus. "With or without a motive, I would never sleep with you. There's a reason you're here alone. Don't wear out your hand tonight, gorgeous," she purred before sauntering away.

Chapter Twenty-One

✯ ✯ ✯

Emily

G's been gone a long time," she mentioned to Jackson over the roar of the music. More than thirty minutes had passed since Ben stalked out, and she retreated to the bar.

"If you're worried, let's go look for her."

"You're so good to me."

Leaning in, she waited for him to meet her halfway. His lips brushed against hers, and the electronic dance music blaring through the speakers dulled to a delicate lullaby, soothing her nerves, and sending her head whirling.

"Do you have to do that everywhere we go?" Ben asked, dropping into the chair next to Jackson, a scowl firmly in place.

In parting, the world resettled on its axis, leaving her lightheaded. "Yes. Get used to it."

"Have you seen Genevieve?" he asked, propping his elbows on the table.

"No. We were about to go look for her." Concern had her placing a hand on his arm. He was distraught over something that had between them. "Want to come with us?"

"I doubt she wants to see me." He picked up the bottle in front of him and raised it to his lips. Disappointed to find it empty, he slammed it down on the table, then waved for the waitress.

"You better stay here," she whispered to Jackson and tilted her head at Ben. "He needs you."

"Alright but hurry up. I'm ready to get out of here and have you all to myself."

"Hallelujah. I'll be back before Ben can finish his next beer."

With a wink, she stood and rushed to the bar, expecting to find Genevieve sulking on a stool. When she wasn't there, she checked the dance floor, the restroom, and outside. Aggravated, she stomped to the car, then searched the packed parking lot and surrounding properties.

When they were younger, and Genevieve got upset about something that happened at the group home or school, she'd often walk it off. She never went far, hoping her best friend would find her and force her to talk about it.

It had been a while since she went on one of her walks. Whatever happened with Ben must have troubled her enough to take a stroll. She should be close, and when

Emily didn't find her at any of the adjacent properties, frustration rooted in her stomach.

"What the hell, G?" she mumbled as she headed back along the thick tree line framing the parking lot. "Yes, you're special, but the world doesn't revolve around—"

"Are you talking to yourself?"

She spun around, expecting to find someone had joined her, but only a frightening, dark void filled the area. Like a scene from a horror movie, fear took over and prevented her from retreating to safety. The one ancient light hanging over the center of the parking lot flickered often, lighting only the small space directly beneath. In that back corner of the lot, she was hidden in darkness and wholly vulnerable. She never should have put herself in this dangerous situation.

Taking a weary step back, two shadowy figures emerged from the tree line, causing her to stumble on the next step. The momentum got her moving faster toward the club. Her frantic footsteps pounded on the pavement in tandem with her heart until she heard a familiar voice, calling for her over it all. She stopped, her name echoing through the fog and seeping into her damp skin to fuel her panic.

"Emily," a male voice said again behind her and closer this time.

She closed her eyes, not wanting to turn around and confirm what she knew to be true. Why was he in Jacksonville? Why was he hiding in the woods behind the same club they picked at random that night? The tone of his voice and the way he lurked in the…

Wait. There had been two shadows.

She whipped around, and her heart dropped into her stomach. Air filled her lungs, held there, and stung as she tried to make sense of what unfolded before her.

"Is she who you're looking for?" Lucas asked, stepping into the dim light of the full moon overhead. He had a firm grip on Genevieve's hair, yanking her around like a rag doll. Her hands were tied behind her back, her ripped shirt exposing her bra. Wet mascara dripped down her cheeks.

"Bastard. Let her go!"

"Emily, run," Genevieve yelled before the back of Lucas's hand landed on her cheek. He yanked her head back with a force to silence her.

"If you run, your hot little friend here will get more than another tap on the cheek."

"Lucas." Emily held up her hands in surrender. "Please let her go, and we'll talk."

"She's staying, and I'm not interested in talking with you, Emily."

"How did you find me?"

"It wasn't hard, thanks to her idiot boyfriend. Too bad you didn't find him," he said to Genevieve and clucked his tongue. "I was hoping to see his reaction to us."

"How do you know Ben?" Emily asked, confused.

"From your sexy friend here. We chatted at the bar about how she's a bitch to him. She was distraught over it, so I offered my company to help take her mind off him."

Horrified, Emily's eyes shot to her.

"It's not like it sounds," Genevieve panted, trying to explain through the searing pain.

"Why are you here?" Emily asked him. "What do you want from us?"

"You know why. You had no business leaving before we finished what we started. And G, here…" He looked over and ran a finger down her swollen cheek, his touch making her yank her head away. "That's what you call her, right?" he asked Emily with a smug grin. "G said I wasn't worth spreading her legs for. I don't like to leave anything undone, and I certainly don't like to be told no."

He stepped forward, yanking Genevieve along until she fell to her knees.

"Nothing was started," Emily continued to keep him talking. "Nothing but your ridiculous obsession."

"I can't help it. I want what I want, and I always get it." He jerked Genevieve's head back. "You hear that? I always get what I want."

Tears of helplessness burned Emily's eyes.

"Fine," Genevieve growled through gritted teeth, her voice hoarse but determined. "Take me but leave Emily alone."

"G, no."

"Isn't this interesting? Two for the price of one." His face lit up. "Why can't you be more like her?"

"Lucas, please. She has nothing to do with this."

"That's where you're wrong. Come here." He held out his hand, but when she didn't move, he looked down and addressed Genevieve. "For your sake, tell her to rethink that."

With her eyes resolute on Emily, she slowly shook her head, urging her not to comply.

"No," Emily answered through a blinding haze of fear and rage.

What happened after that, she couldn't be sure. She caught a glimpse of amusement on his face and heard Genevieve scream before all her senses went terrifyingly blank.

––––––

"Wake up," Emily heard someone yell inches from her face—close enough to smell the nauseating mixture of beer, mud, and cologne.

Groggy, she groaned and reached for her sore head. As her eyes began to focus through the pulsing pain, she noticed Lucas shirtless with his shorts unbuttoned and his knees straddling her hips.

"Lucas," she murmured, her voice barely a whisper.

Where were they, and how did they get there? She could see the starry night through a silhouette of trees above her. Given the mattress of pine straw and leaves beneath her, they were no longer in the parking lot at the club, but she could hear the faint rhythmic thumping of the speakers inside. At least he hadn't taken them far, but with the way her body ached and burned, he hadn't been gentle.

"Where's G?" Frantic, she shifted her head over the crisp ground, finding her lying on her side nude with her hands tied behind her back. Dirt and straw matted in her hair, and her breathing shuddered.

Fury took over Emily's body when she finished processing what he'd done. Thinking of nothing but punishing him, she swung her fists, landing one or two before he caught her arms and held them down.

"What did you do to her?"

"Nothing compared to what I'm going to do to you." Yanking her tank top over her head, he tied it around her wrists, then smiled down at her. "No bra? How convenient and incredibly hot, Emily. I didn't take you for the type."

Lifting her head, she spat in his face before twisting and yanking, kicking and punching in a useless attempt to free herself from the load of him. Her movements only fueled his resolve. Grabbing her arms again as though they were mere twigs, he held them firmly in one hand.

"Your breasts are exactly how I pictured them."

He ran a thumb over her nipple and squeezed a breast in his free hand. Leaning down, he brushed his lips over each before catching a nipple between his teeth. He looked up to see her face, smiled, then pulled the tender skin until it sprang from his lips.

"Lucas, please. I don't want this."

"Yes, you do, and I'm going to get everything you promised the first time we kissed."

"I made no promises."

"Emily." Shaking his head, he sat back on his heels. "You know that's not true. And if you refuse me, I will carve my initials in that whore over there until you cave."

"Why are you doing this?"

"Since getting a taste of you, every other woman has been a bore. You awakened something inside me when you baited me, challenged me."

"All of that is in your vile mind."

"Tell yourself that if it makes you feel better, but you were going to give yourself to me that night. You climbed into my lap, remember? You turned me on, then left me wanting. You started this game. But as you're about to find out, when I play, I always win." He trailed a finger between her breasts and down to the top of her shorts. "It's time to collect my prize."

"You're insane."

"No. I'm finally awakened. You make me feel so alive." He kissed her with force, holding her head still when she fought against it. "Emily," he breathed against her cheek before releasing her and sitting up. "We're doing this my way, or—"

"Help!" she screamed, lifting her hips, and rotating again, but he was too heavy, too strong.

"No one can hear you out here." He scooted down to kiss her belly button. "Go ahead, scream. It will only add to the excitement. And soon, when you're trembling with pleasure, it will be *my* name on your lips." He ran a hand up her abdomen and over each breast before raising his eyes with a satisfied grin. "Let's get started, shall we?"

Straightening, he unbuttoned her shorts, but as he grabbed hold of the waistband, Genevieve rolled over to face them.

"Emily," she whispered, her eyes struggling to open through the swelling.

"G, it's okay."

"Get off her, you asshole!" Genevieve fumbled with the restraints around her wrists and freed herself as Lucas jumped on top of her. She thrashed at him with a new ferocity from seeing Emily vulnerable and exposed. But he collected and secured her flailing arms with minimal effort.

"I did what you wanted. Now, leave her—"

"Shut up," he snarled, turning Genevieve's head by her jaw when Emily's sobs registered. "Emily missed your impressive performance earlier. How about a round two so she can watch?"

"Go ahead but let me know when you're finished. I couldn't feel your tiny dick last time."

"Is that so?" With a few swift adjustments, he freed himself of his shorts, and shifted to see if Emily watched. Instead, he found her on her feet about to lunge at him.

"Stop!" He propped himself up with both hands tightly secured around Genevieve's throat as she gulped for air. "Stop right there, or I'll snap her neck."

Helpless, she retreated, tears flowing fast. This was all her fault.

Lucas sat back on his heels, pulling his shorts up over his hips as he stood over Genevieve. "Get up."

Laboring, she used what little strength she had left and rose to her feet. As she straightened, determination hardening her pretty features, Lucas reared back and delivered a debilitating punch to her stomach. Emily screamed on contact, and watched her friend hunch over, stumble backward, and vomit.

She looked up at Emily with dull, watery eyes, her fight successfully beaten out of her. Reaching for a tree to brace herself, her tired muscles were no match for the pain, and her hand slipped off the trunk. She tumbled to the ground and curled into herself.

"Ah. Alone at last," Lucas announced, strolling toward Emily.

"Please, I beg you. I'll do whatever you want. Just stop hurting her."

Tilting his head, he studied her. "It's about time you came to your senses. You're mine. Isn't that right?"

In a few strides, he stood mere inches away. He pressed her back against a large tree, the jagged edges of the bark scraping against her skin.

"Isn't that right, Emily?" he forced through gritted teeth.

"Yes."

"That's all I wanted to hear come out of your gorgeous lips. Well, I also want to hear you sigh my name when I touch you, but that will happen soon enough." Grabbing hold of her waist, he tugged her hips to him. "Like the first time my hands touched you here."

He turned her head to kiss her neck. Trembling from the sobs she couldn't seem to wrangle, she closed her eyes and prayed. Prayed she could tolerate the pain. Prayed for him not to hurt Genevieve again. Prayed they both lived through this so they could lock him up and throw away the key.

"Stop fucking crying," he hissed. "It's getting on my nerves. All of this is your fault. You gave me a taste of what you're capable of, made me want more, and came out tonight wearing this skimpy little number. I hoped getting you alone would have been a little more exciting, but I grew tired of watching you with him. Watching him have what's mine."

She set her courage. "If I'm what you want, why is Genevieve here?"

"She was the decoy, but when she started mouthing off, she needed to learn a lesson. All sluts should know their place."

"How long have you been following us?" she asked to stall whatever nightmare he had planned while she figured out another escape.

He sighed, and his hot breath floated over her face. "I know you heard me. Stop talking and remove those shorts. I want to see you."

He moved back, and she took off. Weeds and twigs scraped her legs as she ran, but she couldn't feel it. In a blind panic, she sprinted toward the club, and soon saw the bright entrance sign through the branches. A few more yards to go, and she'd have safety and help for Genevieve.

With the parking lot in her sights, an arm reached out from behind a tree and circled her waist, lifting her off her feet. The large frame held her still and covered her mouth with a hand while she kicked and beat her bloody fists against him.

"Emily, it's Ben. Shhh. I've got you."

At the first sound of his voice, she collapsed into his arms, her knees buckling with relief. She'd made it out of her worst nightmare. Sobs poured from her body in waves as he held her.

Angry voices, sounding off in the distance, had her sitting up. "Is that Jackson?"

"Yeah. Don't worry. He's taking care of the problem."

"What? No." Yanking from Ben's arms, she fought to get to her feet.

"What are you doing?" He tightened his grip around her waist. "You're safe here."

"But Jackson's not."

What if he'd brought a weapon she hadn't seen yet? One Jackson couldn't defend himself against, and Lucas hurt another person she loved. What if Genevieve got caught in the crossfire again? She couldn't bear it. Prepared to do whatever it took to protect them both, she tore herself free and stumbled toward the commotion to find Jackson and Lucas in a standoff.

———

Jackson

"I'd hoped we'd meet again," Lucas said with unwarranted arrogance. He had no idea who he taunted. "But I expected it to happen after I had my way with your girlfriend."

Jackson's muscles, on alert for coming face-to-face with Emily's attacker, eased a bit as he stepped forward. He'd gotten there in time.

Lucas mirrored his every movement, maintaining a wide berth between them. "Did you know," he continued, "that she makes the most insatiable noises when she's turned on? When her hips push against you, begging you to touch and explore, the most magnificent sounds ooze out of her like hot wax. Have you heard it, Jackson? Or did she save those just for me?"

In all his years in the military or during arguments with his father, Jackson had never lost control. But there's a first for everything in life, and at that moment, he could see only rage. He lunged with his eyes laser-focused on the target, catching Lucas off guard. His fist connected with bone with a force that knocked him onto his back.

One crushing blow was all it took to secure Lucas until the police arrived, yet he couldn't stop. He lost track of his mission, his morals, and the man he wanted to be. The only thing that mattered was seeing the asshole bleed.

With Lucas as his punching bag, he let loose the stress that had built up during his agonizing search for Emily. His guilt for not being able to save Will. For the loss of his friends and the fear and pain Emily endured alone. He didn't feel his muscles throbbing or the blood on his fists until someone lifted him off the target.

"Buddy, you got him," Ben urged, holding back his arm. "That's enough. If you kill him, he can't pay for what he's done."

Sweat burned his eyes as he stood breathless over Lucas, lying unconscious on the ground. His bloody, swollen face would never be enough punishment. Jerking out of Ben's grasp, he stalked toward the lifeless body until he noticed Emily in his periphery.

Anger melted into ache at the sight of her frightened and fragile. Her arms crossed over her bare chest, shoulders trembling as she cried. Tangled hair framed her red, tear-stained face. Suddenly weak with concern, he rushed to her and folded her in his arms.

"Jackson." She sank into him.

"Are you hurt?"

She shook her head because all she could do was cry.

"It's okay. I've got you."

He took the shirt Ben handed him and slipped it carefully over her head. "I'm so sorry, my love." He bent down to kiss her forehead; guilt over his inability to protect her stinging his own eyes.

"Emily," Ben asked, unease diminishing his voice. "Is this Genevieve's?" He held up a light blue blouse, nearly ripped in two.

"Oh, my God." Suddenly panicked, Emily grabbed hold of Jackson's arms. "G!"

———

Ben

"She's here?" he asked, joining them.

Without a word, Emily took off through the trees, and he and Jackson followed closely behind.

As he ran, fear raced faster through his system. All this time, he assumed Genevieve left the club after their argument. He thought she was blowing off steam somewhere else—some place safe. Now, Emily's frantic search had his imagination spiraling, filling him with an overwhelming sickness. All the ways that maniac could have hurt her flashed through his mind. And where in the hell had he taken her?

"I don't see her. Where is she?" he yelled through the tremors, his breathing erratic with concern. Emily seemed to be wandering, unsure of where to go.

"There!" She pointed and hot bile rose into his throat.

Circling the last tree, the sight of Genevieve lying nude in a shallow ditch turned his thoughts murderous. His imagination on the way there didn't prepare him enough for the truth. For seeing the scrapes and welts on her skin and knowing that monster had put his filthy hands on her.

Ben and Emily dropped to their knees on either side of her.

"G, wake up. G!" She pressed an ear to her chest to be sure and let out a sigh when she heard a beat. "G, sweetheart, it's over. Please wake up."

When she didn't stir, he scooped her up and rushed toward the club. Nothing in his life had ever been as wretched as holding her limp body in his arms. Seeing her ripped clothes littered about the ground like trash and her flawless skin splattered with blood.

The damage Jackson inflicted on Lucas would never be enough. He should've let Jackson kill the bastard when he had the chance. And if his priority at that moment wasn't getting Genevieve to the hospital, he would have finished the job himself.

Chapter Twenty-Two

✮ ✮ ✮

Emily

H ey, buddy." Jackson placed a hand on Ben's back, his head resting on the thin mattress with her hand in his. She'd yet to awaken, and he hadn't left her side for more than a few minutes since they arrived. "You need to eat."

"I'm not hungry."

"What good will you be to her if you pass out?"

"That's what coffee is for." He looked up at Jackson, eyes red and hair unruly from running his hands through it. A three-day-old beard dusted his jaw.

"Come on, man. Emily can sit with her."

"How is she?" Ben asked, sitting up.

It was sweet how he still had space in his broken heart to be concerned for her. "I'm better," she answered, crossing the room to kneel beside him. "But I would feel even better if I didn't have to worry about you, too." She placed a hand on his cheek. "Thank you for taking such good care of her. But you need to go eat and get cleaned up. I'll call you if she wakes up."

Relenting because he'd do anything she asked, he raised Genevieve's hand to his lips and stood. "I'll be right back."

"Are you going to be okay here?" Jackson asked her, not wanting to leave her alone.

"Yes, I'll be fine."

"I love you." With a gentle kiss to her forehead, he rushed after Ben.

What would she have done without him? That tender, thoughtful, cinnamon roll of a man. Not only had he saved her from whatever hell Lucas had planned, but he'd also tended to her every minute since. When the nightmares came, he helped her recover in a way that only he could. He explained how he dealt with the same hauntings or distracted her with tales of his travels or childhood adventures with his friends. Those colorful stories made her laugh and helped her forget, if only for a moment.

But she couldn't relax fully while she worried about him and how he managed his own memories during their hospital stay. He hadn't shown any indication that he struggled, but she had the sinking feeling, he powered through and hid it for her benefit. It wasn't fair to rely on him this wholly, but he insisted, and she needed him.

She could have called her parents to give him a break, but she couldn't bring herself to push the button. Her father would be disappointed she put herself in that situation. Due to his military and law enforcement background, they'd discussed how to avoid exactly what happened at length her entire life. A career-driven, patient-focused nurse, her mother wouldn't understand why she quit her job. She'd be forced to tell them about Lucas and how she failed at handling the situation, resulting in his irrational behavior.

She'd come a long way since escaping the ordeal, but she wasn't yet strong enough to endure seeing disappointment on their faces. Not when she could finally breathe again. She wanted to put off reliving the nightmare with incomprehensible explanations for a bit longer and focus on what mattered most: Genevieve's recovery.

The first step in that mission was getting her to wake up.

"How much longer are you going to hide in there?" she asked and sat in the chair Ben vacated.

Her light gray hospital gown with faded pink flowers blended with her pale skin, bringing attention to crisp white bandages covering her cheek and wrists. Thinking about why she needed those bandages made Emily's anxiety bubble back to the surface.

"Come back to us, G. You're safe now. The staff here have been taking great care of you, and you should see how Ben fusses."

She leaned closer.

"You'd hate it, but it's so sweet. I'm doing okay. Nights are the hardest. I suddenly don't care for the dark. No surprise there. I've had a few nightmares, but Jackson says that's to be expected. Hopefully, they'll leave you be. Harry has called a few times. I feel bad, but I can't bring myself to answer. The house is probably flooded or split in two by a tree. It would be my luck these days."

She took a deep breath, hoping it would ease the helplessness that had filled the space around her lungs. "Whatever the reason, it's probably bad news, and I just can't take any more of that right now." She managed a grin, but when it wavered, she dropped her head to the mattress. "I'm so sorry. This never should have happened to you."

"I'd do it again."

Emily sat up. "Oh, thank God." Raising Genevieve's hand to her lips, she said a quick prayer and stood to see her better. "How do you feel?"

With her eyes closed, she took in a shuddered breath. "Numb."

"You're a little pale but beautiful as always."

"Did they get him?" Her eyes opened despite the swelling pushing them closed.

"Yes. He was discharged and taken to jail yesterday."

"He was here?"

"The doctors had some work to do before he could be arrested."

"Why?"

"Jackson got a hold of him."

Her eyes went blank then glistened before she rolled her head to the side.

"It's okay. No one's going to think less of you if you cry."

"I still hate it."

"No doubt. If it makes you feel any better, I cried for two straight days."

"It doesn't. You cry about everything."

Emily dabbed at the tears forming against her best effort to be strong. "That may be true, but it doesn't—"

"Wait." She turned back to Emily. "Two days? How long have I been out?"

"Since we arrived three nights ago."

"Oh." She took in a breath and let it seep out. "Emily, I need to know what happened. Did he..." She couldn't make herself say it, adding to Emily's guilt.

Before answering, she took a moment to gather her nerve. She hadn't expected to talk about what happened so soon, but she couldn't deny Genevieve the answers she needed. "No."

"Thank God." She squeezed Emily's hand. "Did Jackson find us? Is that how we got out?"

"Yes. He and Ben."

At the mention of his name, her eyes darted around the room.

"We forced him to go eat," she answered so Genevieve wouldn't have to ask. "He hadn't left your side since we were admitted, and he won't be able to stay away for long."

"They're still here?"

"Of course. Why wouldn't they be?"

"Last time..." She swallowed hard. "They left."

"Oh, sweetie. That was different—the situation, our relationships. Everything was different then. They're not going anywhere until we're ready. We'll walk out of here together, stronger."

"Like a family," she whispered as her eyelids slowly closed.

"Yeah, like a family. Get some rest, and I'll—"

Emily's gaze snapped to the muffled sound of Genevieve's cell phone vibrating inside her purse. She ignored it until a text message announced its arrival immediately after. Assuming it was Genevieve's assistant, Emily dug out the phone to turn off the ringer. But the caller I.D. displayed *Unknown*, and the name in the message caught her attention.

Lucas Oliver.

Her knees softened, and she lowered into the chair.

"Was that my phone?" Genevieve asked, her voice hoarse and labored.

"Yeah. The prosecutor called, then texted when you didn't answer."

"What does it say?"

"Lucas was denied bond. We're safe."

———

Ben

Being away from Genevieve felt like a tequila hangover. Nothing felt right inside, and he was too nauseous to be hungry. He'd barely put more than coffee in his system for the past three days, but Jackson wouldn't let him out of timeout until he ate. In minutes, he forced down a soggy sandwich and chips from the cafeteria and took the stairs two at a time back to Genevieve's room. The half-chewed meal churned with his anxiety like the morning after a good party on every leap.

Stepping back into the room, he found Emily staring absently out the window, her arms crossed over her belly, and Genevieve asleep. After three days of silence, he wasn't surprised nothing changed in his absence, but hope managed to wiggle into a corner of his heart anyway.

Without a word, Jackson took Emily in his arms, and Ben reclaimed his position at Genevieve's bedside.

"She woke up, but it was for only a moment," Emily informed them and that's when he noticed her red-rimmed eyes.

"Damn. I knew I shouldn't have left."

Minute by painful minute, they waited together for Genevieve to return to them. He lost track of time, and his back ached from hunching over the bed, but he couldn't leave her again. Not even to find a more comfortable chair.

But when she stirred and grimaced and Emily sprang to her side, he retreated to the opposite side of the room. And he had no idea why. What was wrong with him?

Emily must have wondered the same since she narrowed her eyes at him before giving her attention to Genevieve. "We're here. It's okay."

Her soothing voice sounded more like a jet engine in his short-circuited brain. For two and a half days and three nights straight, he begged Genevieve to wake up so he could see her enchanting eyes again. But now that she had, he felt paralyzed. Their last conversation not only seemed like a lifetime ago, it ended miserably and set off a terrifying chain of events that never should have happened.

Genevieve rolled onto her side, her arms springing around her stomach with a groan, and Ben's rage sharpened. He was losing the battle to control his spiraling temper the more he thought about how she got those aches and bruises.

Then, she reached for him and nothing he wrestled with mattered anymore. Sitting on the bed, he carefully placed a hand beside her hip and pressed a kiss to her forehead.

"I'm sorry for the way I acted," he whispered. The sparkle in her emerald eyes had been dulled by pain, and regret clawed at his heart. "I was sorry the second I stepped away from you."

Curling into his arms, she locked hers around his waist and let her eyes close. "You did nothing wrong. I'm sorry."

Finding Emily on the couch, he silently pleaded with her.

"I think I'd like to get some food," she said suddenly to Jackson.

"Sure. I know where to find some tomato soup and grilled cheese."

"Comfort food. Perfect." She smiled at Ben. "We'll be back in a little while."

Sliding an arm under Genevieve, he climbed into the bed beside her, content to lie with her while she dozed.

"Why are you still here?" she asked moments later.

"What do you mean? Where else would I be?"

"I'm sure you heard what happened. What I did. Why are you still here?"

"Genevieve, you didn't do anything. You're the victim." Placing his hand under her chin, he lifted her face. "I want you to listen. Look at me and promise me you'll open your stubborn ears and listen."

She nodded and held his gaze.

"I'm here because I care about you, and don't you dare try to push me away. We will get through this together. Got it?"

A tear trailed down her cheek, and suddenly, he was no longer falling. She buried her face in his neck, and he held her tight. Every ragged sob and shudder of her body that followed emptied him. But knowing she sought comfort in his arms filled him again with a feeling unlike any other pleasure. Better than that first buzz from tequila. Better than the thrill of flying through an endless blue sky. Better than sex.

From that moment on, whatever it took, whatever she demanded, he would do it to have the chance to earn her love in return.

———

Genevieve

When thoughts of Lucas and all that was left unsaid with Ben wouldn't stop poking holes in her lungs in the deafening silence, she leaned back and strained for air. "I need to tell you something."

"That's not—"

"No. I have to," she interrupted and took his hand, holding it against her chest. "It's not an excuse—I should have said no to the guy who approached me on the dance floor—but I'm not used to having…" She paused, searching for the words. "This. Us."

He brushed his knuckles lightly over her cheek. "I know."

"Despite how it looks, I didn't want to be with anyone else that night, especially… him. I offered myself to protect Emily."

"Sweetheart, you don't have to explain. What you did was selfless and brave, and all that matters is that you're safe now."

"But it matters to me. I need you to know the truth, and your feelings matter. That's another new one for me. I hope you can bear with me while I figure all this out." She shifted slightly to press a gentle kiss to his lips. "And stay."

"I'm not going anywhere. You're stuck with me now."

Not knowing the right thing to say, she settled on showing him instead. With her head on his chest, she melted into his arms and treasured him. For him, she shoved every doubt and misconstrued perception she'd ever had about men and relationships into her mental garbage disposal. Because this man, the one holding her like she powered the moon even after the pain she caused, deserved that and more. He deserved to hold all of her.

Chapter Twenty-Three

✯ ✯ ✯

Jackson

Over the two weeks it took to reach St. Augustine, Emily slowly reclaimed the pieces of herself she lost in Jacksonville. But because the bruises and lacerations lingered, she worried about her parents noticing and demanding to know what happened.

As his path brought their reunion closer, she often talked about taking an easier route to explain her injuries. Maybe she slipped off the treadmill, swam through a swarm of jellyfish, played dodgeball against a professional team.

Jackson often got involved in the brainstorming sessions, conjuring up outlandish stories to make her laugh. It became his go-to distraction technique whenever she succumbed to the memories or woke up in a panic and couldn't fall back to sleep. She'd come a long way, but until Genevieve's spark came back, the guilt over what happened would continue to haunt her.

"It's perfect and so them," she said, taking in her parents' new house from the driveway. The small ranch house had a white brick exterior, dark blue shutters, and a bright red door. Sleek and modern but still warm and inviting. "I can see them sitting in those rocking chairs, enjoying the warm, salty air each morning with a cup of coffee." She took a long breath to let it soothe her as well. "Okay. I should probably stop stalling."

"Take all the time you need. There's no rush." He could empathize with her hesitancy since he had the same reaction to visiting Will's parents' house in Murfreesboro, North Carolina, the second stop on his journey. Unsure of how they would react and unprepared to face the hard conversations sure to come up, he stood out front for the longest time, trying to muster the courage to knock on the door.

"I'm ready to see them. Whatever happens, I can handle it."

"Yes, you can."

With her hand in his, she led him to the front porch and rang the doorbell. "I love you so much."

"I love you, too." He kissed her fingers and tamped down his nerves with the feel of her skin. He'd survived basic training, war, hazardous situations with his reckless friends, and multiple major surgeries. But none of that compared to the anticipation of meeting Emily's parents for the first time.

She fidgeted, sighed, and fidgeted some more until footsteps could be heard on the other side of the door.

"Momma." With a squeal, she lunged into her mother's eager arms.

"Emily, darling." Her mother squeezed her tight, then held her at arms-length to look her over. "What are you doing here?"

"It's a long story, but Momma, this is Jackson." She took hold of his arm and leaned in.

"Nice to meet you, Mrs. Robertson." He reached out a hand, but Emily's mother only stared, giving him a moment to study her. A tall, slender woman, she would look more like Emily's sister if it weren't for the gray streaks in her sand-colored hair.

She glanced at Emily and then back at him. "I'm sorry. Don't mind me. Eden," she corrected, taking his hand. "Please, call me Eden. Come in, come in."

Making their way to the living room, Emily cast him a wide smile over her shoulder. It soothed him to see her happy.

"Where's Dad?"

"You know."

She sat next to her mother on the small beige couch. "Fishing?"

"Every day. I'm so sick of eating fish I could scream." Leaning into her daughter with a laugh, she collected her hand, the tender gesture so natural and easy. "I've missed you, sweetheart. How are you? Apparently, a lot has happened since we last spoke."

Emily flashed an unsteady smile, then looked to Jackson for encouragement. He had claimed the armchair nearby. "Well, that's the long story I mentioned earlier."

"I don't expect your father home for a while, so…" A smile matching Emily's turned in his direction. "She only told me you existed and that you met in Myrtle Beach."

"When we last spoke, I was so busy with G's recovery and work," Emily said in her defense. "I neglected to tell you about a lot of things." He noticed the tiny shake of nerves in her voice and wondered if Eden did as well. "Like Jackson's mission. He's running to Orlando."

The usual what-in-the-world expression covered Eden's face. "Why on earth would you run across multiple states in the southern summer?"

"Tell her, Jackson." Emily reached out for his hand.

He watched his thumb trace the delicate curve of her knuckles while searching for the words to begin. For this moment, he'd give anything to be more articulate. But unfortunately, they don't teach Marines how to tell their girlfriend's mother about complicated personal stories within a few minutes of meeting her.

"It's another long story," he started as the back door slammed shut with the ocean breeze.

"Eden, sweetheart," a deep male voice yelled from the other room. "We're going to eat good tonight! Fire up the grill and—" His list of instructions halted when he entered the living room and laid eyes on Emily. Judging by the tears of love in his eyes, he must be her beloved father, Charlie.

"I'd love some grilled fish for dinner," she declared and waited for him to cross the room to her. She stood in time to be swallowed in his embrace. "Hi, Dad."

He smelled of saltwater, sweat, and fish, his gray hair flowing in all directions from the damp ocean wind. But he looked healthy and happy. That fact alone, Jackson knew, would bring Emily deep relief and satisfaction.

"I've missed you, my sweet. Look at you. You get more beautiful every time I see you." He pulled her close for another hug before noticing Jackson standing beside them. "Who's this fella?"

He held out a hand. "Jackson Vane, sir. A pleasure to meet you."

"Her boyfriend," Eden whispered to her husband's back.

"Boyfriend?" He looked Jackson over, and without warning, threw his arms around him, slapping him hard on the back. "Man, you're built like a tank," he added, releasing Jackson enough to squeeze his biceps.

"Daddy," Emily scolded with a roll of her eyes. "Sorry. My father's brain isn't wired to filter his thoughts."

"Pay her no mind," Charlie dismissed. "Come. I'll save you from all the women talk, and you can help me with dinner." He led the way to the kitchen. "Are you a beer, wine, or liquor kind of guy?"

"No preference. In the military, you learn to like anything you can get your hands on."

"You're a military man? Which branch?"

"Marines." He watched as Charlie collected items from the kitchen cabinets. After setting two martini glasses, a silver shaker, and a bottle of gin on the counter, he grabbed tall stirring sticks from the drawer and a jar of olives from the refrigerator.

"I was a paratrooper in the Army. Served in Vietnam. Got the scars and a bad hip to prove it," he said over his shoulder as he reached into the freezer and tossed a few ice cubes into the shaker.

That explained Emily's affinity for Army references, Jackson mused.

"How long were you in?" Charlie asked.

"Eight years. Would have been more had I not been injured." He watched as Charlie swiftly poured the gin and other ingredients into the shaker without measuring.

"I respect anyone who serves country above self. Especially career. Takes steel balls to want to do all that shit for life. Got a pair of those myself." Without even a smirk at the comment, Charlie closed the lid on the cocktail shaker. He gave it several hard shakes then filled the glasses.

"How long did you serve?"

"Twenty-six."

"Colonel?"

"Damn, straight. What about you?" Charlie asked, dropping an olive into each expertly prepared cocktail.

"Sergeant. I was up for a promotion when it happened."

With a nod of respect and, more importantly understanding, Charlie handed Jackson a martini and raised the other. "To our ladies, our freedom, and our country. God bless the U.S. of A."

Happy to have someone to talk to who spoke his language, Jackson joined in the salute. The clear cocktail sparkled in the light and looked not only delicious but fully capable of squashing any lingering nerves that remained from earlier. As Charlie sipped and admired the flavor, Jackson brought the glass to his lips. But the moment the liquid graced his tongue, he doubled over, choking on coughs that seemed to have claws and a mind of their own.

At the clatter, Emily and Eden rushed into the room.

"Daddy, you didn't," Emily accused as she filled a cup with cold water.

"What? He's a Marine. I thought he could handle it."

"You're impossible."

Jackson raised his watery eyes in time to see a smirk flash across Charlie's face and Emily stifle a chuckle. But he could concentrate on nothing except washing away the sand in his throat, draining the cup of water Emily handed him in one gulp. "What in the hell was that?"

Emily slapped a hand over her belly in a wild burst of laughter. Although her parents attempted to hide their amusement, albeit not very well, they soon caved. Both laughed along with Emily until she could hitch her laughter long enough to speak.

"It's called a dry martini. It's Dad's specialty, but he takes it to the extreme." She patted Jackson on the back and kissed his forehead. "It's absolutely undrinkable."

"No." He met Charlie's amused eyes and grinned. "I never turn down a challenge."

"My kind of guy. Grab your glass, and let's go prepare the fish for dinner. You know how to gut a fish, don't you?"

"Yes, sir," he got out before another short coughing fit took over. "I spent a lot of time fishing at our family lake growing up."

"Well, let's get to it. I'm starving."

———

Emily

"Have fun," Emily handed over Jackson's martini with a lively smile before he left the kitchen with her father. Seeing them together was better than she expected it would be.

"Alright, spill it," Eden demanded and removed a bag of brown rice from the cabinet beside the stove.

"Spill what?"

"Don't play dumb with me, young lady. I see the way you look at him. What's up with this relationship. How serious is it?"

"Oh, Momma. He's the one."

"Really?" She poured the water she'd measured into the pot and set the gas stove to flame. "How can you be sure? It's only been what, a couple months?"

"I knew the moment I saw him at this ridiculous country bar. He made me feel things I've never felt before… all with a simple glance." Although, a look from Jackson was anything but simple. It did inconceivable things to her body she'd never be able to put into words.

"He's very handsome. And those blue eyes."

"Tell me about it. But it's so much more than that. He's different."

Eden placed a hand on hers. "I've never seen you like this. He brings something out in you. Confidence, I guess it is."

"You have no idea. I barely recognize myself anymore."

"I'm happy for you. So," Eden began, grabbing two glasses and a bottle of wine from the cabinet, "where in the world did you get those scrapes on your legs?"

And there it was. The question she'd been dreading. Emily focused on a thread of gold in the stone counter and thought about how disappointed her mother would soon be. She'd made every effort her entire life to ensure that look never graced her mother's pretty face.

"Emily?"

"Huh? Sorry." She took the glass of wine her mother poured for her and drank for a little added courage. Using one of the wild stories she and Jackson created on the way there crossed her mind, but she settled on the truth instead. She'd never been good at lying, anyway. "We had an incident in Jacksonville about two weeks ago."

"In Jacksonville? What were you doing there?"

"I was with Jackson."

"You're not traveling to meet him when he stops, are you?"

"Well, I…"

"What about work? I doubt you have many days left to take off after your vacation."

"It's not an issue."

"Not an issue? What do you—"

"I quit." She blurt out the words, knowing it was the only way to keep from chickening out.

"What? Why? Don't tell me you quit to travel with him."

"No. I didn't."

"Then, why did you do it? You loved that job."

"I did. Once." She took another sip and braced for the sting. "Unfortunately, some things happened, and although he didn't know until afterward, Jackson gave me the courage I needed to stand up for myself for the first time in my life." When the tears came, she silently cursed how weak they made her feel.

"Oh, honey. What happened?" Leaning on the counter, she took Emily's hand.

"It was awful. I put up with it for so long, thinking I could handle it."

"Put up with what? You're worrying me."

Emily took a deep breath. "One of the doctors at the practice—" she couldn't bring herself to say his name, "—was harassing me, sexually." She paused on her mother gasped.

"You reported it, right?"

"Yeah. Little good that did. The HR Director all but said it was my fault and that I was lying." She flashed a shaky smile, lifted her shoulders, then let them fall.

"Emily, I'm so sorry. What hell that must have been."

"You have no idea, but that's not all."

"Isn't that enough?"

"Apparently, not." Wiping the tear that escaped, she continued. "I decided to join Jackson not just because I missed him. Someone's been breaking into my house. It's happened twice. At least, those are the times I know about."

"My goodness, Emily."

"With all that's happened, I haven't had a chance to tell him yet."

"I won't say a word. You should talk to your father," she said over her shoulder on her way to the stove. "He can help."

"The Savannah P.D. are doing all they can, and I don't want to disturb his retirement. He deserves to not be a detective right now."

"Fair, but he'd want to do all he can to ensure you're safe."

She already felt safer with Lucas in jail. At the time, Emily hadn't considered Lucas a true threat or suspected he could be the one breaking into her home. But thinking about his possessive and frightening behavior following her vacation and in Jacksonville, she realized now that she barely knew him and what he was capable of.

Maybe he had been the one going through her things to torment her. She wouldn't put it past him and wished she had given the officer his information when she reported the first break-in. Maybe they would have questioned him, seen he was unstable, and arrested him, preventing Jacksonville from ever happening.

"But that still doesn't explain the scrapes. What happened in Jacksonville?" Eden leaned on a stool beside her daughter and glanced down at her marked legs.

"He came unhinged."

"Who did?"

"The doctor harassing me."

"What are you talking about? Unhinged how?"

"He tracked me down in Jacksonville and—"

"No." Eden's hands sprang to her lips.

"He only roughed me up, but he did horrible things to G." Sobs rose into her chest and choked her. Saying it out loud hurt more than thinking it.

"Oh, my God." She pulled Emily into her arms.

"Jackson saved us before I…"

"I'm so grateful. What happened to G? Is she okay?" she asked, releasing Emily.

"What he did to her was so awful, I can't…" She trailed off, wiping her nose with the tissue her mother passed her. "She tried to distract him from hurting me. She was at the wrong place at the wrong time and paid for it. I've never seen her like this, Momma. Everything about her is broken. It kills me."

"That hurts my heart. Emily, I have to ask. Did she get her test results?"

"What tests? What are you asking?"

"AIDS, STDs, pregnancy. All the tests they run after… such an incident."

"Oh. I didn't think to ask her." But after all the in-depth conversations she and her mother have had through the years about injuries, diseases, and medical treatments, she should have. "We've been focusing on happy things to help her cope, careful not to mention anything that might be a trigger."

"Where is she now? She should be here with her family."

"She wasn't ready, and Ben's taking good care of her at the hotel."

"Who's Ben?"

"He's traveling with Jackson on his trip. Oh, remind me to show you some of the photos he's taken along the way. They're amazing."

"Okay. It's nice of him to take care of her."

"Not just nice. Things like that are on the list of boyfriend duties."

"You're lying."

"Nope. Head over heels... both of them."

"Will wonders never cease?" She shook her head and held both of Emily's hands, her eyes softening. "Why didn't you call us, sweetie? I hate that you and G went through this alone."

Emily's shoulders drooped with hearing the disappointment in her mother's tone. "We weren't alone. We had the guys. Jackson's been through far worse and knew what we needed to start healing. I didn't want to worry you."

"Worry us? We're your parents. Worrying about you is our main job."

"I know, but please don't tell Dad about this."

"Emily," she said firmly, standing to pace. "That's not fair."

"Please. Just until I'm gone. I won't be able to handle seeing pity in his eyes right now. I just want to enjoy our weekend together. Please, Mom."

"Fine. But you'll have to deal with more than pity when he finds out you kept this from him."

"I can live with that."

Eden leaned over the pot to check the rice through the clear lid. "What will you do after Jackson's trip?"

"Not sure yet. We haven't talked about our future in any sort of detail. All I know is that he'll want to go home. He's got a lot of friends in Richmond."

"So do you in Savannah."

"Only G, really," she corrected. "And I'm not sure I will ever feel safe in Savannah again."

"Sounds like you've already made up your mind."

"I think so, but I still don't know what he wants."

"Do you love him?"

With a timid grin, she nodded. "More than I thought possible."

"Does he love you?"

"Yes."

"Then, talking about your future is the next step."

As if on cue, Jackson entered through the kitchen door. "I was sent for the butter and seasonings. He said you'd know which ones."

"Yes, of course." Eden gathered the requested ingredients and handed them over, along with a butter knife.

"Everything okay out there?" Emily asked when he smiled in her direction.

"It's great." Strolling to her, he pressed a kiss to her forehead. "How about you?" he whispered. When she nodded and looked up at him, he understood her signal to keep the status quo going. "Charlie has some interesting stories."

"He'll talk your ear off if you let him," Eden chimed in.

"I've gotten a few words in here or there," he winked and exited the back door to rejoin Charlie at the grill.

Jackson

"Glad to see you survived interrupting the girl talk," Charlie joked when Jackson passed him the ingredients.

"It was touch and go there for a while. I got out just in time."

"Ha." Charlie unwrapped the stick of butter, cut several slices, and dropped them onto the filets. After closing the lid on the grill, he watched Jackson take a reluctant sip of his martini. "If you'd like a beer, there's a stash in the cooler over there." He motioned toward a small outdoor refrigerator near the door, grinning when Jackson didn't budge. "You did well, son. Challenge completed."

"Oh, thank God," he said, already lunging toward the refrigerator. With a long pull, he leaned back in the chair and enjoyed the cool liquid on his throat.

"Tell me, Jackson. How serious is this situation with my daughter?"

"Actually, that's something I wanted to talk to you about."

"Oh, yeah?" Sensing the implications of the statement, Charlie snatched his drink from the table and claimed a seat. "What do you want to talk about?"

"Emily means the world to me. I'm in love with her." He took in an unsteady breath when Charlie remained silent. "I want to marry her one day in the near future, and I was hoping to have your blessing."

"I see." Charlie sipped on his martini. "I have to say, I wasn't expecting that."

"We've been together only two months, but the moment I saw her, there could never be anyone else for me."

"She is special, but how do you know?"

Jackson considered the question for a moment. "I can't answer that. I just do."

"And she feels the same?"

"She does."

Sitting up, Charlie rested his elbows on his knees. "Look, I like you, but I need more time. How about I give you an answer before you leave?"

"You have reservations, understandably. What can I do to put your mind at ease?"

"Tell me about home. What do you do?"

"There's not much to tell. One of the purposes of this trip is to help me figure out what I want to do with the rest of my life."

"You don't have a job?"

"No, sir." *Damn.* This conversation wasn't going to plan.

"How are you going to support my daughter?"

"You and I both know Emily will not want to rely on me for that but supporting her is not a problem."

"How? You said you don't have a job."

"I understand your concern, Charlie, but Emily will be well taken care of. You have my word."

"We just met, Jackson. I don't know you or the value of your word yet."

Sweat began to bead on his back, and it wasn't from the blinding summer heat. He'd never been comfortable talking about his inheritance and hadn't even discussed it with Emily yet.

"Sir, my father passed away last year and left me his entire estate. His house, business, savings, investments. All of it. Emily will have the financial freedom to follow her dreams and do anything she wants."

"I'm sorry for your loss."

"Thank you."

The fish sizzled on the grill, stealing Charlie's attention. He stood to check it and add seasonings. "Where will you two live?"

"Well, I hope she will move to Richmond."

He twisted to look over his shoulder. "You two haven't discussed where you'd live?"

"It hasn't come up. Everything's happened so fast."

"Hmm." Scooping up the filets, Charlie transferred them to a clean plate. "These are ready. Let's eat."

———

During dinner, the wine and conversation flowed easily, helping Jackson relax from his awkward moment with Charlie.

"Oh, Jackson. You were interrupted earlier by a rude fisherman and didn't get to tell me about your trip." Eden cast her husband a playful smile, but Charlie remained stoic.

"That's right," Emily rested her chin on her hand and encouraged him to begin with adoring eyes.

How could he resist her when she looked at him like that? He talked briefly about how he was injured, Will, and his recovery, focusing more on why he started the journey and what he hoped to accomplish.

"My journey took a turn for the better in Myrtle Beach when I met your daughter." Reaching across the table, he held out his hand for hers. "I was beginning to doubt my capacity to finish what I started. My symptoms were debilitating, but she took all that away and became my guiding light."

She mouthed *I love you* before her eyes widened with realization. Rising from her seat, she pointed toward her parents on her way out of the room. "I need to show you something." She returned moments later and handed Eden her phone. "Ben, Jackson's friend, is traveling with him and documenting the journey. Look at these beautiful pictures he took."

As she watched her parents huddle together, scrolling through each photo and reading the descriptions, Jackson watched her. Through her eyes, he could see her heart swelling with every one of their reactions. He ran for her and to see that look in her eyes as much as he ran for himself.

In response to a photo, Eden looked up at him, her eyes glistening with unshed tears. "Jackson, I barely know you, and this is going to sound weird, but I'm so proud of you." She let out an uneasy laugh and held up the phone before handing it to Emily. "These are beautiful, and what you're doing... It's amazing."

"I appreciate that, especially coming from you," he said, touched beyond words.

———

After dinner, Emily and Jackson took a walk on the beach, returning after her parents went to bed.

"I feel like I'm in high school and just successfully snuck my boyfriend into my parent's house."

"Sounds like you have experience in that area," he teased.

A laugh escaped her lips before she could stifle it. "That's funny. No, I don't have any experience sneaking a boy into the house. I was just saying, being with you, in the same bed, in my parent's house... It's awkward knowing that they know."

"I know," he added with a wink and attempted to keep his system from revving when she smiled back. The happy, authentic kind that always made him stop in his tracks.

They hadn't been intimate since reaching Jacksonville, and seeing her relaxed and carefree again, he never ached for her more. He'd been cautious not to rush her. When the time came, it was important that it be on her terms.

She seemed to read his mind and moved closer, circling her arms around his waist. With her head on his chest, he softly rubbed her back, breathing in tandem with her as he'd done many times over the recent weeks.

She leaned back and held him captive with her gaze. "Make love to me, Jackson."

"Are you sure?" Tucking her hair behind her ear, he searched her face for any uncertainty. He needed her to have zero reservations. "You don't have to—"

"I want to be with you and feel normal again."

He held her palm to his lips, then kissed the inside of her wrist and felt her melt into him. Nothing he'd ever done had prepared him for the sensations that rocketed through his body every time he touched her. Even after all they'd been through, those explosions hadn't lessened. If anything, they intensified with every new and profound understanding of each other.

Guiding her arms up, he took hold of the bottom of her shirt and gradually gathered it in his hands until she stood before him bare. But without her thin armor, her arms folded over her belly.

Guilt poured over him as if he stood under a waterfall. If it hadn't been for her pleading eyes, calling for the safety she found in his arms, he would have backed away to give her space. "We don't have to do this. I'll wait, however long you need."

"It's not that. The bruises are so ugly."

Relieved to know his latent desire hadn't influenced her request, he lowered to his knees and kissed the purple and yellow marks covering most of her stomach. As he rested his head there, her hands glided into his hair, welcoming his touch. "You're beautiful, and I love you."

"Show me," she said on an exhale. Cupping his elbow, she led him to his feet and closer until their bodies came together. "You're the only one I want, Jackson. The only man I will ever love."

Chapter Twenty-Four

✮ ✮ ✮

Jackson

Following breakfast, the group gathered the necessary supplies and snacks, then headed to the beach.

Along the way, Charlie grabbed his fishing supplies and an extra pole from the back porch. "Want to join me, Jackson?" he asked on his way to the shore without waiting for a response.

"Absolutely."

After a few minutes of baiting and casting lines into the waves, Charlie broke the awkward silence.

"I've been doing some thinking about what you asked me yesterday."

Jackson turned to face him, but Charlie continued to stare out over the ocean, his expression unreadable. "Sir, I—"

"Let me finish."

He nodded, worried Charlie might crush his hopes without fully understanding his intentions.

"Ever since Emily started dating, I've prayed for her to find a good, honest man who would love her the way she deserves. A man she adored and made her happy." He reeled in the line and sent the bait flying again. "I believe that man is you, Jackson, and I'd be honored to call you family."

"I don't know what to say. Thank you, Charlie."

"I can see how much she loves you. Just keep making her happy, and you and I will be copacetic."

"It's all I want to do for the rest of my life."

"Glad that's settled. So, when will you pop the question?"

"I haven't thought that far out yet."

"And you haven't talked about where you will live." It wasn't a question but a reminder of all the things yet to be decided about their future. "I'm sure you will figure it out, but can I give you a piece of advice?"

"Please."

"Have these talks and get on the same page before you propose," Charlie got out before his pole jerked and the reel spun with the pulled line. "Hell, yeah. Got one!"

––––––––

"Mom and I called G while you were fishing," Emily told Jackson as they walked along the surf hours later.

"How is she?"

"She had a rough night. Nightmares."

"I'm not surprised, but Ben will help her through it."

"Yeah. I'm so glad she has him."

"Does she need to go home?" He bent to pick up a butterfly-shaped shell, turned it over to see the deep purples and ivory colors inside, then tossed it into the waves. "It might be easier on her if she can relax in a familiar space."

"Actually, I think traveling helps. It gives her something to take her mind off what happened. Plus, Ben would never leave you, not this close to the end, and she needs him. Even she knows that."

Emily took a deep breath, glancing out over the ocean. The soft orange glow of the setting sun highlighted the trepidation in her eyes.

"What is it," he asked.

"Have you thought about the end and what you'll do afterward?"

"A week left to go, and I still don't know. It's starting to get to me. Your father asked me that, too." He smiled as her head snapped to him.

"He did? Why?"

"You know, guy talk."

She gave him a playful nudge with her shoulder, knocking him off stride.

"We talked about the trip, and what I hoped to gain by the end. I had to admit that I don't have an answer." And it pestered him more with every passing day.

"There's still time. Even if you don't figure it out by then, at least your family will be together, and you have me."

Stopping suddenly, he pulled her close. Her big blue eyes widened an impossible amount with the surprise ambush. "Come with me. After Orlando, move in with me in Richmond."

"Yes," she said, nodding fast, tears springing free.

Picking her up, he spun her around. She buried her face in his shoulder as she hung on. "That makes me so happy." He set her down and brushed a thumb over her wet cheeks.

"Me too. It's about time you asked," she teased and placed a hand on his chest, his heart slamming against her palm with eager anticipation.

"Sorry. I procrastinated, trying to tell if you would move away from Savannah and Genevieve. I couldn't bear it if you had any hesitation. I need you to be sure."

"I'm sure. One hundred percent. Anyway, G's already given me her blessing."

"Oh really? You two have discussed this?"

"I wanted to be ready to answer—without hesitation, as you put it—if you decided you wanted me there."

"*If* I wanted you?" His overactive heart came to a screeching halt. "Did you doubt that I would?"

"A part of me did." She lowered her eyes, shying away from him.

"Why?"

"I can feel how much you want to be with me, but you don't talk about Richmond or your life there. I worried that you thought I didn't fit into it."

Wishing he could go back to all their previous conversations and find the words to set her mind at ease, he resigned to doing it then. "Please know that never once crossed my mind. I want you with me always, whether that's in Richmond or someplace else."

"I feel the same, but there is no other place for us. When you told me about your family, I knew your place was with them in Richmond."

"My place is with you." He bent to place a gentle kiss on her lips. "But what about Savannah? Are you sure you're ready to leave?"

"I love the city, and I have a lot of fond memories there. I'll miss G, of course, if she stays." She flashed him a hopeful grin. "But being with you in Virginia feels right."

"Then, it's settled. After Orlando, we'll pack up your house and start over together." He brought her hand to his lips, expecting to be enthralled by her excitement over their plans, but her smile faded as she sunk into her thoughts again. "What's bothering you?"

"I have a confession to make." She forced herself to look into his eyes, and he nearly dropped to his knees when he saw worry in them.

"What is it?" He held his breath, waiting for her to set his rambling mind to rest.

"I've already put the house on the market."

"Wow. You really are sure." The stale air in his lungs leaked out, and he took a clarifying breath of relief. "The way you were looking at me, I thought you had something more terrifying to say."

"Yes, I'm sure." She grinned, but it didn't last. "Moving isn't the only reason to sell it." She looked around. "Can we sit?"

After locating a secluded spot in the dry sand, she tossed her long braid over her shoulder, turned to him, and took his hands into hers.

"You're worrying me," he said, rubbing a thumb over the tops of her trembling hands.

"I know, and I'm sorry. That's why I didn't want to tell you."

"Tell me what?"

"Someone's been breaking into my house. It's happened twice. Once while you were in Savannah and again after I joined you."

Tension snapped into his shoulders at the confirmation of his suspicions. He thought about the dresser drawers, the broken window, Lucas. "Did you call the police?"

"Yes."

"Did they catch him?"

"Both times, there were no fingerprints or signs of forced entry. Well, except this last time."

"The window."

She nodded, and he drew his hands free. Pulling his legs up, he rested his elbows on his knees.

"Was it him?" he asked without looking at her. He didn't have a grip on his emotions yet.

"I don't know."

"How long has he been harassing you?"

"Jackson…"

"Answer me, please. I've been wanting to ask but didn't want to upset you. I need to know."

"It started after I learned about Joey's suicide. He was there for me, and we kissed. That's all," she said quickly when his hands balled into fists. "But afterward, he pursued me, aggressively, even though I told him repeatedly that I wanted nothing to do with him."

He'd figured there had been more to her history with Lucas than she originally said, but knowing the facts cut far deeper than his imagination and assumptions. He sucked in a long breath through his teeth. "That only fueled his obsession."

"Yes. He wouldn't take no for an answer. He said in Jacksonville... that he enjoyed the challenge."

What a sick, piece of—

Shooting up, he stalked to the edge of the surf in search of something to calm his hazardous thoughts. Why had she shut him out and endured this dangerous situation alone? Didn't she trust him? As he focused on the waves pushing sand over his feet, his head pounded at his temples with each ragged breath. The darkness he thought he'd conquered seemed to be taunting him from the murky depths of the ocean beyond.

"Jackson."

He jumped when she placed a hand on his back.

"At the time, I thought he was harmless, and I wanted to save you from this heartache. If I'd told you about Lucas or the break-ins, you would've been just as angry then, and you would have returned to Savannah. As much as I wanted you with me, I refused to get in the way of your journey."

"Yes." He squared his shoulders, tears blurring his vision. "I would have been upset, and I would have gone back, but that should have been my decision. This feeling I have now." He dug a fist into his stomach. "This helpless feeling and sucker-punch to the gut…" When Jacksonville re-entered his thoughts, the unmistakable burn of regret rose into his throat. "I might have been able to prevent it."

"You can't know that, and thanks to you, I'm safe. We're together."

"I could have protected you."

"I'm sorry I didn't tell you, but this journey means so much to you and so many people, including me. I didn't want to ruin that."

He looked away and crossed his arms. "This is worse." His voice was barely a whisper over the ocean breeze. "This is far worse than anything I could have felt or the time I would've lost."

She stepped around to see his face, but he continued to stare blankly over her. *I could have prevented it*, rattling around in his head like a spiked pinball.

"Sweetheart, will you look at me?" she asked, her voice wavering and ripping him in two.

He took a deep breath that did nothing to calm him and lowered his eyes to her.

"I love you so much. Please try to look at it from my perspective." She caught the tear, tracking down his cheek, with her thumb.

He turned and pressed his lips to her palm. "I know you were looking out for me, but no more secrets. We tell each other everything and make decisions together, no matter how difficult it may be."

"Deal."

He kissed her with a sweetness that had tears springing from her eyes and spilling over.

"Don't do that. Please." Pulling her close, he held her until her shuddering body calmed and the tension had dissolved for them both. "I need another promise from you."

"Anything."

"I need you to never go back to Savannah or your house alone. Promise me."

"I promise."

Chapter Twenty-Five

★ ★ ★

Emily

"Did Jackson leave already?" Charlie asked when he found his daughter sitting by the front window staring out into the distance, a cup of coffee in her hand.

"Yeah. About twenty minutes ago."

"You know," he said as he took a seat beside her. "Seeing you sitting here takes me back to when you were a little girl. You'd sit by the window for hours waiting for your mother to come home from her shift." She smiled at the memory, but it was unsteady. "What's wrong, my sweet?"

"Every time he leaves, it hurts. I'm scared something will happen to him."

"Don't. He's a Marine. Those bastards can survive anything."

"Not helping."

Charlie held up both hands in surrender. "Sorry. Why don't you tell me what's really got you down?"

She should have known he'd see the truth. "I got a call this morning from my neighbor. You remember Harry, don't you?"

"Yeah. Short, round, bald guy."

She nodded, grinning at his out-of-commission filter. "He's taking care of the house while I'm away and has been a Godsend." With a sigh, she set down her coffee mug on the nearby table. The news he gave her left a sour taste in her mouth, ruining her relaxing morning routine.

"What is it? Did something happen to the house?"

"It was broken into and ransacked." The tears she'd been fighting since receiving the call pooled in her eyes and stung. After Jacksonville, she'd convinced herself that Lucas had been responsible for the break-ins. It allowed for space to breathe and heal. Knowing someone else lurked in the shadows allowed fear to reclaim her heart, and once again, she was drowning in it.

Crossing her arms over her aching stomach, it suddenly churned with ferocity. She jumped up and ran to the hallway bathroom, making it to the toilet before the convulsions took over. Her father followed, held her hair, and whispered soothing encouragements.

"Thank you, Daddy," she said, sitting back and accepting the damp towel he passed her.

"You're welcome, Baby. Come on. Let's go talk." He helped her up and led her to the living room couch, grabbing a bottle of water from the refrigerator as she curled around a pillow.

He waited while she drank, then got down to business. "Now, start from the beginning," he instructed, his no-nonsense cop persona already switched on.

"Missing your detective days?"

"Old habits die hard."

She wanted to laugh, hoping it would make her feel better, but fresh tears gathered instead. Giving her a moment to compose herself, he strolled to the small desk in the corner. The same one she'd used in elementary and middle school before outgrowing it.

He opened the large, battered drawer on the side. She'd kept all her school supplies in that drawer and broken it in the sixth grade, slamming the day she received her first B on a test. For hours, she cried uncontrollably until he came home from work and mended both the drawer and her bruised confidence with his hammer and quick humor. He always knew what to say, and he'd never let her down. The pending conversation, she suspected, would be no different.

"There it is," he murmured. Reaching inside, he pulled out a small black notebook with a pencil still secured through the metal spiral and a box of tissues before returning to her.

"What's that for?" she asked with a sniff.

He set the tissues down on the couch beside her and claimed a cushion, waving the slender notepad in the air. "Old habits require the ole' trusty notebook."

A laugh rumbled to the surface and kept the tears at bay for a moment longer. Knowing it wouldn't last, she yanked out a tissue and recounted what she knew about the break-ins while Charlie scribbled on the tattered, yellow notepad. To not worry her father with unnecessary details, she skipped over the assault since Lucas couldn't be a suspect from jail.

"S.P.D. must have found something this time, right?" he asked, exasperated with concern.

"Harry called while they were there, so not sure yet." She fidgeted with the label on the water bottle while her promise to Jackson weighed heavily on her mind. She wasn't looking forward to adding more stress to his journey with this new development.

Charlie stood sharply. "I'm going up there. Harry shouldn't have to deal with this."

"What?" She shifted to the edge of the couch. "Are you sure?"

"Yeah. And I bet your mother could use a break." He laughed. "And I don't want you to worry about anything. I'll take care of the house. I dare that asshole to make an appearance again."

She went to him, dampening his shirt with grateful tears. His cedarwood scent filled her with nostalgia, years of seeking safety and comfort in his arms replenishing her ragged soul.

"I'll find him, Baby, and he's going to pay for what he's done."

As they parted ways to pack for their individual trips, he stopped inside the doorway to his bedroom. "Oh, Emily?"

She stepped back into the hallway. "Yes?"

"I like Jackson. He's a good one."

———

Ben

When Emily arrived at the hotel, Ben met her in the lobby and took the luggage she carried.

"How's G?" she asked.

"I'm worried, Em."

"Why? What's wrong?"

He rolled her and Jackson's suitcases to a couch in the corner of the lobby and wished he'd had any sleep in the past two days to help him get through at least the next two. "The nightmares are absolute hell, and she won't talk to me. I'm completely helpless."

She placed a hand on his knee. "But you *are* helping, Ben. Just being there, making her feel safe, is what she needs most." She glanced at the clock on the wall behind the reception desk. "When do you expect Jackson to arrive?"

"Any minute now."

"Why don't you wait here for him, and I'll go sit with G for a while? Take some time for yourself."

They stood together, and as she wrapped him in a hug, his arms felt empty around her. His spirit had been beaten down by exhaustion. From constantly pulling Genevieve closer while she pushed him away.

"Hang in there. You're doing everything you can."

He handed her the room key and suitcases before retreating to the adjacent bar. After ordering a bucket of beer, he claimed a table near the entrance to watch for Jackson.

"Looks like you plan to be here for a while," a silky female voice said as the bartender dropped off his order.

His eyes flew up to find her leaning on the empty chair across from him, her deep auburn hair flowing in waves down her back. Her low-cut green tank top showcased her youthful, hourglass figure. Two months ago, he would have been happy to entertain her, but all he could see when he looked at her were reminders of the woman he loved.

"Yeah." He yanked a bottle out of the ice bucket and took a long pull, ignoring the sultry look she gave him under her lashes.

"Mind if I join you?"

"He does," Jackson answered from behind her.

Straightening, her eyes covered him from head to toe and back again with a hungry nibble on her bottom lip. He'd strolled in shirtless, his skin still damp from running in the Florida sun, and she didn't bother hiding her pleasure from the interruption.

Without a word, Ben tossed him the extra shirt he'd brought as Jackson stepped around her.

"Still attracting them like flies to rotten meat, I see," Jackson joked when she got the hint and let them be. He slipped on the clean shirt and claimed the empty seat. As Ben absently stared into his beer, he motioned for the bartender to bring him a glass of water. "How's Genevieve?"

"She's had better days."

"Why are you down here?"

"Emily's with her," he said before draining the bottle and grabbing another, "and I needed a break."

The water arrived, but Jackson didn't drink. Instead, he leaned on the table to survey his friend. "What's the matter, buddy? Talk to me."

Ben shook his head. "The more I give, the worse it gets."

"She's been through a lot, and she already doesn't like to lean on others for help."

"I know. I just thought we were past it, that's all."

"Sorry, buddy. I think she's going to need a lot more than a couple weeks to break that cycle and heal."

"But I'm scared she'll have a nervous breakdown before then."

"Why?"

Ben slumped back in the chair. "She's distant and won't talk to me. She jerks away or cringes when I touch her, and the noises she makes during the nightmares, they're fucking gut-wrenching."

"She wasn't doing that when we left for Emily's parents' house. What changed?"

"I think it's whatever she sees in her sleep. It's getting worse. She doesn't realize it's happening or understand what she's seeing, but it affects her." Removing the top of the fresh beer in one swift movement, he tipped it up and drank half. His frazzled nerves leveled out a little more with every gulp, but he needed something more than a decent buzz to get him through. "How did you handle it, you know, after your ordeal?"

Leaning on the table, his hands circling the glass of water, Jackson sighed. "Not well, at first. I honestly don't know how I made it out. But I know if Eleanor hadn't been there, I'd still be lost or dead by now."

"What did she do?"

"Even when I didn't make it easy to be, she was always available when I needed her. She was patient, positive. God, she was frustratingly positive, and she listened whenever I wanted to talk."

"That doesn't sound too hard." Ben contemplated the subtle advice. Being available to Genevieve was the easy part. He was committed to her for as long as she'd have him, and probably after that if his history proved how deep his loyalty had rooted. Listening and being patient, he could do. But staying positive seemed as impossible as breathing underwater whenever she recoiled from his touch.

He missed her and the sound of her laughing at his stupid jokes. Whatever he had to give to see her eyes sparkle again—even if they sparkled for someone else—he'd do it without question. And he wished he didn't spend every available minute planning out, in strikingly clear detail, what he would do to the monster that hurt her.

"Ben." Jackson slapped the table to get his attention.

"What?"

"You blacked out. And you need to stop."

"Stop what?"

"Squeezing the bottle like that. You're going crush it. What were you thinking about?"

"Oh." Flexing his fingers, he rubbed each sore knuckle. "Just envisioning the asshole's neck in my hands."

"Yeah. That was incredibly satisfying," he empathized, garnering a scowl from Ben.

"I bet. I wish you would have saved me a piece of him." Rolling his shoulders, Ben sulked in his thoughts until realizing he'd been a selfless jerk since Jackson arrived. "I'm sorry, man." He set down his beer and ran his hands over his face.

"For what?"

"For being a terrible friend. How was meeting the parents?"

Jackson grinned. "Where's Eleanor when you need her?"

"Ouch. That bad?"

"No, actually. It was fine. Her dad's protective, so he wanted to make sure I wasn't a bum or a serial killer."

"Don't blame him."

Ben watched him take a deep breath, looking uncharacteristically nervous. "I asked for his blessing."

"Blessing for what?" Snatching up the bottle he opened earlier, he raised it to his lips, then slowly lowered it to the table again, his eyes widening with understanding. "No shit? Marriage?"

"Her dad was friendly until I mentioned it. Dead silence after that."

"Damn. What happened?" He leaned on the table, enthralled by the major left turn Jackson's life would soon take.

"The next day he gave it to me, but I was sweating bullets for twenty-four straight hours."

"Wow. I'm speechless."

"I doubt that."

"No, really. You started this trip three months ago with no interest in dating or sex or anything remotely feminine, and now you want to get married. What the... Oh, hi,

Emily." He smiled, draping an arm on the back of his chair to look like he hadn't just been told the biggest news of the summer.

Based on Emily's skeptical glare, he hadn't pulled it off.

"There you are." She ran a hand over Jackson's back and leaned in for a quick kiss.

Despite his frustration and concerns with his own relationship, he couldn't help being happy for his new friends. They both deserved the bliss they'd found in each other. "How is she?" Ben asked her.

"Still sleeping. She took some pain meds that knocked her out, so I thought I'd come check on you."

"I guess I'll head up, then."

"Ben." She placed a hand on his arm as he stood. "Thank you for what you're doing. She needs you whether she can admit it right now or not."

The sweet sentiment might have sunk in if defeat didn't cover him like a sheet of suffocating plastic. He'd never been one to pray, but that's all he could do as he headed upstairs. He was going to need all the help he could get.

Chapter Twenty-Six

✧ ✧ ✧

Jackson

"A re you excited?" Emily asked as she rested in his arms. The lights from the bustling city outside their hotel room lit the walls and cast abstract shadows above the bed.

"Mmm. I'm excited about a lot of things right now."

A muffled laugh escaped her lips, and she stifled it by nibbling on his shoulder. When she did that, he could only think of having another taste of her.

"Come on. Tomorrow's the biggest day of your entire trip." Adjusting for a better view, she folded her arm on his chest and propped herself up. "You must be excited."

"I am, but it's the end. I'm not sure I'm ready."

"Ready for what?"

"To go back with no plan. No answers."

"But you ran the entire distance and honored your country and friends. The future isn't going anywhere. Enjoy this moment."

"I thought you were a physical therapist, not a psychotherapist." He laughed when she rolled her eyes playfully. "You're right, as always. Tomorrow, I'm going to savor what I've accomplished and not think about what I didn't."

"Good."

Running a hand over her hair, he kissed her on the forehead. "I couldn't have finished this without you. You saved me, just as Eleanor said you would."

"She did? When?"

"After letting Avery go, it felt like I was incapable of loving someone."

"Oh, Jackson. You were still healing from so much trauma."

"At the time I couldn't see through it. I was so empty and lonely. My heart a remnant of what it used to be." He paused to let the ache settle. At least he'd gotten better at anticipating and managing the effect his memories had on him. "Even though I didn't believe her at the time, I never forgot what she said, and it all makes sense now."

"What did she say?"

"That my heart would open when I found the one for me." He held her hand to his chest. "And it did the second I saw you."

———

Emily

The next morning, they showered together and ate breakfast in the hotel lobby before packing. It was the last time she'd have to say goodbye and watch him disappear over the horizon. He had just over ten miles to go before their forever could begin.

Only ten miles. Why was she so damn terrified?

"Shhh," he soothed while she cried in his arms. "Why the tears?"

Shaking her head, she covered her face with her hands. "I cry at everything. Ask G. She hates it."

"That's a cop-out. It's me you're talking to."

"I know."

After softly removing her hands from her face, he held them to his chest. "What is it?"

"I hate watching you leave," she admitted, lifting her lashes to look into the eyes that always made her insecurities and troubles melt away. "I don't want to bring you down, but it gets harder every time."

"The good news is this the last time. After today, I'll ever have to leave you again. And two hours after that, we can have some fun at the park and act like kids again. I'd love to see you in a Cinderella costume." He smiled when she did. "What?"

"It's fitting that I should be your Cinderella. You've been my Prince Charming all this time, and you rescued me from my boring, wretched life."

"Wretched?"

"Well, maybe it wasn't that bad, but it was certainly boring. I'm so grateful you chose me for your happily ever after." Rising to her toes, she waited for a kiss.

"I will always choose you. But I wish I had a glass slipper handy for dramatic effect."

She felt for the necklace he gave her in Savannah and pinched the diamond heart between her fingers. "This is better. A glass slipper sounds very uncomfortable."

He snorted out an unexpected laugh. "Good," he said and kissed her forehead with a loud smack.

"Will your official stopping point be Disney World?"

"Yeah. I thought it was the perfect spot since it symbolizes my journey."

"How so?"

With the most carefree and brightest smile she'd seen on him yet, he took her hand and led her to the small couch beside the bed. "From coming home to being here with you, the journey was a wild rollercoaster ride with a fairytale ending."

"Clever."

"Thanks. Plus, it's a place the boys and I often visited when we were young. So, it fits."

"I can't wait to see you on the other side. You did it, sweetheart." She draped her legs across his lap and snuggled closer, warming herself with his love. "Can you believe it?"

"If you'd asked me that question two months ago, I would have said no. But since Savannah, I feel like I can do anything."

"Damn right, you can."

Leave a Review

If you enjoyed Book 2 of The Journey Series, *A Journey To Love*, please consider leaving a review at any or all of these platforms: Amazon, Goodreads, BookBub, Barnes & Noble, social media (remember to tag me) , and others. Reviews are vital to new authors and help us reach more readers.

Keep reading for a sneak peak of book 3, *A Journey Home* (Jackson's story finale) . And don't forget to read The Journey Series prequel novella, *A Journey Worth Taking,* for a look back at Will and Sydney's love story.

Alexandra Grace

Keep reading for an excerpt from
Book III in The Journey Series

A JOURNEY HOME

by Alexandra Grace

Emily

"Come on, Emily. We've got to go," Ben yelled from outside her hotel room soon after Jackson left for his final run. After nearly 900 miles of running in honor of his fallen comrades and veterans, he'd reach his destination of Disney World in Orlando, Florida in the next couple hours. She, Genevieve, and Ben planned to be his welcome party.

"Okay. Okay. Hold your horses," she called and opened the door to let him inside. "What's the rush?"

"Trust me. We need to go."

"Fine," she exhaled. "Take Jackson's suitcase." She handed him the luggage before grabbing her own and followed him out the door. "Where's G?"

"Already in the car."

"She talking to you yet?"

With a scoff, he pushed the button for the elevator, and the door opened immediately. "Can't touch her either, but at least she doesn't cringe as much. Just avoids me."

"I'm sorry. I thought she was getting better."

"Maybe she is and just doesn't want me to know it." As they stepped out, he stopped at the edge of the lobby and lowered his voice. "Emily, I'm not sure how much more rejection I can take. After today, the trip will be over, and we'll be free to go our separate ways. It seems to me that's what she wants."

"Ben." She rested a hand on his arm and studied his face. The hurt he'd endured over the past several weeks was present in the bags under his eyes. He hadn't been sleeping—too worried, frightened, desperate, and near his breaking point. "She just…"

"I can't do this right now. We have to go." Without waiting for her, he rushed to Genevieve's tiny yellow sports car, waiting under the awning.

"Can you please tell me why we're going so early?" She huffed when she finally caught up to him.

He loaded their luggage in the back seat then held the driver's side door open for her. "The keys are in the ignition. Follow me."

Irritated at his ignoring her again, she sunk into the driver's seat and watched him jog to the other car. "Do you know what's going on?" she asked Genevieve, sitting in the passenger seat.

Genevieve responded by buckling her seatbelt, still silent, distant, and in her head.

With a sigh, Emily started the engine and followed Ben out of the parking lot. In less than thirty minutes, they were parked in the back of a large, packed lot near the Disney World theme park entrance.

"Ben, slow down," Emily huffed. She and Genevieve were having trouble keeping up with him as he hurried through line after line of vehicles. But as soon as they reached the street, she saw it. A huge festival of red, white, and blue.

They stood at the edge of the crowd in awe of the magnitude. Thousands of people were everywhere, holding U.S. flags or balloons, visiting colorful exhibits, and enjoying food trucks, vendors, and a live band. The amusement park could be seen off to the right.

"What is this?" Emily asked, her hand rising to her heart as she took in all in.

Before Ben could answer, a thin blonde woman with bouncy curls and porcelain skin waved and approached them with a wide smile.

"Ben! It's so great to finally meet you in person." She stretched out her hand.

"Yes, it is."

Emily watched Ben place his hand in hers and linger for a moment. The woman's big dark eyes held his gaze without acknowledging Emily or Genevieve, standing beside him. Not appreciating their unspoken familiarity, Emily cleared her throat, then forced a grin when they turned to her in unison.

"Hi, I'm Emily, and this is my friend, Genevieve. How do you two know each other?" She looked to Ben for the answer.

"Samantha is the Assistant to the Orlando Mayor. She contacted me through social media several weeks ago and organized all this."

"Speaking of that. What is it?" Impatience smoldering in Emily's belly. Genevieve was disengaged in the conversation, barely making eye contact, and Emily worried she'd read Ben's reaction to Samantha the same way she did.

"He didn't tell you?" Samantha asked, her eyes widening with her playful smile, as she smacked Ben on the arm. "Shame on you."

"How about you tell us?" Emily suggested, then narrowed her eyes at Ben.

"This is for Jackson. We've been following his journey through Ben's beautiful photos and wanted to give him the finale a hero deserves."

Emily's eyes filled with tears. She looked over Samantha's shoulder at the festivities with a new understanding and saw more than she had before. In the distance, she saw banners welcoming Jackson to Orlando, dozens of exhibits for veteran's services, and patriotism abundant in every direction.

"It's absolutely amazing."

"It was our pleasure. Come." Samantha took Ben by the arm, then beamed a smile over her shoulder. "It's almost time."

"Time for what?" Emily yelled as they entered the noisy crowd.

"You'll see."

They shadowed Samantha and Ben's hasty path to the edge of the stage where the band had played just moments before. Stopping in front as she directed, they watched Samantha climb the stairs and take the microphone.

"Good morning, fellow Floridians." She waited for people to gather around before continuing. "Thank you for coming out today to honor our nation's veterans, and especially one special veteran who's on his way here right now." The crowd erupted into applause, and she motioned for them to quiet down. "Jackson Vane fought through near death, paralysis, and unfathomable loss. He worked hard, refused to give up, and has run over 900 miles to bring awareness and pay tribute to veterans everywhere. He is a true patriot and hero to us all."

The crowd roared again, and Samantha had their undivided attention. If tears weren't blinding her vision, Emily would have been right there with them.

Samantha soon held up her hand to quiet the noise while she answered a phone call. Emily's excitement boiled over and she could barely contain herself. She linked her arms with Ben and Genevieve on either side of her and waited for Samantha to continue.

"Good news," she announced and placed the phone in her back pocket. "He's almost here! You know what to do. Let's give him a hero's welcome to Orlando."

"What's happening?" Emily asked Ben when the crowd began dispersing quickly down the street.

"I'm not sure. She didn't give me any details when we talked on the phone."

With how friendly he and Samantha had been, she wondered if they flirted more than they'd discussed the event. She looked at Genevieve who appeared ready to bolt the second Emily released her.

"Isn't this exciting?" Samantha clasped her hands under her chin, her eyes laser-focused on Ben.

"Where is everyone going?" Emily asked.

"To line the road and cheer for Jackson as he enters this area."

Emotion consumed Emily once again.

"Are you okay, honey?" Samantha placed a hand on Emily's arm and turned to Ben when tears flowed down Emily's cheeks.

"She's Jackson's girlfriend. They met during his journey," he explained.

"Oh, my goodness. How romantic! Come on, we have a few minutes. I want to show you something you're going to love."

She followed Samantha to a T-shirt stand nearby. There were generic shirts for Orlando and patriotic shirts in red, white, and blue. Then, Samantha pointed to a dark green one hanging high above the rest.

JACKSON, ORLANDO, and USA were intermingled together in a crossword puzzle-like pattern with black ink. Decorating the inside of the O in ORLANDO was the flag, and the O in Jackson's name was replaced with a red heart.

"It's perfect."

"She'll take two," Samantha announced to the teenager behind the table. "You look like a woman's small, and what size does Jackson wear?"

"Large, I think," she answered, though her voice garbled with new tears.

She handed the bag with the shirts inside to Emily and passed a fifty-dollar bill to the attendant. "These are on me." She shuttled Emily back to the edge of the crowd and motioned for the others to join her. "Right there is the spot where his journey will officially end." She pointed to a roped-off area between the stage and crowd. "You'll be able to see everything from here."

"Thank you, Samantha," Emily said, gathering herself. "For the shirts and for organizing all this. You were right. He deserves this."

Samantha gave her a quick hug before leaving the group to tend to more event logistics. As she walked away, she didn't bother hiding the I'll-be-seeing-you-later look at Ben. Emily scolded him with her eyes for not discouraging it. Yes, he was lonely and frustrated, but his lack of concern for Genevieve's feelings agitated Emily's already fragile state.

"I'll see you later." Ben announced. He stepped away before she could ask questions or say something he obviously didn't want to hear.

Speechless, Emily stared after him until the noise from the crowd rose suddenly. She turned toward the commotion to see a patriotic balloon arch rise at the end of the road. People screamed and waved small colorful flags on sticks, while a marching band played an upbeat song.

Her heart pounded in her chest. Jackson must be approaching, and she was beyond happy for him. He'd worked hard for this moment. He'd endured so many hardships and so much pain. He'd made sacrifices and difficult decisions along the way. But he also helped and inspired so many people, all while finding both healing and love for himself.

In just a few minutes, his journey would officially end, and she had the best view to see the culmination of it all.

———

Jackson

The sun was high and bright, causing Jackson to squint when he checked his watch. Close to the end, he had just over a mile to go, but he was behind schedule. During the run, he had to stop several times to rest his sore knee or stretch to work out the cramps. It was as though his body knew the end approached.

Near the one-mile mark, he noticed a sign stuck in the ground with *Thank You for Your Service* drawn neatly in black paint. A few yards further, he found another sign. This one said: *Welcome.* Must be the work of some friendly residents, he assumed, and smiled.

Then, another sign caught his attention, and he stopped in his tracks. *Congratulations, Jackson.* Maybe that friendly resident saw his journey on social media and planted a few signs. Orlando had been the right destination for his journey, and these signs confirmed it.

But what about the next step when the journey was over?

Marry Emily, obviously, but that was third on the to-do list after asking her to marry him and moving her to Richmond. The details of the first task were still a blur. He'd only thought as far as deciding the proposal would come that night. The words, he hoped, would arrive in the moment. At least, he already had the ring. All he needed now was the right moment to make it memorable.

He snapped a quick photo of the sign to show Emily later and took a moment to look around, feeling proud of how far he'd come. But it was odd not to see hustling traffic and people everywhere. He was less than a mile from Disney and there should be cars lined up on that road waiting to get in. Where was everyone?

Continuing down the road there were several more signs, and finally, as he rounded the bend, sounds of life— people, movement, action, and excitement. The entrance to Disney World would be just over the horizon.

Emily would be waiting for him by the entrance. They'd embrace, enjoy a day of amusement rides and ice cream, and have dinner together that night to celebrate. The following day, they would head to Savannah as a newly engaged couple, and then to Richmond to start their lives together. He couldn't wait.

Then, something in the distance caught his attention. The haze and humidity from the mid-day Florida sun on asphalt made it difficult to make it out. He shielded his eyes from the glare, the blurry shapes sharpening into vibrant images as he approached.

There were thousands of people lining the street, clapping, waving, and cheering. All for him, he realized, and it stole his breath. Overwhelmed, he doubled over, rested his hands on his knees, and gulped for air. The crowd soon began to chant his name, giving him the energy to straighten and walk toward the dedicated finish line.

Making his way through the aisle of people, he studied their faces, the waving flags, and the veterans proudly displaying their service, and wondered. Why had someone gone to all this trouble for him? He was no one special. But if his mission inspired these people to come out and support veterans that day, then, mission accomplished.

Drawing strength from them, he crossed under the arch, surprised by the band revving into a song beside him. Several people patted him on the back or crowded him for photos. Reporters with mics and recorders swarmed him as the suffocating anxiety did.

He needed space, peace, air to breathe, and a moment to regroup. He took a sharp turn away from the commotion near the stage, but a bubbly woman with thick, golden hair intercepted him.

"Jackson! Welcome to Orlando."

"Thank you, but—"

"I'm Samantha," she yelled over the band and held out her hand. "Please come with me. I'd like you to meet someone."

"Sure, but I need to—"

"Don't worry. This will only take a minute."

"I'm sorry," Jackson began, following her. "Who are you again?"

"Samantha Peterson. I'm the Orlando Mayor's Assistant. He wanted you to have a hero's finale and was responsible for this celebration. What do you think?" She motioned to activities behind her.

"It's…"

"Jackson, my boy. Welcome!"

A short man, plump around the middle, waddled towards them with a wide smile. Strands of long hair once secured over the top of his bare head blew wildly in the breeze.

"Jackson, it is my pleasure to introduce you to Mayor Kennedy," Samantha provided.

"Nice to meet—"

"Come. Let's give the people what they want."

Mayor Kennedy grabbed Jackson's arm and pulled him to the stage where the crowd had gathered. He noticed Emily standing on the opposite side with Genevieve, but he couldn't get to her. She blew him a kiss over the sea of heads, making him desperate for the calm she always gave him.

Because of the excitement, his nerves were fried already, and his heart rate had yet to stabilize after his run. He paused at the top of the steps leading to the stage to catch his breath.

"Come on. We shouldn't keep them waiting." Mayor Kennedy yanked Jackson onto the stage, and the crowd cheered. "Friends," he said to quiet the group. "It's my pleasure to present to you, U.S. Marine veteran, and our hero, Sergeant Jackson Vane."

He placed a hand on Jackson's shoulder. "Jackson, we are so happy you chose our beautiful city as your destination. We've been following your memorial run for a while now, and it's been exciting to watch. How's it been for you?"

He thrust the microphone at Jackson, rendering him speechless and frozen in fear. Put him on the battlefield with a sea of Marines, but not this. He felt exposed, naked emotionally, and sinking fast. What could he possibly say to the hundreds of people staring at him?

"Just speak from the heart, son. They're here to support you," Mayor Kennedy whispered.

Jackson nodded, and with an unsteady hand, accepted the microphone, wishing to be anywhere else.

"I don't know what to say."

He ran a hand over his hair, trying to calm his pulse and stop it from hammering in his ears. He couldn't think. Being forced to face a silent crowd, hanging on his every word, transported him back to his best friend Will's funeral. As he'd been that day, he was vulnerable and drowning in the darkness, treading wave after wave of heartbreak and hopelessness. Sweat beaded on his back and stagnant air stung in his chest. He had no idea where to begin, since the words he needed to say kept getting tangled with a dangerous storm of emotions.

"Semper Fi," someone yelled from the crowd and that was all it took to remind him of his purpose, why he started this journey, and how he finished it.

Will had saved him from the burning Humvee that tragic night in the desert and guided his path from Richmond to

Orlando. Because of that, he wanted to honor their fallen friends and fellow Marines, Billy and Josh, give back to other veterans, and prevent losing any more to mental illness, addiction, or suicide. He thought of Harrison and Eleanor, who raised and supported him when his own parents wouldn't. They, along with Avery, saved him from himself during recovery so he could have this opportunity. And then there was Emily and the light she cast over his life.

Without all these pieces, he wouldn't be standing there, kicking himself for not having the words to express his gratitude.

"Oorah," he responded, causing an uproar in the audience.

Mayor Kennedy raised his arms to quiet them again, allowing Jackson to continue.

"It's been a long journey since returning to the states. Doctors said I'd never walk again, but Marines never give up." He paused when cheers rippled again. "I lost my three closest friends to war and PTSD, and I also struggle with the disease. But thanks to my family, the support I received on social media, and the amazing people I've met along the way here, my life was saved. This trip may have been mine, but it was for all veterans. If my journey keeps one person from giving up the fight, then it was a success. Thank you for this." He waved over the crowd and toward the festival behind them. "It was completely unnecessary and definitely unexpected, but I'm grateful to share the conclusion of my journey with all of you."

As he handed the microphone back to Mayor Kennedy, reality slapped him across the face. It was over. The running, the traveling, the mission. All of it had become his life over the last several months. What purpose did his life serve without a mission?

While Mayor Kennedy addressed the audience, Jackson looked for an escape and located the stairs they'd climbed earlier. He hurried off the stage, stumbling on the last step before stopping his momentum against a nearby tree. Deep breaths, he reminded himself, and closed his eyes to the tumbling ground under his feet.

"There you are," he heard Emily say behind him.

Straightening, he took her in his arms.

"Everything okay?" she asked. He was acting as he had in the hospital at Myrtle Beach and worrying her.

Reluctantly, he pulled back, framed her face with his hands, and pressed his lips to hers. He needed her to set things right again. Show him how to exit the dark tunnel he'd entered.

"Sorry," he managed and rested his forehead against hers, his eyes still closed to block out the chaos around them.

"Why are you apologizing? What's wrong?" He felt her searching his face for the answer, but all he could give her was uncertainty and fear. "I have something for you," she said to provide a distraction.

Reaching into her purse, she removed a T-shirt and held it up. She watched while he studied the design. "It's perfect, right?" she asked when his emotions cracked again.

"Yes. It's perfect."

"They're selling them at the festival, and all proceeds go to the Warrior Angels Foundation. See?" His eyes snapped to hers, then back to the shirt. She flipped it over and pointed to the words WARRIOR printed in small block letters on the sleeve.

When he had no words, Emily softly wrapped her arms around him and ran her hand over his back.

"Sweetheart, there's more." She leaned back to see his face. "They've been fundraising for the Foundation since learning about your mission and raised over $100,000. All of it, along with proceeds from the T-shirt sales, will help so many veterans. Jackson, the donation," she placed her free hand on his cheek, "will be made in your name. The mayor's going to make an announcement later."

Consumed with emotion, Jackson reached for the tree to steady himself. When he slid down the trunk to the ground, she knelt in front of him and rested her arms on his knees.

"Jackson, look at me." When he didn't budge, she continued. "Do you remember what you said soon after we met? You said that you can find peace in my eyes. Look at me," she instructed gently. Slowly, he lifted his eyes, but they were filled with tears yet to be spilled, blurring his view of her. "You did it, my love. You accomplished what you set out to do, and it has helped and inspired so many people."

"What you've done is extraordinary. You deserve this. You and so many veterans didn't get the fanfare that you deserved when you came home. If you don't want this celebration to be about you, let it be about them."

She was right, he knew, but it didn't make pushing through the chaos any easier. He nodded, wanting to make her proud, and wiped his eyes with the back of his hand. "Where's that awesome shirt?"

Reaching into her bag, she pulled out the shirts. She handed him his and pulled on the other.

"You look handsome." She ran a hand over the soft fabric covering his chest and met his gaze. "Now, it's time to have some fun."

His stomach knotted. "Okay. Will you stay with me?"

"Always."

Printed in Great Britain
by Amazon

41974904R00219